INSURRECTION:
APPALACHIAN COMMAND

Dan Santos

To Greg Milhiser

a soldier after my own heart

Hooah!

Dan Santos

5/17/14

Table of Contents

Dedication

This book is dedicated to Ofelia Gutierrez de Santos,
the love of my life.

Acknowledgements

This novel would not have been possible without the love, support and hard work of my wife Ofelia. What an amazing woman. First I drag her through a string of Army posts, where she heroically kept the family together even through the night of the 13 tornadoes in DeRidder, Louisiana. Later, she braved earthquakes, foreign penury and terrorist threats at seven different US diplomatic posts all over the world. She was always there for me and our daughters.

A very special mention is in order for my friend Jaime Posada for sharing his extensive kayaking expertise on the Potomac River, especially the capabilities of the versatile Klepper kayak.

Our country owes a tremendous debt of gratitude to the men and women of the US Secret Service, the Central Intelligence Agency and the Department of Homeland Security. It is thanks to their professionalism and love of country that Al Qaeda's evil designs have been thwarted.

Finally, I'd like to convey my heartfelt appreciation to the selfless women and men of the US Armed Forces and the American Foreign Service. This country will survive thanks to them, not the politicians. May God bless and protect the United States of America.

CHAPTER 1 — The Shot that Calmed the Breeze

"Death, be not proud, though some have called thee
Mighty and dreadful, for thou art not so..."
"Death Be Not Proud" John Donne

1827 hours, January 8, 2018

The sniper under the Ghillie blanket melted into the brush that lined the knoll. The moonless night made it even more difficult to see the former Army Ranger aiming his instrument of death. No one could see him, and no one could sense his tortured soul.

He was prone, motionless and totally receptive to the night's smallest disturbances. The silence around him was so intense that he thought he could hear the vibrating parts of his middle ear in their natural sequence ...hammer, anvil, stirrup...hammer, anvil, stirrup. Or was that only the beating of his heart?

There was a slight rustle in the river breeze, and he calmly drew in a deep breath to check out for smells. Deodorant, soaps, tobacco, booze and food can betray the fighter in the bush. Jude thought that it was harder to sense the approach of a teetotaler, and he smiled imperceptibly under the camo face paint at the thought of that old-fashioned name for people who had sworn off of alcohol.

From above, Jude would have seemed just like another part of the knoll that overlooked the deer trail. The bend in the deer trail before him was just the right spot to funnel tonight's Militia patrol into the cross hairs of the ATN PS22 night scope mounted on his XM-2010 sniper rifle.

The Provos had been running Militia patrols on a predictable schedule along the Chesapeake and Ohio Canal to check Rebel incursions from across the Potomac. Instead of just harassing the enemy behind the lines, Jude's mission tonight was to create a diversion. He thought it was funny how killing a man could be called a "diversion."

The former Ranger was counting on the Militia's poor training to overreact and make a lot of noise to give the Sibley Hospital snatch team a chance to cross MacArthur Boulevard undetected.

The snatch team could then sneak through the nearby suburban development toward the famous hospital. The Rebel National Headquarters out in Colorado had agreed with the Appalachian Command that kidnapping the Provo Intelligence Chief, a patient at Sibley Hospital, would be a significant blow to the usurpers of the American government.

1829 hours, January 8, 2018

The sound of a distant boot on the dry and frozen vegetation alerted Jude. The scents carried by the night breeze hit him even stronger than he had expected, making him shudder momentarily. His senses came alive. His skin crawled. His eyes scanned from left to right with rapid side-to-side movement; a Ranger technique used to penetrate the shadows of the night. His right finger caressed the trigger's notched steel as a helmeted silhouette slowly rose on the defile.

Even at that distance Jude smelled the heavily perfumed soap mixed with sweat. The patrol's point man was about to pay for bad Provo training. The cross-hairs acquired the forehead slowly. Jude exhaled silently, and gently squeezed the trigger.

The puff of the silenced shot broke the tension of the night, quieting all the critters instantly, eerily. Even the leaves stopped swaying in the rustling breeze, as if there were a natural law which froze everything in place when a .300 Winchester Magnum round flew through the air. The flight of the fully jacketed bullet turned the C&O Canal air gray and oppressive.

Jude knew what was coming. Every fiber of his being knew. He longed to start his exfiltration. But the sniper's tradecraft called for additional steps before he could slip away.

Later he would recall that before all hell broke loose, his hyper-sensitive hearing picked up a human hiss that could only have been a last sigh. The Provo's soul had escaped his body, giving Jude a sort of finality for tonight's kill.

1829 hours, January 8, 2018

The rubber soles gripped the ground gently as they stopped at the bottom of the upgrade. The patrol leader's breathing was controlled and tense. He cursed the pebbles and loose dirt under his feet. They could betray his presence. The curse was mute, but there was fire in his eyes. You could have seen the tension on his face if there had been sufficient light; which there wasn't.

His left hand tugged twice on the string connecting the canvas harness to the man behind, and he dropped slowly and silently on one knee; so did the other nine men in the patrol.

Yazid had asked Mohsen if he could take point. Taking point on a night patrol on the Potomac was a rite of passage, a way for a green trooper like Yazid to "make his bones." Now Mohsen thought that maybe the guy hadn't been ready after all. Maybe he should have chosen Rashid.

Mohsen knew that his men were not ready to take on the Rebs. He had been a Farsi translator for the US Army in Afghanistan. He had not been trained to fight, but he had seen enough patrol action to get an idea of how things were done. He could tell good infantrymen from bad infantrymen. Yazid was not a good one, but the battalion commander was his uncle.

The patrol leader was more afraid than he would admit to his men. The Rebels were dangerously unpredictable, more than the Taliban had been when he served in Afghanistan. Who would have thought that the Rebels would rely on Viet Cong (VC) guerilla tactics? That stuff was over 50 years old.

Provo high technology was no match for primitive fighting, and the Rebs knew this. Provo iPhones had no Apps that could see trip wires attached to a grenade, or sense loosely packed vegetation over a hole in ground. Yet, either one of those ancient VC traps could kill or maim.

Each of his troopers had a personal radio with an earplug and a mouth mike, but the humidity by the river short circuited them. The regulars had given the Militia radio model variations designed for the desert. Moreover, the waters of the Potomac River and the C&O Canal amplified sound at night, including their whispers into the microphones and the metallic responses in their ears. The enemy knew a Militiaman was coming from the loud static that his radio emitted.

So Mohsen had ordered his patrol to maintain strict radio silence. When you give that order you expect your men not to talk on the radio. You do not expect them to shut the damn things off. They did. Now he couldn't raise any of them. Nothing worked. It would have been funny if it weren't so tragic.

The Iranian-American patrol leader had read in the Patrol Manual that you could use a string to increase command and control in a night patrol. So his troopers were connected to each other with string. What he forgot to do was to set up a code of string tugs so that his fighters would know what he wanted them to do when he tugged at the string once, twice or three times.

When the string segment that connected him to Yazid went slack, he had tugged the other end twice. He was hoping that his fighters would understand that he wanted them to stop and take cover. It was just a guess, but it worked. It probably helped that the rest of the patrol was too damned close to him and saw him drop to his knee.

Mohsen could sense there was some sort of trouble ahead when the segment of the string that connected him to Yazid had gone limp and unresponsive. He tugged and Yazid did not tug back. Mohsen guessed that Yazid had to be down in the prone position.

1830 hours, January 8, 2018

Mohsen was thinking how the Rebels had been stopped at the Potomac River a while back. But Provo intelligence had reported last week that the insurgents were increasing their incursions into the capital region; maybe in preparation for resuming their attack. And he worried. He knew that despite their loose organization in the Appalachian Operations Area the Rebs were great fighters.

The Rebs decided when and where they would bring the war to the Provos. This was the same advantage Al Qaeda fighters had enjoyed in Iraq, and the Taliban in Afghanistan. With the exception of the foreign fighters who had joined the Rebel forces from countries far afield, the insurgents fought at home. They were familiar with terrain and environmental conditions.

No matter how much money Tehran poured into the Militia and its equipment, it fought at a disadvantage. It was mainly made up of recent immigrants to the US, poorly trained and motivated only by religion. Mohsen had no trust in their ability to apply the quick basic training they had received. And he knew and resented that Greco was using the Militia as cannon fodder, saving the regular units for more "important" work. That fact did not contribute to the morale of his men.

Mohsen's Militia unit had been tasked with securing the area around the Carderock Naval Surface Warfare Center which was now a POW internment camp, and therefore a high value target for the Rebs. So the Militia put out frequent patrols to protect the approaches to the facility.

He and his fellow patrol leaders had been briefed on how the Rebel Appalachian Command was fighting the Militia using the primitive methods that had been used against US forces almost a half century before in the jungles of South East Asia.

Just minutes ago, Yazid had almost plunged into a 40-foot drop which the Rebs had concealed with indigenous brush. A boy from last night's patrol had been impaled by a sharpened branch sprung by a trip wire. Last week a patrol leader had stepped into a 'punji' stake trap. While the sharpened bamboo sticks smeared in human excrement had not gone through the reinforced boot sole, they pierced his ankle as it slipped into the hole.

The Rebs were not just killing them. They were killing whatever Militia spirit there was with their psychological warfare.

Provo Intelligence told them, and Mohsen agreed that they were facing the Appalachian Command's infamous Ghost, a Rebel commando who had escaped after being taken prisoner by the Militia during a battle in which his unit was ambushed and destroyed. There had been at least seven hits attributed to him in the past 45 days. He didn't know how Intel could determine that it had been this Ghost guy, but it didn't matter. He had a job to do, and fucking Yazid was not responding to his tugs.

1831 hours, January 8, 2018

Mohsen knew that Yazid was not too bright, but if he had hit the ground, it must have been because he had seen something. If he was just unsure of what was ahead he would have just dropped to one knee, just as he had done.

Mohsen had heard what sounded like Yazid exhaling hard when he dropped. The idiot must have been out of breath. He had to get these guys to do their daily exercises and get them in better shape.

After a little while, Mohsen decided to try whispering into his radio's microphone and breaking the radio silence he himself had ordered. He hoped that Yazid's radio was on. No answer. He waited a few more seconds, not daring to use the radio again, and crawled carefully towards the point man's position.

Yards of rocky trail ahead, he reached Yazid's prone figure from behind, expecting some sort of reaction when he touched the man's boot. Nothing. Yazid was just lying there.

It hit Mohsen that Yazid hadn't dropped: someone had dropped him.

The Militiaman moved up to Yazid's head and saw the hole on the forehead and the brain matter squishing out from the under the helmet. Oh, God, Yazid was dead. Yazid was a *real* dead man; the first one Mohsen had seen.

Mohsen jumped up, yelling for Allah and emptying his magazine against the unseen enemy all around him.

Predictably, his troops followed suit and responded to their leader's reaction with a cacophony of small arms fire; the common response of poorly trained soldiers who are scared shitless.

With friendly fire flying all around and miraculously missing him, Mohsen's radioman brought up the PRC-155 manpack radio, and handed him the handset.

Remembering bits and pieces of his training Mohsen reported the patrol was under attack. He then keyed in an 81mm mortar fire mission.

1830 hours, January 8, 2018

For a nanosecond, Jude remained prone at the base of the promontory: the sniping tradecraft's preferred position. Not only did his Ghillie blanket and weapon blend invisibly with the surrounding plant growth, but his green grease-painted flesh blurred his handsome features, making him look like part of the ground cover on which he lay.

The air that left his nostrils in the aftermath of the trigger-squeeze disappeared into the musty stillness of the EENT; the End of the Evening Nautical Twilight. The EENT was the best time of the evening for denying the enemy a clear sighting. Religious practitioners of at least two world faiths would measure this time by holding a white thread against the waning light. Scientists and photographers used sophisticated light meters to determine its arrival. Normal people blinked, squinted and called it dusk when it was just too dark to see.

With the remarkable discipline that had kept him alive before, during and after his kills, he took stock of every centimeter of his body, making his brain run through a list that was not too different from the one that pilots run pre-flight. In nanoseconds of practiced efficiency he went from the hair stubs on the top of his head all the way down to toenails encased in thick wool socks and soft-sided boots.

As the biological inventory progressed, he allowed his eyes some freedom of movement…left…then right…up…then down…and finally back to the newly formless clump slumped beside the distant oak: the clump that used to be a human being, the Provo. He had never been able to dehumanize his kills. Frankly, it helped his psyche to absorb that he was killing 'one of them'.

At the end of this anatomical checklist he focused his senses on potential enemy responses to the kill: he first checked with his hearing, and then with his sight. The former Army Ranger listened for the tell-tale rustling of vegetation, the crushing of dried leaves and twigs under the weight of a foot, or the metallic clink of an unsecured rifle sling or helmet strap. There was nothing beyond the stillness of the night and the initial thump of the patrol noisy stop as they lost sight of their point man.

Next, he did the smell check. Human sweat mixed with adrenaline in a stressful situation smells like bittersweet decomposition. Jude had learned to tell the difference between his own sweat and the enemy's. His own musk was rendered almost neutral by a strict diet of nuts and dried fruits for the three days preceding an infiltration or a hit. At the end of the scenting exercise his nose sent a reassuring message to his brain. The only sweat he could identify was warm, comfortable, and above all, *his*.

His enemy's sweat usually smelled like battery acid mixed with fear. Yes, the human animal's stench was very different from other animals. There was no human sweat within fifty yards. Then Jude projected his sensing exercise beyond the hundred-yard mark. He was reassured: there was nothing. The patrol had not moved. The enemy was still motionless and remarkably silent.

Jude could also tell the difference between the acrid smell of his own freshly burned gunpowder from enemy shots. He loaded his own rounds mixing in tiny amounts of wild mint. His shots left a minty smell. His enemy's shot smelled like the crushed, burnt pepper stench of regular gun powder. Provo intelligence had tagged the minty smell as his trademark. He was glad that they knew it was him, and that they knew he was paying them back.

CHAPTER 2 — Cell 786 Infiltration

"The pieces of the bodies of the infidels were flying like dust particles. If you had seen it with your own eyes, your heart would have been filled with joy." Osama Bin Laden's ode to the attack on the USS Cole in Yemen, composed on the occasion of his son's wedding.

2305 hours, June 13, 2013

Ahmed Alawi's blue-green eyes pierced the darkness on the American side of the Rio Grande. Their hired Mexican coyote's crumpled body lay at his feet and Alawi's hands were gooey from the carotid blood that coated his blackened blade. He clicked the springy metal of the toy clacker in his left hand, piercing the night air with what sounded just like another bug living in the thick and thorny river brush. His team froze into the stony stance they had mastered at the Algerian camp. The jihadists' breathing was silent and controlled, despite the recent sprint across knee-deep water.

The irregular shadows on the Mexican side formed a backdrop to their dark clad figures which made them almost invisible to the US Border Patrol's 4x4 that was playing with its spotlight not twenty meters north of them.

The light from the Tahoe had pinned down the decoy group of braceros to the Migra's left, just as Alawi had planned. The decoy would keep the Americans just busy enough for Alawi's group to breach the border and infiltrate the Texan countryside from the right. It would also justify the remote ground sensors going off in the

Border Patrol Command Center during the last few minutes.

Charlie Owens jumped off the Tahoe just as the real Mexican illegal migrants made a move to escape. The tall Texan fixated on the more obvious prey and missed the jihadist group crouched only yards to his right. Charlie drew his Beretta 96D, holding it in a two hand stance in the general direction of the pollos. Sometimes Mexican cartel drug dealers and other such vermin would hide among the illegal immigrants, so Charlie was not about to take any chances. The spotlight's beam glued the illegals to the ground they stood on, just like deer caught in a car's headlights. Some of the decoy real Mexicans had seen Ahmed's group, but would say nothing to the Migra in solidarity with what could very well be a luckier group of compañeros. Maybe those other pollos would be able to make their way to Los Angeles. They could still have a chance to get a good job in America.

As for the real Mexicans, the gringos would take them back across the river and hand them over to the federales. The federales would collect an appropriate mordida of about $100 from each of them and then set them free. The pollos would try to sneak in again as soon as their friends and family could put together enough money to pay a different coyote to take them across the river. Such was the eternal monotony of the majority of illegal migrants who risked their lives on these journeys in order to feed their families.

2320 hours, June 13, 2013

The Palestinian fighters remained as still as the barrel cacti on the dark ground around them while the approaching Bureau of Prison's bus moved closer and packed in the pollos. The whole thing took place in a matter of minutes with an eerie economy of words and sounds. It was regular routine and both the Mexicans and the Migra were used to it. The pollos were unhurried as the Migra plastic-tied their hands and herded them into the bus. The old-timers in the Migra were no longer angry or excited or rushed. They handled their prey with the tired gentleness of the hunter bagging his legal limit of rabbits.

Once the bus carrying the prisoners and their captors faded into the distance, the jihadists let out a slow, silent breath but remained frozen in their places. Alawi's clacker emitted a double click, which brought all eyes onto him. He raised his hand in slow motion pointing in the direction he wanted them to go. It was time to move. The ground sensors would soon be reactivated to detect the next group of unsuspecting migrants.

2324 hours, June 13, 2012

The next two miles were dusty and silent. In the shade of the moonlit rock outcropping, Alawi slid slowly into a crouch, glancing furtively at the GPS and piercing the mist with his trained eyes, until he spotted the silhouettes of the three camouflaged Humvees. The squat monstrosities had the stenciled markings of the Texas Army National Guard's 36th Infantry Division.

The jihadist leader stepped soundlessly toward and around one of the vehicles and stood behind its drivers' field of vision. The waiting drivers all seemed to be in the stupor of boredom, their faces betrayed by the dim light of cigarettes dangling from their lips.

The lead driver's heart stopped as Ahmed's painted face rose slowly in the corner of his left eye. He had to face the fact that an apparition had materialized on the other side of the Humvee's window. He turned rapidly and gave Alawi an embarrassed, nervous smile. He guessed he should have done something soldier-like, but vacated lungs, a rapidly palpitating heart and frozen limbs could not do soldierly things.

Alawi's crocodile grin appeared slowly on his face. Strangely, it had a calming effect on the livid terrorist. The driver's blood began to circulate again, and oxygen resumed its trek to the man's red blood cells. He wanted to stand at attention or salute, or something that would let Alawi know that he was acknowledging the jihadist leader's authority. But the only thing that came out of his mouth was the high pitch 'Saha' greeting of the Algerian camps.

Alawi had a fleeting thought that all these guys from the Algerian camps were too deferential to authority. Someone should have grabbed them by the neck and woke them up to the fact that they were in the land of the Great Satan. It was time to act like a professional.

The jihadist leader thought with relish of all the possible punishment he could inflict on these three sons of she-goats when their usefulness ran out. That would be best left for later. He chose instead to trade the recognition signal, which he followed by a friendlier Allah this, and Allah that.

2330 hours, June 13, 2012

The members of Cell 786 donned US Army uniforms bearing Texas National Guard 36th Infantry's downward arrowhead shoulder patches quickly and silently. The transformation was complete within minutes. They now looked like Guardsmen on the way to the yearly two-week training camp. Some of them could even muster a Texas accent if pressed.

On Al Qaeda's orders they had been selected by their former sleeper cell leaders not only for their skills and dedication to the Holy Jihad, but for their lighter skins and "crusader eyes." Their English flawlessly matched their American personae since most of them had been born in or moved to America when they were very young children. The larger group of forty was then presented to Ayman Al Zawahiri himself. Osama Bin Laden's successor personally chose all twelve cell operatives.

Within minutes they were ready to navigate any Border Patrol checkpoint they might find in Big Bend National Park along the way towards the airport at Midland. The only thing that could raise suspicion was that there weren't any African-Americans or Latino's among them.

It took them what was left of the night to get to a safe house in the outskirts of Panther Junction. After a couple of hours of restless sleep they headed north to Midland International Airport on Texas 385 and US 20. Houston's Cell *Isra* had helped Alawi's brother "procure" a Spanish Casa C-212-M series 200 transport aircraft that could carry and drop the jihadist team on the drop zone in Maryland.

0734 hours, June 14, 2013

The morning drive to Midland International Airport–Alawi thought that only a redneck could have called it

"International"– went off better than expected. The stolen C-212's turbo props were idling when the three Humvees drove into the civil aviation section of the airport, thanks to professionally doctored military tarmac passes. The squat beasts pulled up by the hangar's rear gate and the terrorists dismounted in one well-rehearsed movement. They and the drivers headed for the men's locker room. Twelve jihadists came out dressed in jeans and light windbreakers, and carried their weapons and "civilian kits" in utility bags. The drivers' bodies and their vehicles would not be discovered for another day, along with the plastic bag of heroin left behind to make it look like a drug transaction gone bad.

All except Alawi boarded the Spanish built aircraft through the rear door; the same one out of which they would jump over the Washington County Maryland countryside.

Alawi went in through the crew's entrance and embraced his brother.

"Peace upon you, Mohammed." Ahmed held his brother tightly against his chest.

"May the peace, mercy and blessings of Allah be upon you, Ahmed," responded the eldest brother effusively as commanded by the Holy Quran.

"How's our father?" From Ahmed this was a double-edged question. His physician father had immigrated to the United States and been almost totally assimilated by the all-pervasive greed of the Great Satan. Ahmed had never approved of his father's distancing himself from the fight of the Palestinian people, and his father had never approved of Ahmed's dedication to Holy Jihad.

"He's well. His practice is making him richer. Dollars are dollars, as you well know," said Mohammed with characteristic scorn. As the eldest, he should have been at the forefront of his family's contribution to the fight against America. Al Qaeda had determined, however, that his contribution to the struggle would be behind the scenes. Logistics, propaganda and coordination are as necessary to a military operation as the actual fighting, but much less glamorous than what Ahmed was doing. Ahmed had always been the most athletic of the brothers; less talented in the matters of commerce that Mohammed carried out so well.

"Any trouble getting the plane?" asked Ahmed with trepidation. He had taken a calculated risk in assenting to Mohammed's "going wet" in the killing of the Casa's assigned corporate pilot. But it had to be Mohammed. There was just no one else available. And Ahmed knew that his letting Mohammed participate as a fighter would strengthen the brotherly bond which his sibling's envy had weakened.

"No trouble at all. The American pilot won't miss it. And very few people will miss him", he said with a smile that disguised how shaky his hands felt, and how horrible it had been to take his first life.

Ahmed knew it had been difficult for his brother to kill a man. He purposely changed the conversation to something more mechanical: "Do we have clearance to take off?" Given an opportunity Mohammed would have bragged endlessly about his prowess, fabricating details, and generally complicating the situation.

"We'll get it within seconds" responded the brother somewhat disappointed that Ahmed would not learn how bravely his brother had performed. "I filed the plan only 20 minutes ago. We are transporting cargo to New Jersey with a refueling stop in Tennessee. We timed it well."

Ahmed turned his head toward the rear of the plane, where his men had quickly secured their equipment and were seated on the floor, holding on to the cargo straps.

Alawi looked down the center isle until his eyes locked on Hussein Malaki and said, "Ready, Hussein?" Al Qaeda had appointed Malaki as his deputy to promote the participation of the organization's Iraqi branch in this operation. 'Al Qaeda in Iraq' had not seen action since the Americans had turned tail and abandoned the fight in their country. Ahmed thought sarcastically that Hussein's only contribution to the mission was that his given name was the American president's middle name.

Palestinians had been resettled in Iraq since the creation of Israel in1948. But Iraqis had always seen them as refugees forced on them by the Brits and the French. On their part, Palestinians had always felt as strangers there, and had looked with contempt at Al Qaeda's Iraqi fighters who had been defeated so easily by the Americans. So Alawi was not inclined to have kind thoughts about the Iraqi.

"Ready Ahmed" responded the Iraqi perfunctorily.

And then to his brother who was already at the pilot's seat, he said, "Let's go Mohammed." Mohammed had originally obtained a commercial pilot license to immolate himself if Al Qaeda so commanded. Instead of a suicide mission he would be flying the Casa to the drop zone over Maryland and then on to the New Jersey landing strip. Or so Mohammed thought.

1634 hours, June 14, 2013

The cabin center red light went on, and the Palestinian fighters helped each other strap on modified

T-10 parachutes. They remained standing, eyes fixed on their leader's arms, which would soon start the series of paratrooper commands that would get them to hook up on the static line, shuffle to the door and throw themselves into the void over the field next to Maryland Route 632 and Rench Road, just outside of Hagerstown, Maryland. A fictitious parachutist school had arranged permission for its students to jump into the Washington County LZ.

The Casa would later crash on a Pennsylvania field. Al Qaeda had secretly ordered Malaki to ensure the aircraft's destruction after it had served its purpose. "The Organization" had determined that Alawi would be more motivated by his brother's "accidental" death. In addition, there had been a real danger that Mohammed would have bragged to someone about his part in the mission and about killing the pilot. He was just not the disciplined type.

A Philadelphia sleeper fighter from Cell Gaza, who would later blow up Independence Hall and the Liberty Bell Center, had stolen a tourist bus that morning in Pottsville, Pennsylvania. He was waiting in the stolen bus a few hundred yards north of the LZ. He picked up the fighters and their gear, and drove towards Gaithersburg, taking the back roads of the Maryland countryside. The driver deposited half of the team at the Shady Grove metro station, and the other half further down the Red Line, at Rockville. He then took the bus back to the same shopping center where he had stolen it. The company that owned the bus had not even missed it.

The commandos rode separately in the aluminum subway cars of the Metropolitan Transit Authority. They changed to trains from the Blue and Orange lines at

Metro Center, winding up within minutes of each other in the middle of the George Washington University campus, at Foggy Bottom station. Reunited in pairs, they left the campus on foot following Alawi at inconspicuous intervals. Minutes later, they arrived at their destination, three rental apartments on 26th Street NW. From here, they would bring about the demise of the American Republic.

CHAPTER 3 –Evil Works in Secret

"No enterprise is more likely to succeed than one concealed from the enemy until it is ripe for execution."
Niccolo Machiavelli.

1014 hours, June 15, 2013 to 2006 hours, January 8, 2015

Alawi walked out of the apartment on 26th Street NW at midmorning. As he neared the traffic of K Street, he was picked up by a white panel truck driven by one of his operatives, and painted with the logo of a Rosslyn Virginia flower shop. Once across Key Bridge, the van drove into a parking garage near Fort Myers. The vehicle slid into a narrow parking spot between two columns. Neither Alawi nor the driver said a word while they waited.

They had been there about 15 minutes when a man came out of the concrete shadows, opened the rear doors and climbed into the van's rear. Alawi knew better than to look at him, and the stranger never raised his eyes or the brim of his baseball cap.

The man asked Alawi softly "Ayna ajedu Makkah al-Mukarramah?" in Arabic meaning "how do I go to Mecca?" It referred to Islam's Holy City appropriately as "Mecca the Honored," a small security device an infidel might miss.

Alawi gave the countersign "Imshy ala tool, thumma 'arrij yaminan" which means "go straight ahead and then turn left," an answer that made no sense but which resulted in the man handing him two sheets of paper: one with 18 dead-drop addresses in the Washington metropolitan area, and the other one with the location of 26 subterranean accesses.

Next to each dead-drop address, there was a date and a time where Cell 786 should pick up packages containing pre-measured quantities of octanitrocubane, each destined to be placed in strategic locations reachable only through the subterranean entrances. Four of these underground locations had passageways that led them under the White House and the Capitol, unbeknownst to its occupants and all their highly touted security measures.

The rest of the underground locations were selected to ensure the destruction of infrastructure supporting the targets. The subterranean entrances would lead them to a vast array of underground locations corresponding to utility, sewer and disused nuclear shelters.

The octanonitrocubane charges included a detonating mechanism that could only be activated from the pre-set detonating point near the National Cathedral, to reduce the chances of premature activation.

Octanitrocubane

Octanitrocubane was first synthesized at the University of Chicago in 2000. It was later tested and verified by the Naval Research Laboratory in Washington D.C. The United States Government assessed that octanitrocubane could be more powerful than any other non-nuclear explosive.

One of the densest compounds in existence, octanitrocubane is built only of carbon, nitrogen and oxygen. High density is crucial to the strength of an explosive, because the pressure of the detonation increases tremendously with the increased density of the explosive.

In 2012 an even denser form of octanitrocubane was obtained, which permitted its manufacture in sufficient quantities to become a viable weapon. A Libyan scientist of Palestinian background working on the project shared the classified formula with his Hamas connections. Hamas in turn, transferred the formula to Al Qaeda's Sleeper Cell *Medina* in Los Angeles, where it would be easier to manufacture in the quantities needed.

Cell *Medina*'s chemistry experiment was successful beyond belief. The test at the Luray Caverns in Virginia proved it.

Once the needed amount was ready, its jihadists drove the highly stable product cross-country to trusted contacts who would pass it on to the action operatives. For the Washington phase, which was the principal part of the coordinated attack, the product was distributed to 18 operatives in quantities tailored and cryptically labeled for each of the 26 detonation points.

Cell *Medina* engineers had selected redundant detonation points so that if the federal authorities discovered one or more of them they could still carry out the task. The Cell also provided operative legends, including elaborate background information, to the 18 guardians of the caches to disguise their true objectives. Discovered operatives would be ready to confess to targeting smaller objectives, ensuring final operational viability.

The transfer of these lists to the main action cell took place in that Rosslyn garage.

Underground Washington

Alawi's first task was to personally check each one of the underground passages for operational viability. Of course he trusted the Medina engineers, but the responsibility for the success of the Washington operation was his and his alone. In the manner of effective managers he made it a habit to "trust, but verify."

Like Underground Atlanta, Underground Washington arose as a result of military conflict; the former at the hands of Union General Sherman, and the latter begun at the creation of the nation's capital.

While Underground Atlanta began to be exploited commercially in the late 1960's, the nature of Washington tunnels did not lend themselves to making money, especially since most of the tunneling under the capital city remained either unknown or classified. The recent tunneling, such as the Washington Metropolitan Transit (Metro) was widely known to the general public. Infrastructure tunneling for utilities and sewers was less conspicuous, but still a matter of public records, even accessible on the internet.

Everyone knew where the Washington Metro tunnels were buried. The myriad security organizations in the capital had to vet each one of the Metro tunnels. Those which passed under critical infrastructure such as the White House or the Capitol, or even areas occupied by other government buildings, had been vetoed by the Secret Service and or the Capitol Police. The Capitol, however, had its own underground rail shuttle system to transport legislators between the many office buildings and the Capitol.

Al Qaeda's research organizations had compiled a comprehensive breakdown of tunnels that were not so obvious and well-known. Countless times throughout the history of the capital, city tunnels under Washington had been discovered, often when digging up the earth prior to laying the foundations for new buildings.

While Architect Pierre L'Enfant was credited with digging the first few underground passageways under the capital city to link the National Mall, the Confederacy's major objective of capturing the Union's capital prompted a rash of secret tunnels construction by Union engineers, whose objective was keeping the government working should the city be seriously threatened by Rebel siege. World War Two in the 1940's and the Cuban Missile Crisis in the 60's prompted further tunneling for similar purposes.

By the time Cell 786 was ready to exploit them the tunnels had been selected and classified by a jihadist board of engineers, architects and physicists for the explicit objective of destroying the essential working parts of the American government.

Putting it together

Alawi kept the list of tunnels to himself in his iPhone; a risk he had to take for the sake of the operation's success. For the data's safety he had prepared his iPhone for octanitrocubane destruction with a simple two-symbol code which would blow up the fake extended battery attached to the phone. The smart phone's explosion would kill him also, enhancing operational security for whoever took over as Cell leader. To instill compartmentalization, he would release the locations to his men as needed, when the time came to place the octanonitrocubane in them. But for now, he undertook personally the identification, casing and exploration of each of the tunnels he would use.

It was a dangerous mission in itself because many of the tunnel access points were in very public places. These included McPherson Square, the Metro Center Station, the Renwick Gallery, Lafayette Park, and the Botanic Garden. He had to physically try out each one of the 42 tunnels he planned to use. For this purpose he established multiple legends: botanist, PEPCO inspector, spelunking aficionado, Army Corps of Engineers officer, and even an identity of a homeless person seeking shelter underground from the weather.

His commando team had been trained by some of the finest explosive experts jihadist money could buy. All of them were committed to the cause and all had received redundant bomb-making training at least two international terror facilities. Their skill level was optimal.

The octanonitrocubane charges had been shaped into rectangles labeled as 'play dough' and kept disconnected from the control mechanisms until the very last minute to prevent unplanned explosions.

They would remain at their storage points, as far from the actual objectives as the intricate logistics plan would permit, until they were picked up by Cell 786 operatives. These operatives would then place the charges at the designated objectives after Alawi had finished his recon.

Even then, should one of them go off prematurely through the misfiring of a detonator, redundant devices would ensure the destruction of the target, depending on how premature the explosion took place. If the preemie happened days or weeks before the date, the Al Qaeda media organizations would make sure that it was identified as a failed attempt on an innocuous target by some lone-wolf terrorist. If the premature explosion took place hours or less from T time it would only serve to create a distraction. But the level of expertise with which the preparations had been made would preclude that type of accident.

Alawi also used his different identities to identify official travel patterns that would contribute to the scheduling phases of the explosions. He became familiar with presidential movement techniques and the use of advance teams of agents to secure destinations. Before he entered the US he had been trained by retired Secret Service agents employed by commercial security companies who thought they were training a VIP bodyguard from a friendly Arab country. He put those lessons to good use, and spent long hours observing actual travel with trained eyes to detect changes in techniques and patterns.

He then set out to plan the transportation and insertion of the octanonitrocubane charges. While it was true that the explosive was touted by the scientific community as highly stable, it was fairly new. Alawi recalled that Saddam Hussein used to say that surprise is the mother of failure.

So he had to ensure that the routes and methods were chosen carefully, and how early the charges could be placed to preclude detection by routine tunnel inspections. His masters had inserted him with plenty of time, but Terror (T) time had been set and meeting it required efficiency, dedication and a lot of luck.

The best laid plans

Alawi came closest to being discovered while inspecting the access to the tunnel that ran from the Botanic Garden to the US Capitol's rail shuttle, where the charge would ultimately be placed, in this case disguised as several boxes of solid tree food spikes.

For this particular target portion Al Qaeda had prepared a legend of a visiting botanist from the prestigious botanical department at Cambridge University. Alawi found that preparing for this particular identity was a challenge. He knew almost nothing about plants. In fact, the closest he had come to the field was during his youthful visits to a family olive grove in Palestine. But the Al Qaeda technicians had been very thorough and prepared reading material for a limited area of expertise on which the professor wished to develop a thesis: the construction and maintenance of green houses.

While Cambridge had recently finished an ambitious project in the area, it was always trying to find improvements for future remodeling and maintenance. The Conservatory at the US Botanic Garden was situated directly across the US Capitol. Unbeknownst to that fine institution, it also sat atop a 19th Century tunnel that was discovered during one of the Capitol rail projects. The project engineers had closed off access to the system, but they also left a detailed description of the tunnel's location and exploration. The detailed plans had been available on-line at the Library of Congress, so it presented an enticing early target for Al Qaeda planners.

Years before Cell 786's arrival, Al Qaeda had sent in a team to run through the tunnel's potential for an attack on the Capitol. The exploration and construction of an access port to a Capitol rail tunnel had been halted in late August, 2001, when Bin Laden decided to use one of the hijacked planes to destroy the Capitol building instead of the tunnel. United Airlines Flight 93 was originally destined to destroy the US Capitol when its heroic passengers immolated with the aircraft into a field in Somerset County, Pennsylvania.

The Al Qaeda team withdrew prior to 9/11, abandoning the original plan, but not before it had built a concealed access to the Capitol's rail system that could be put to good use for some future operation. The organization's stored record of its location turned out to be very useful to Alawi.

A jihadist sympathizer at Cambridge took care of introducing Professor Viktor Sokoloff to the US Botanical Garden's Conservatory's management. There were a series of letters and emails which originated from Cambridge requesting access to construction and maintenance files for the 'Professor', a Russian émigré to the UK. Of course, the permission was granted in due course and the visit was arranged.

'Professor Sokoloff' arrived by taxi on a Wednesday morning and was given the VIP treatment by the unsuspecting US Botanical Conservatory management officials. Al Qaeda had even gone to the extent of creating an identity for the Professor at Wikipedia, identifying him as a promising scholar with a 15 year history in the field of botanical greenhouse construction. His particular area of interest was climate control for different types of greenhouse environments ranging from Amazonian rain forest to frozen tundra. Conservatory maintenance officials were most obliging in granting

Alawi access to the known underground infrastructure. After two days of the Professor asking incessant questions, the maintenance officials left him to ponder greenhouse architecture on his own.

While inspecting the Garden Primeval fern exhibit during a lunch hour, Alawi opened the trap door he had earlier identified as the entrance to the tunnel. He climbed down and walked the length of the tunnel until he reached a concrete wall that separated the Conservatory's foundation from the Capitol's rail tunnel. He found the entrance concealed behind a movable concrete slab and slid it sideways, revealing the access to the rail tunnel without any difficulty, at precisely the time that a shuttle sped by the entrance. The shuttle scraped the access door's sliding supports slightly, producing a scratch on the shuttle's body that would remain a mystery to shuttle maintenance employees. The shuttle's noise had masked any noise resulting from its unfortunate encounter with the secret door.

Still shaken after the train's vacuum almost sucked him into the tunnel, Alawi waited a few seconds and leaned his head tentatively into the tunnel, entering it sideways and shuffling to the precise location where the charge would be placed. That done, he backtracked to the secret access point and secured the panel in place so that it would remain undiscovered. He then negotiated his way back to the Conservatory's trap door, and lifted it smoothly to regain access to the Garden Primeval display above ground.

"Hey, Professor, what the hell you doing down there? That trap door is condemned and it ain't suppose' to go anywhere."

"Oh. Hi, Hank," said Alawi recovering quickly. It was Hank the plumber, who oversaw the basement's myriad tangled pipes that carried the water for the plantings above. He assumed his British absent minded professor demeanor and told the plumber, "Well, as you can see, I am a nosy fellow, what? I think about trap doors in the same manner that alpinists look at mountains. I go through them "just because they are there", you know?"

Alawi's mind was grappling with the close call and how to salvage this important walkway to the objective. He quickly decided that Hank had to go. "I did find something most unusual down below, though," improvised the Palestinian. "Your water pipes may have a leak. It appears to be small now, but who knows what damage it could do if left unrepaired? Come take a look."

"I don't know, Professor," said the ever-cautious Hank. "That trap door had a 'condemned' sign on it and I don't want to break the rules. Maybe I should talk to Mac and get permission before I go down there?"

"As you wish, but if I were you I would see what the problem is first so that you can tell Mac in detail. You know how testy he gets when things don't go quite right, eh? It will just take a minute. In fact, the leak can be seen a couple of meters from the entrance ladder." Alawi saw further hesitation on the part of the plumber cloud his visage, so he added, "And, if worse comes to worst, I will break the news to Mac myself to keep you out of it. But I think you must see this so that either you or I can point it out to Mac."

Still munching on the academic's plan, but believing he owned the problem, Hank told Alawi. "Uh, that makes sense Professor. Let's go take a look."

Alawi held the trap door open for the plumber and descended the access ladder right behind Hank, closing it after they were in.

Hank started to turn towards Alawi to protest the suddenly darker passageway but he didn't get the chance. Alawi broke his neck before the man had finished his turn. The Palestinian dragged the body to a pile of lime which had been left over from the original construction. Alawi had given it a wide berth when he first explored the tunnel but now saw its obvious potential to hide his crime. He donned the heavy working gloves Hank had stuck under his belt and piled lime over the dead body with his hands. The lime would hide the stench and speed up decomposition. The secret entrance to the tunnel would not be discovered due to the decomposition of Hank's cadaver.

Alawi made his way back out into the physical plant beneath the Conservatory, ensuring that the trap door appeared undisturbed. Hank would certainly be missed. But this was Washington DC, which featured a crime rate that could account for anyone's disappearance. From now until they blew up the Capitol, he and his team would keep an eye on crime news and body discoveries, just in case. But his instinct told him that this portion of the attack was still a go.

Preparations completed

As T time drew near, Alawi had taken great care in pairing the right people, taking into consideration his detailed knowledge of each of his fighters. For instance, there was a tunnel accessible through the basement of a liquor store. For that particular tunnel, he chose a two-man team that did not have any hang-ups about alcohol. The situation required professional control, not religious rage.

By New Years Day, 2015, all the charges were in place. In a move that could have been criticized as risky by Al Qaeda security, Alawi went back into each tunnel one more time after the teams had all done their jobs and personally inspected all 26 detonation points and their charges. The Palestinian did not mind the risk of blowing himself up ensuring that the operation had a chance to succeed.

0800 hours, January 8, 2015

On the morning of America's destruction Alawi began to execute the meticulously planned exfiltration from the Foggy Bottom area.

He and his team found anonymity in the five commercial vehicles that they had rented over the two preceding days: two U-Haul moving vans, two Budget panel trucks and one Home Depot small flat bed pickup. U-Haul moving vans were commonplace in the George Washington University dorm community around the main campus. The panel trucks were disguised with magnetic signs bearing the logos of local businesses. And the Home Depot flatbed pickup was an everyday fixture in this upwardly mobile brownstone neighborhood of do-it-yourselfers. The jihadists would be transporting nothing but their original equipment bags out of the rented apartments on 26th Street NW, but commercial vehicles attracted less attention in that neighborhood.

The moving vans were parked adjacent to the Columbia Plaza high-rise apartment and office complex, the panel trucks were positioned across from the infamous Watergate building, and Alawi personally drove the Home Depot pickup, keeping it moving around the area in counter-surveillance mode.

The jihadists spent the morning and a good portion of the afternoon "sanitizing" their living quarters. They cleaned the apartments thoroughly, even dusting under the furniture just in case they had left behind any by-product of their terrorist activities. All surfaces were wiped clean of fingerprints. Bathrooms and kitchens were scrubbed clean to prevent DNA collection. Instead of disposing of the removed waste in the buildings' garbage chutes, they bagged it and put the bags in their vehicles for disposal far away from the neighborhood. It was important that all their neighbors and landlords remembered them as nice, quiet GWU students.

By 1700 all jihadists had left the apartments and boarded their assigned vehicles. Precisely at 1702 Alawi signaled the departure, and all vehicles except his pickup started moving in different directions toward a common objective: the Gaithersburg Square Shopping Center in the Maryland suburbs, where the next series of non-descript exfiltration vehicles were parked.

Around 1800, satisfied that there they had not been made, Alawi dialed a remote computer that had been set up to transmit at his command a coded digital signal that would prepare for the triggering of the simultaneous explosions. The computer responded by arming the digital connections with the 26 detonation points, ensuring their readiness to receive the detonation command.

Alawi then drove up Wisconsin Avenue to the National Cathedral. Once in the Cathedral's area, he found a parking spot behind the school from where he could tune to the traffic cam on Pennsylvania Avenue and Jackson Place, which his team had repositioned to observe the White House north portico.

As the time approached, security vehicles predictably signaled the upcoming presidential movement. At 2005 hours the TV lights that permanently haunt the portico went on, a sure signal that the Commander in Chief was coming out. And so he did at 2006 hours, the very moment that Alawi dialed the control computer and punched in 9-11-2001, the very symbolic code which would detonate the octanonitrocubane charges.

By 2007 hours it was all smoke and rubble.

2006 hours, January 8, 2015

People in the area of the National Cathedral felt the rumble of the collapse of their patriotic symbols. The Cathedral's expensively restored gargoyles that had tumbled down in the 2011 Virginia earthquake again took a dive. Darkness enveloped Wisconsin Avenue as Alawi calmly pulled the pickup truck into the dinnertime traffic.

It took the jihadist leader over an hour and a half to make his way north on Wisconsin, which turned into Maryland Route 355, to the shopping plaza where the team awaited in fresh exfiltration vehicles. The team, now grouped in three vehicles, took US Interstate 270 north, and then US Interstate 70 west all the way into the hinterlands of the America they had destroyed.

CHAPTER 4 —Closure?

"When they reached the threshing floor of Atad, near the Jordan, they lamented loudly and bitterly; and there Joseph observed a seven-day period of mourning for his father." Genesis 50:10

0715 hours, January 15, 2015

After seven days his eyes were painfully dry, the convulsions on his chest merely light aftershocks. He vaguely remembered eating and sleeping because it was all a blur. Maybe there was something to the Jewish mourning period they called Shiva. Wasn't that also the name of a Hindu goddess? His mind struggled briefly with the concept, and settled around the finality of "seven days." The ancients must have been aware of some paranormal context to the number seven: seven days to the week, Seven Wonders of the World. Focus! He shook his head and his brain screamed for focus: What now? What next?

The day after the attack that destroyed America, Thursday, January 9, 2015, he had gone to the Fort Myer make-shift morgue and claimed her body so that he could bury her –both of them- properly. The Old Guard had kept Specialist Brown's word and paved the way for an expedited burial at Arlington due to Jude's veteran status. Because of the large number of 8 January casualties most formalities were waived or postponed. Angie and baby boy Winthrop were laid to rest in a niche at the newest Arlington National Cemetery expansion that Saturday morning, January 10, 2015. Maybe that would bring him some sort of closure, he thought. Hamlet's tortured "consummation devoutly to be wished."

Five days after their burial, he felt the track of one more tear make its way down his right cheek, followed by a cadence of muted sobs from deep in his chest; a chest that also held explosive anger.

He stumped down the carpeted steps to the first floor foyer, and almost tore the townhouse's front door off its hinges on his way out. Funny, there was no squeaking this time. The squeaking of the fake brass hinges used to wake up Angie in the mornings as he left for work. The squeak would wake her up and trigger another bout of nausea. He would curse the cheap bastard who built the house; and then himself for forgetting again to put some WD-40 on the damned things. And, now that it didn't matter anymore, the freaking hinges did not squeak. Go figure. If only the squeak still mattered!

He jumped into his battered brown Wrangler with the faded canvas top and coaxed the engine to start. And, it did, as if it knew that this was not the time to mess with Jude. He put it in gear and the Jeep found its own way out of the townhouse complex and on to Falls Road. He did not remember how he got there, nor if he had heeded the four stop signs that usually slowed the ride into the Potomac artery. At the speed he was driving it was a good thing that Falls Road was deserted except for one or two furtive, non-descript dark cars, and those were speeding too. Not a single Montgomery county cop could be seen, which was just as well.

He followed Falls Road west to where MacArthur Boulevard entered Great Falls Park, and then south into the northern entrance to the Clara Barton parkway. This was the long way, but he sought the familiar comfort of the trees that sheltered the drive. The leaves were all gone, and he would have usually missed them in the winter. But he didn't this time.

Entering the Parkway, he passed on his left the long warehouses with the curved top of the Carderock Naval Surface Warfare Research Center. He clicked on his favorite radio station, WTOP, like he always did, as if the "traffic and weather on the eights" mattered at this point. Fussing with the radio controls, he totally missed the unusual level of activity at the eternally quiet naval facility. He didn't notice that the Wrangler was the only car on the road. And there was music playing on WTOP; something quiet and classical. It did not register with him that the station was normally all news and weather and traffic. He wasn't quite listening anyway. He just wanted continuity and white noise.

He headed south on Clara Barton towards Canal Road, the scenic Maryland twin to Virginia's George Washington Parkway. The bushy parkways lined both sides of the Potomac River as it spread out from the nation's capital and the Northern Virginia shore. These roads were arguably the most beautiful in the world, although they were hell when it rained or snowed. Clara Barton and its continuation, Canal Road, ran along the Chesapeake and Ohio Canal, built in the early eighteen hundreds to take the barge trade from Washington and Northern Virginia all the way to Ohio.

In the 18th and 19th centuries, the Potomac's basin was a major tobacco distribution area. The Potomac could not be used for the trade because of two sets of falls north of the capital area: Great Falls and Little Falls. So it was decided to build a canal that could carry the trade up to Ohio. By 1850 they had completed 74 of the canal's locks which would permit the barges to navigate to the northern markets. The Canal extended north from Georgetown 185 miles to Cumberland, Maryland. Its construction stopped there because it could not compete with the Baltimore & Ohio railroad. Instead of tobacco, it was switched to transport coal until the 1920's. These thoughts rang out in Angie's voice, and he wondered if she had pointed out this little piece of history to their visitors from Algeria.

When he stopped at the red light at Chain Bridge, the radio station came alive: "The US Provisional Military Government requests that all State Department employees, repeat, all State Department employees report to the Harry S Truman building this morning. Department Annexes throughout the city are closed. Employees should report to the C Street entrance of the Truman building. They will be directed from there to their temporary duty stations. There will be announcements concerning other government departments within the hour."

The Chopin mazurka came back and filled the void of his thoughts.

Hey, hold on! At that instant, with almost a jolt, the fact that the news radio station was playing music and the intrusive announcement registered in Jude's mind. The cynical curl that appeared on his lips heralded thoughts of other times and other places.

He remembered other radio stations in other countries. West Africa came immediately to mind. He would fly into a given area for urgent State Department missions-mainly refugee coordination-during military takeovers. People who lived there had learned to read the signs that a "coup d'état" and the imposition of martial law was taking place. Normal programming in radio and television stations would be preempted. The radio and TV stations oozed martial and classical music, interrupted sporadically by official announcements asking people to remain in their homes, or imparting pertinent instructions to government workers. From time to time the military junta would broadcast its takeover rationalization to the citizens, usually rampant corruption and crimes against the people. There were also dire warnings for those who failed to obey the new authorities.

But this was America. Coups d'états don't happen here. We don't get dire warnings from the government and instrumental music in news stations, he told himself. We get news.

What was it in that announcement that stuck to his mind…temporary duty stations? What was the meaning of "All employees to report to the Harry S. Truman building?" Why wouldn't they go to the normal sprawl of State Department annexes? These questions bothered him.

He was confused, and the fog of his consciousness lifted just enough for him to realize that he was confused. He had to stop and think.

He saw the break in the stone barrier of the road and twisted the Wrangler's steering wheel into a sharp right to the road that went down to Fletcher's Boat House on the eastern shore of the Potomac. He found the quiet he needed in the deserted parking lot, shook the cobwebs from his mind, and tried to figure out why he had such a bad feeling about all this.

CHAPTER 5 – Flashback

"...the heart's memory eliminates the bad and magnifies the good, and that thanks to this artifice we manage to endure the burden of the past." Gabriel García Márquez, <u>Love in the Time of Cholera.</u>

1245 hours, January 8, 2014

Jude looked out of his Foggy Bottom fifth floor window with intense boredom. On his desk was the text of a demarche to the German government on something or other concerning the environment. He was amazed that some of his colleagues in the Bureau of Oceans, Environment and Scientific Affairs would think only about their provincial issues, blinding them to the real problems of nurturing major European economies.

And all for what? At end of the day, some lowly "Beamter," civil servant in Berlin would accept the not-so-earth-shattering demarche from a too polite mid-level officer from the American embassy, with the usual cynicism. Funny thing about these demarches: from the old French to "take steps to" they had turned into the daily fare of diplomacy, with armies of diplomats from all countries "demarching" foreign ministries and each other. They ranged from the ridiculous to the sublime. This diplomatic crap made him yearn for his simpler Army days: the job of the US infantryman was to find the enemy, kill him or capture him, and then do it all over again.

From his 5th floor window he looked across to the other sidewalk on C Street – a city street which, like many others, had been blocked since September 11, 2001. There was a band of demonstrators chanting into a megaphone against American interference in the affairs of their former country.

Another person would have been mildly interested, but Jude had more important things on his mind. For one thing, Angie was somewhere nearby serving as tour guide to a couple they had met and befriended in Algiers. He smiled at the thought that the Abdelkaders had made good their threat to visit Angie and Jude when they got to Washington.

He was back in the States for the first time in the five years since he was sworn in as a Foreign Service Officer. Foreign Service Officer. That was the modest title the tax payers gave American diplomats, to prevent their heads from getting all swollen at the world-wide admired status they enjoyed. It was the closest one could get to some sort of an American title of nobility.

At the end of his five years as an Army Ranger officer he had taken the unbelievably hard written test, followed by the exasperatingly difficult oral exam and the final medical security and "suitability" scrub. This last obstacle consisted of a thorough examination of his qualifications and travails by wizened old owls whose job it was to predict whether Jude would do well as a member of America's most exclusive club. He had passed with flying colors and was sent immediately to the hot spots in North Africa and the Middle East.

After completing compulsory "career enhancing" tours in Afghanistan and Algeria he was back in Washington, where he had bid and landed the job of Assistant Desk Officer for Germany. He was theoretically supposed to help coordinate American foreign policy with that country. In reality, the phalanxes of junior officers like him were just mere "gofers" for their regional bureaus, in his case the Bureau of European and Eurasian Affairs.

The Bureau was in turn a collection of gofers for the Undersecretary for Political Affairs…who ran errands for the Secretary…whose job was to take crap from the White House and distribute it evenly around the State Department building and annexes. As he pondered this scatological table of organization, the demonstrators outside his window got louder, and then his phone rang.

"German Desk, Jude Winthrop speaking" his voice was almost bored in anticipation of some other meaningless task thought up by the Department's bureaucracy.

"Hi baby" Angie chirped brightly, immediately improving his outlook.

He sat up in his chair at the sound of her voice. "Hey Angie, how is it going with our tourists?"

"Going great, Honey. We are at the Air and Space Museum right now having a blast. Listen, do you think you could tear yourself away from your desk to have dinner with us tonight, after I drag them out to see the illuminated White House?"

"I don't know, Babe," Jude answered, putting on the tone of the exasperated bureaucrat. "I am working on a document on which rests the very fate of the world. My boss would probably have a stroke at my leaving the office earlier than 10 p.m. when most normal people are happily at home, sitting in front of the tube. He is probably sharpening his pencil right now looking forward to correcting my draft on the environment, changing "happy" to "glad" and rearranging commas and periods."

He laughed out loud and chuckled "Get real, Winthrop! I'd be so fucking glad to get out of here before ten that I can taste it. I can't wait to break bread and sip wine with my favorite girl and our friends. Seriously, with any luck my last meeting will end a little before eight and we could meet somewhere downtown. Where would you like to meet?"

"There is always Georgetown. Clyde's comes to mind," she said in a honey-laced voice, taunting him hesitantly. It was more of a rascally provocation than a suggestion. Angie knew how much he disliked Georgetown and wanted to egg him on.

"Right!" he said in an indignant voice with rising exasperation. "All day long they shove me around this building's endless hallways, and you want me to get pushed around some more by the preppy crowds in Georgetown-after-dark?"

Then, realizing that she was just playing him he conceded more calmly, "OK, you got me. You always know how to push my buttons!" You could literally 'hear' his smile as he capitulated to his favorite prankster.

"OK, how about this? We could take them to the Taverna del Alabardero on 17th Street. It's pricey, but we owe these guys a bunch of meals. Besides, they do those garlic shrimp you love; only, no ice cream with them, or some other pregnancy weirdness, OK?"

This last phrase came out more lovingly scolding than forbidding.

"Yummy!" she squealed. "Shrimp and ice cream. You read my mind!" He heard her laugh with that deep, throaty sound that turned him on. "Seriously, Jude," she said almost mockingly. "I promise to be entirely normal."

"OK," he said. "I'll put this demarche thing through the clearance process, go to the inter-agency meeting, and meet you at the Taverna around eight. Deal?"

"Deal! We'll look at some more spaceships, and then wander over to the Indian Museum. We'll grab lunch there. I've been dying to try the cedar roasted salmon at the museum's Café. Jesus! Before the baby comes out I'm going to blow up like a balloon; all this food!" she stopped imperceptibly while she seemed to salivate and then compose herself

"OK. As I was saying: after the Indian Museum we'll do part of the Smithsonian on American painters or something. The exercise will do the baby good, and we should reach the White House around eight or so. The Abdelkaders want to see it from the outside. We didn't get a chance to register for the morning tour because it was cancelled due to the government sequestration. They don't want to leave Washington without seeing it, even if it's only from the outside. From there we'll take a cab to the restaurant. How does that sound?"

He thought that Angie had really warmed up to her role as tourist guide, like everything else she did. "Sounds good to me, Babe. See you tonight. And Angie, you all might be better off walking to the restaurant instead of taking a cab. Don't forget tonight is the State of the Union speech and even if you do find a cab the streets are going to be gridlocked."

There was a pause followed by a very soft "Jude? …I love you."

"I love you more…" almost whispering their old give-and-take…

1948 hours, January 8, 2014

After an endless interagency meeting on the third floor, Jude rushed back to 'the Desk' and grabbed his trench coat from behind his office door. He waved goodbye at Lakeesha, the Director's Office Management Specialist who was busy on the phone, and who smiled with envy at Jude's being able to go home 'so early'. Despite the lateness of the day, he pointed to his cell phone, signaling that he was leaving the building but could still be reached. One never knew what crisis could come up for which they needed a 'junior gofer'. Just last week there had been another Caucasus earthquake and the predictable 24 hour working group at the Operations Center.

Relieved at his temporary freedom, he stepped into the Washington winter night through the Diplomatic Entrance on C Street, the entrance reserved for important foreign diplomats and high level American bureaucrats from other federal departments. Once out the door, he headed left on C Street through the maze of concrete barriers put there to prevent car bombs from being driven into the building.

He followed C Street dashing through the hubbub of busy traffic on the side streets of the nation's capital, even at this hour. As he turned left into 17th Street from the alley on the north side of the Organization of American States building, he caught sight of the euphemistic 'Old Office Building' in the corner of his eye. It was probably the ugliest building in Washington, but it housed the NSC and other random White House staffers. Just as he thought, the place was a zoo due to that night's State of the Union speech.

2006 hours, January 8, 2015

There were black limousines lining the streets. He also saw globs of 'nondescript' but actually very obvious black Secret Service SUVs with tinted glasses and blue lights. Close by there were plenty of police: police on horses, police on bicycles, police on foot. His sense of humor was coming back after losing it during the inter-agency meeting from Hell.

The thought occurred to him that he could become rich right then if only he had a doughnut stand on this corner. He was about to think up a sequel to his mental joke, when the ground shook up…and down…and sideways.

Jude felt his body lift up into the air and fall back down smacking the hard sidewalk. Then, and only then, he heard the blast…and all became a surrealistic scene. The incredibly loud roar. Then the silence. He saw people mouthing unheard screams and felt wet stuff running from his ears. It was a total out-of-body experience.

The Victorian NSC building crumbled as slowly and awkwardly as a fatally wounded cowboy in a class B movie. The roof with the ugly dormers was the first to cave in. Then the northern facade, the one on Pennsylvania Avenue, hit the ground. The gray structure was whole for an instant, then in a powdery smoke the next. The blocked-off stretch of Pennsylvania, the one in front of the NSC and the White House, was sucked into a giant void underground, a giant elongated sink hole. Further ahead and to the right, white portico columns toppled on the White House's grounds, darkening the television lights that had been illuminating them. The sink hole must have crushed the underground utilities because the city went dark.

From his vantage point on the sidewalk, lying on his back, he thought he could see stars in the sky. They were many and they were bright - brighter than the city lights would have allowed. Then darkness came.

2012 hours, January 8, 2015

Slowly, Jude reemerged from the darkness in a daze. His eyes tried to focus and look around in the haze, and could only discern faint things in the dark, the dust and the smoke. A man loomed over him and asked him something he could not really make out, but it felt as if he was asking if he was OK. He nodded more automatically than stoically and the man rushed off to check the next person on the sidewalk. At that point the thought hit him: Angie and the Abdelkaders! They could have been walking by on the way to the restaurant. Oh, God, no!

He felt every muscle in his body hurt at the strain of trying to get up. He couldn't hear a thing. Evidently, the explosion had busted his eardrums. He ran his hands over his ears and felt the twin sticky rivulets of blood that ran tracks down his neck. With a lot of effort he turned his head, then his body towards Constitution Avenue. If Angie and the Abdelkaders were going to look at the White House from the outside, they would have been walking on Constitution and taken the blocked E Street by the Ellipse. That was the best angle for pictures, by the wrought iron fence.

He made his legs move, slowly at first, but then he was running, looking at the human remains strewn along his path. At one point in the carnage that assaulted his consciousness he had to concentrate to remember the telltale signs he was looking for, including what Angie looked like. He searched for the familiar silken golden locks, the turned up nose and the provoking smile. And a slight curvature of the abdomen, especially now. At that thought he broke into a sprint. In his mind he heard himself calling for her, but his mouth only produced silence.

He turned a corner, and the sight shook his heart. Between the Ellipse and the White House's rear fence there was another deep, dark trench. All around it, and sticking out from its shallower segments there were bodies and parts of bodies, some bloody and in strange stages of quivering. Others corpses lay quite still and dignified even in their impalement on the remaining segments of the wrought iron fence. Still some others were awash in death's deep silence, even if the ragged flesh crumpled in horrific little mounds. There, on the left an old man stood in death, supported by a lance from the White House fence through his chest. He had a curious expression on his face, as if wondering how this could have happened to him. Jude helped him to the ground gently, in painless death, and closed his eyes.

He turned to the right and began a mad rush from heap of human debris to heap of human debris. Here was a head with the shoulders still attached; there laid a hand clutching a handbag. He felt somewhat morbidly relieved with every strange mound of flesh and blood and bone he examined and decided that it wasn't her.

Maybe they had made it to the restaurant, or maybe they were rushing to this area, thinking just as he did about them: that Jude could have gotten hurt on the way to the restaurant. He risked looking into the dark trench.

It was useless. It was darkly filled with great chunks of concrete and asphalt, and more quivering flesh.

A 'first responder', recovery team had arrived and was working through the desolation. In what seemed like hours but was more likely just minutes, Jude began to detach himself from the anxiety of finding Angie and thought the decent thing to do would be to help the responders. He approached a blood-stained paramedic and heard himself-hey, his hearing was coming back-ask what he could do to help. The woman looked him up and down with a funny look, mostly with a sense of incredulous pity as if saying "lay down on a stretcher, you fool, you full o' blood." The words remained unsaid because somehow she knew that he was not the type to take that type of rejection despite the shape he was in.

But she felt his need to do something and pointed to a box full of plastic triage labels. "Grab those red tabs and drop them on top of people you think are still alive," she said. He took a full box and her eyes followed him as he embarked on his almost meaningless quest.

Other ambulances were arriving, police cars, fire trucks. There seemed to be a uniform bending over each person on the ground. Amazed, he noted there was already what looked like at least twenty body bags on what was left of the sidewalk. How long had he really been out?

The noise of sirens was deafening, as if he needed that. From around the corner ran four men with Uzis, all dressed in dusty dark suits. Jude's first thought was, "Right! Secret Service. Who are they rushing to protect?"

The foursome ran directly toward the firefighters and the medical personnel and loudly ordered them to cut across the White House's garden, which was still intact and beautiful, and to report to the Secret Service coordination center.

When one of the line backers in dark suits arrived at the woman who had given him the triage labels he growled at her in the heat of the moment: "This means you!"

The woman medic calmly looked up at him as she moved away from the child who had just stopped responding to CPR and said in an annoyed voice "Can't you see I'm busy?" The G-man's temper exploded in the solemnity of the moment. "I'll tell you when and where you get busy, EMS. Grab your bag and move across that garden, right now. There are people out there who really need your help. The ones out here are done."

The statement was so matter-of-fact in its violent connotation that it sent a chill through the medic's spine, and through Jude's. The linebacker turned to Jude and asked, "What the fuck you looking at?"

In the confusion of the moment Jude's response was to fumble for the State Department plastic smart ID hanging from the chain on his chest. He showed it to the USSS man, who shook his head. "The last thing we need now is a State Department asshole", he said sarcastically and added: "We don't have any champagne and caviar to feed you. Clear this area!"

A mounting tsunami of hot blood roared rushing through Jude's head, drowning the junior diplomat and waking up the dormant Ranger captain. The powerful inner self that littered the battlefields of Iraq and Afghanistan with enemy carcasses shone alive in Jude's eyes and pierced the USSS man.

The Ranger instructor the trainees called Uncle Bernie came to his mind's eye. Then he heard the soft menacing warning the NCO used to hiss to make his point to POGS, 'personnel-other-than-grunts': 'the US taxpayer paid for me to learn to kill you in more ways than you can imagine…with pain…without pain, silently…loudly…slowly or quickly…I'm just considering which way you gonna go.'

The G-man saw the look in his eyes and understood the unsaid message respectfully – even though he was the one with the Uzi. The agent turned around and left in silence, never taking his eyes off the strange dude from State.

Putting the incident aside as a lower priority, Jude resumed his silent trek dropping red tags on those he saw breathing or heard moaning. He reached the first row of the black, heavy nylon bags. He was about to turn around when the third bag in that row caused him to freeze in his tracks.

Not fully zipped, it revealed a familiar woolen maternity frock, gray with little flowers. His feet stopped moving. They refused to go further. He forced them to move forward. His heart levitated somewhere outside his chest and hovered over the black plastic.

He knelt by Angie's side and with a trembling hand smoothed the silky strand of blonde hair resting impudently on her forehead. The blood stains were drying over the elegant arch of her brow. He gently ran his right hand over her eyes, closing them. It slid to the belly in a caress so intimately tender that it would have made her sparkle with love if she were alive.

After much discussion on the pros and cons, tomorrow she was going to get an ultrasound that would tell them whether the baby was a boy or a girl.

Even kneeling, his legs refused to continue to hold him upright. There was really little reason for remaining on his feet, nor for anything else. He slowly buckled into one last embrace, with sobs following the primal snarl of great loss.

2035 hours, January 8, 2015

In time, it seemed forever. The first signs of a smoky, hazy dawn enveloped the Washington monument and brought a pair of camouflaged legs to crouch by him and lay a gentle hand on his shoulder.

"Are you OK, sir?" The voice was young. The tone was caring.

He looked at the boy with pitiful, red eyes and continued sobbing into his chest. What the Hell was he going to tell this boy in uniform? The camouflaged legs knelt by him as if in prayer and a hand out of nowhere pushed a paper into Jude's hand. "Sir, I'm Specialist Brown, from the Graves Registration Unit at the Old Guard, The Third Infantry Regiment at Fort Myers. I'd like to get your name and address on this label, so that tomorrow or the day after you can claim your…wife...OK?"

Jude took the boy's pen and mechanically filled in his name, address and phone number in the Next of Kin card; and handed it back to him. The boy, or young man Jude supposed, gave him another piece of paper. "Call this number tomorrow and we will help you out."

It sounded like a well-rehearsed speech, with the finality of all such impersonal speeches from strangers who deal with the dead. But he was young and soft spoken. And Jude felt that the boy knew somehow the gut wrenching pain going on inside him. Jude nodded, and allowed Brown to pull him up. The soldier's eyes stared at Jude's face with concern, and then went over the rest of Jude's body as he helped him to his feet. "You best get yourself looked at, Sir. You've got blood all over. Some seems to have come from your ears."

"Thanks, Specialist." The tone with which Jude said 'Specialist' hit Brown. It was the 'take command' tone of the Army officer. Brown recognized it immediately and it stiffened him, not at attention, but reclaiming the respectful anonymity he wanted to give this superior he had surprised crying. Jude straightened up, still looking at Angie's final plastic shroud. He felt the sobs wanting to return, but a certain inner strength gripped him and he kept them inside. He knew there were things to do. Instinctively, he went into the 'what do I do now' mode ingrained in Fort Benning long ago: observation, orientation, decision, and action (the OODA-loop). That was just what he needed to begin to see things clearly and deal with the chaos of the moment. But first he had to do something about this young man holding him.

Specialist Brown felt the Ranger's muscles coil inside the man he was propping up, and so he let him go as if he had suddenly realized he was holding onto a hot ember. "You're welcome, Sir. There is a cracker box…an ambulance…right there. The guy's cool. He'll help you out."

He was convinced that Jude would not listen to him, but he had to move on to the next victim. There was so much to do, Oh God.

Jude looked into his eyes and said softly, pleading. "Right. Are you going to take care of her?"

And the boy knew just what to say "Yes, sir, personally. I'll take good care of her. I'll be gentle."

Jude was all business now, even though his eyes kept flickering back to Angie's body bag. "Thanks, Specialist." He quickly wrote in the graves registration label Angie's name, and repeated the information he had written in the Next of Kin card, telling the boy "And, there may be two foreign nationals nearby. They were with my wife. They should both have been carrying Algerian passports with the name Abdelkader, Dr. and Mrs. Abdelkader. If you find them, you may want to notify State's Office of Foreign Missions, and they will take care of calling the Algerian Embassy.

"Yes, Sir." The boy almost saluted as the man's shoulders pulled back and his legs began to move toward the ambulance, his eyes still glued on the woman in the black bag.

CHAPTER 6 — Wake Up Call

"When it comes time to die, be not like those whose hearts are filled with the fear of death, so when their time comes they weep and pray for a little more time to live their lives over again in a different way. Sing your death song, and die like a hero going home." Chief Aupumut, Mohican. 1725

0750 hours, January 15, 2015

The iPhone had probably been ringing a while.

"Hey, Steve, what's up?" The caller ID showed Steve O'Neal. Jude answered stretching out of his mental fog, and grabbing for the Wrangler's steering wheel.

"Jude, are you on the way in?" The dry question carried a sense of urgency that was just not like Steve. His buddy would have started less abruptly.

"Yeah, I'm on Canal," Jude said, uncertainty creeping into his tone. He was strangely unwilling to say on the phone that he had been parked at Fletcher's Boat House.

"Listen; let's meet for coffee before you get to the building." Jude's awareness rose. Steve's voice was different. His friend would have normally phrased the question including a jovial deprecatory remark, such as 'the Fog at the Bottom' from the building's location at Foggy Bottom, instead of just 'the building'. Something was up. Otherwise Steve would have suggested the State Department's basement cafeteria as a meeting place. His buddy loved a gooey, sticky pastry they sold there.

"I don't know Steve, WTOP has been broadcasting..." Jude started to explain.

"I know. Forget that. Turn left on Canal and come back up Reservoir to the Starbucks in the supermarket Marti and Angie like to go to. And, Jude...*do it now*."

The phrase that was full of authority also held the click of finality.

The command '*and do it now*' went back to their time in 'the sandbox' the American fighter's nickname for Iraq and Afghanistan. The phrase meant he was dead fucking serious, and he was not giving Jude an option. If Jude had not been altogether awake on his way to the office, then that phrase coming from Steve woke him up. Something was happening that his friend was not free to tell him about on the phone.

Jude hung up without another word, which would indicate to Steve that he had understood the need for secrecy. He turned left on Canal, instead of veering right towards the Whitehurst Expressway. Just as he turned, three Army Humvees thundered by him towards Georgetown at full speed.

0805 hours, January 15, 2015

Steve O'Neal worked at Diplomatic Security and had been assigned as Jude's RSO (Regional Security Officer) counterpart for in-country missions he would conduct to negotiate with Afghani tribal leaders. What could have been a rocky relationship-common between diplomatic officers and security officers in 'the sandbox'-had developed into a lasting friendship.

Years before, Steve had been a Military Police Officer in the Army with assignments that often paralleled Jude's unit or Area of Operations (AO). They didn't know each other then, but they knew of each other through the reputations they had built.

Both had left military service at about the same time, coincidentally landing jobs at the same civilian department. It was kismet, the Turkish word for fate or destiny. Even weirder, they wound up renting neighboring townhouses in the Washington suburbs of Maryland. Steve and his wife Marti began to spend a lot of social time with Jude and Angie. Marti and Angie, homemakers without kids, became the best of friends.

As Jude pulled into the supermarket's small parking lot Steve walked rapidly from his official sedan to the Wrangler, almost dragging two heavy gym bags with one hand as he juggled two hot coffees on the other. At the Wrangler, Steve passed the hot containers to his friend and then threw the bags on the back seat. The heavy clunk of the bags told Jude that there was some heavy artillery in them. Seeing the questioning look in Jude's eyes, Steve sat down on the passenger's seat, signaling "later" with his eyes and buckling his seat belt, while Jude inserted the two coffees into the cup holders.

"How much gas do you have in this thing?" Another strange question from his buddy. Boy, Steve was really going to have to do some heavy explaining.

"I filled it up last night." Jude responded with a growing sense of curiosity and exasperation at Steve's mysterious demeanor.

Steve held his words to a minimum despite there being no discernible prying eyes or ears nearby. "OK, head north and get into MacArthur Boulevard. We then take River off of Falls Road and continue north from there. Clear?"

Jude put the Wrangler into gear and joined the trickle of traffic on Reservoir. Steve was his buddy, but there was just so much that Jude could take on faith. And Steve knew it. So the Special Agent signaled calm with both hands as he began a phone conversation into his Bluetooth headset. He knew that Jude would only get half of the conversation, but he also knew that Jude was savvy enough use that half of the conversation to begin drawing a mental picture of what was going on.

"Marti? I just dumped the official car at the supermarket and got into Jude's Jeep. How far are you?...OK... Sure it's OK to take 70 all the way. Don't stop for gas until Hagerstown if you can manage without. Can you manage? Awesome. OK Sweetie, I'll tell Jude you said so. I'll call you as often as I can, and don't forget to turn off the GPS."

Steve looked at Jude as he said this.

Jude understood immediately and turned off his iPhone's GPS while holding the steering wheel with his other hand. "I gotta go now. Don't forget that I love you, and we will be together soon. So long, Sweet Pea.

As the Wrangler rolled north on Reservoir, Steve faced him and said, "OK, Judeman, hear me out until I finish and then you can ask all the questions you want." There was a quick 'putting-it-together-in-my-head' pause and then "First of all, Marti sends her love." And he continued:

"The Provisional Military Government asked DS to hold you and several other "potentially dangerous" people on account of your Ranger background; that, and your reputation for being a pain in the ass."

He grimaced humorously at the insult. "I had gone to the DS command center before going to Langley this morning, and was the one who answered the phone. So I just said 'Sir, yes Sir', and rushed to the locker room to retrieve some supplies," He pointed at the gym bags behind him "that I had stashed along with my 'bug out' bag. Lucky for me I had parked the official car in front of the building…"

And so Steve brought him up to date as they continued on their journey north.

CHAPTER 7 — The Love and Thanks of Man and Woman

"These are the times that try men's souls. The summer soldier and the sunshine patriot will, in this crisis, shrink from the service of their country; but he that stands it now, deserves the love and thanks of man and woman." Thomas Paine, Pennsylvania Journal, December 19, 1776

America Groans

Steve had been working overtime in the aftermath of the bombing. Confusion reigned, but not so much as to confound the thinking man. While Jude decompressed in the townhouse after putting his wife and unborn child to rest, official Washington was collectively shaken by the developments. Everyone understood that they had been left without a government, but more importantly, without a Commander-in-Chief.

In seven short days the word had spread like wild fire about Admiral Greco. He had put together a group of yes men-and women-whose only attribute was that they were hungry for power and saw the collapse of the republic as their only chance to rise to prominence.

The DS Special Agent had been working as a State Department Security Liaison at the CIA Operation Center in Langley. From his perch on top of the world as seen by the CIA, he could see and understand the state of the country. It was not only Washington that got hit. Most major patriotic symbols in the US had been destroyed by the Iran-supported terrorist cells.

But what was even scarier than that, Steve saw Greco consolidating his position, something that didn't smack of democracy and the American way. Among the many tell-tale signs that tipped him off was a scary order issued by Greco's circle to put the Second Amendment on hold. He ordered the ATF to confiscate all registered weapons nationwide. The FBI was told to coordinate with state police forces to disarm all holders of concealed carry permits. Military Police Units were dispatched to confiscate arms and ammunition at gun shops and National Guard armories.

As these orders whisked by his screen, Steve kept thinking to himself how all these directives went against the very grain of freedom and individual liberties that he loved so much. It was clear that all power would consolidate in the military government that Greco controlled. Civilian agencies like State would be neutralized, at best. The six-foot-four Irishman knew what he had to do. This situation went counter to all he believed and all that he and his friends had fought for.

Had Greco wanted to do so, he could have taken immediate, effective steps to restore civilian government to power and renew American democratic institutions. Despite the terror attacks on the national symbols, the state Governors could temporarily appoint new members of Congress through the state legislatures. The military services had efficient regulations in place to replace on an 'acting' basis those who had died in the Capitol until a reconstituted Senate could confirm them.

The Judicial system could still function up to and including the District Courts and the Court of Appeals. Matters requiring the Supreme Court could wait until new Justices were appointed. The civilian departments had deputies who were in the 'acting' category to replace the Cabinet secretaries. A civilian government could be put into place in a short period of time and restore normalcy.

But it soon became clear that Greco didn't want to restore democracy. Steve could not believe how freedom was snatched so swiftly from the hands of the one people on this earth who, better than any other, was the repository of the flame of liberty. He had to do something, and he knew just who among all his friends he could trust to do what was needed. And Steve was not alone. Many people in America knew what they had to do.

The things Steve had told him made Jude snap out of the funk in which he had lived for the past seven days. A warm blanket of outrage enveloped him and thawed the despondency which started when he first laid eyes on Angie's mangled body. Here was his call to action.

Steve was doing the right thing. For this to work there would have to be more than two persons willing to oppose Greco, and to restore freedom to America. Americans had a big job ahead of them.

Jude turned to Steve and told him he was going to cut across the Chain Bridge into Virginia. That it was Steve's turn to be quiet while Jude made a few calls of his own. There was big machinery to be put into operation.

A national resistance and insurrection

Jude and Steve were not the only ones in the country who felt the vibes and were resolute in protecting American freedom.

Faster than anyone would have predicted, entire Reserves and National Guard units organized themselves into commands that were independent from the National Command Authority in Washington, and independent from any other command authority, such as the State Governor or regional alliances. The first units to secede and succeed were in the West, where confusion reigned after the Republic's collapse. A group of independent military units tentatively organized themselves into what would later be called the National Rebel Command and assume the mantle of authority over non-Greco forces.

The National Rebel Command set up headquarters at the foot of the Rockies, in the buildings of the former Lowry Air Force Base, in Aurora, Colorado, near Denver. It took a while to gain control, to coordinate and decentralize personnel and property records so that the Rebs could take stock of the available personnel and equipment. The pluses for this location included the tenancies of the Defense Finance and Accounting Service (DFAS) and the Air Reserve Personnel Center. The new command would use both as data platforms for reconstituting personnel and financial systems essential to the running of a defense establishment.

That also meant that Greco's forces were deprived of their services, dealing a substantial blow to their ability to operate. The toughest call for the former general officers was to ignore the frantic orders coming out of Washington. But before long they had restored some sort of support bureaucracy for the anti-Greco resistance in America.

The Navy was the one arm that stood solidly behind Greco for the longest time through a combination of loyalty and 'what else can we do at sea?' syndrome. This obedience lasted until Greco gave the Pacific contingent orders to yield control of the seas to "our Chinese friends, who will join us in protecting America during this emergency". That was something that few old-time sailors could swallow. But the Chinese had taken swift steps to neutralize a naval response by landing in force at most key naval installations on the West Coast, even before their beachhead in America was stabilized.

Credit must be given to private enterprise, which kept essential infrastructure working. This included utilities and communications; some banking, health care, as well as food distribution. Private concerns also established a system of expanded credits which would allow them to function with near normalcy in the expectation of national recovery. Everyone made sacrifices.

Citizens were the last to respond to the emergency and the subsequent insurrection as a group because they just were neither prepared nor organized to do so. Sure, there were the radical militia and other extremist groups who rapidly took to the hills. A large number or "survivalists" also took to the hills, but due to their lone-wolf approach they were the last to integrate into the Rebel forces.

As the provisional government took additional steps to consolidate its power, such as confiscating personal weapons and banning the sale of ammunition, a number of 2nd Amendment groups and associations organized themselves into urban and countryside guerrillas.

Police forces in a number of small to medium-sized communities put up a credible fight against the advancing Islamic Militia, but the cops were crushed in the end by the sheer numbers of the Militia which had assumed the responsibility for local law enforcement in

Greco-held territory.

CHAPTER 8 — Greco

...And I know if I'll only be true
To this glorious quest
That my heart will lie peaceful and calm
When I'm laid to my rest

And the world will be better for this
That one man, scorned and covered with scars
Still strove with his last ounce of courage
To reach the unreachable star.
"The Impossible Dream" from MAN OF LA
MANCHA (1972)

Humble beginnings

The grandson of poor Italian immigrants, Joseph Greco graduated from the Naval Academy at Annapolis with honors. Its engineering curriculum was no match for his mathematical talents, and its leadership training was no match for his ego. He maintained a 4.0 average and graduated as brigade commander, the top midshipman grade. His main challenge at Annapolis was taking orders from upperclassmen when he was a plebe…and, oh yes, taking orders from female midshipmen…or were they supposed to call them "midshipwomen?" That had sounded to him like a reference to pirate wenches tied to the main mast awaiting sexual punishment by the crew.

Greco had taken careful note of those who carried out the traditional hazing. He would deal with each and every one of them throughout his 30 year career, including the women; especially the women. Joe Greco was not one to forget.

A week after graduation and commissioning day Joe married Martha Huntington, a Maryland heiress who had instinctively known 'her place', and who brought lots of extra money into the marriage. She had also known how to take care of her man, her kids and her home, while he sought on the high seas the glory he knew he deserved.

As time went by, Joe realized that Martha wouldn't fit the role of First Lady. A Greco First Lady had to be young and beautiful, like Jackie Kennedy. During the first week of his appointment as Chief of Naval Operations (CNO), Admiral Greco informed Martha that after thirty years of marriage she would not be attractive enough to handle the role when he got elected. He dumped her for the young and beautiful Amanda Wellington and he was glad he did, too. What a great piece of ass Amanda was!

Destined for bigger things

Joe Greco had always been an opportunist. When he got appointed CNO he knew that this was as much power as the Navy could give him. He immediately began a cunning and systematic courtship of Washington power-brokers on both sides of the aisle.

It wasn't strange for a military man to aspire to high civilian office. George Washington began that tradition, although if historians are to be believed, he had served as president almost reluctantly. Of the 43 presidents since Washington, only 12 had not served in the military. This list included Obama, Clinton, FDR, Hoover, Coolidge, Harding, Wilson, Taft, Cleveland, Van Buren, John

Quincy Adams and his father John Adams. So Greco decided to play up his military service for all it was worth.

Like so many flag officers before him Washington society courted Joe Greco. Many of the powerful people he met suggested a natural progression to the House or even the Senate. Some spoke of governorships. But Greco only had eyes for the top of the heap.

He really didn't have a party preference. When he was with Democrats he was a loyal minion to President Obama. When he met with Republicans he would roll his eyes at the mention of the Commander-in-Chief. By the time Al Qaeda blew up the White House and the Capitol, Greco had built himself a political base within both parties that would support his presidential bid when he retired from the Navy.

In fact, he had really stayed away from the 2015 State of the Union Speech not because his head cold was all that bad, but because he didn't want to have to stand up to applaud Obama and piss off the Republicans, or to remain seated at the wrong moment and piss off the Democrats.

Opportunity comes knocking

Admiral Joe Greco was preparing to sit down comfortably before the TV set and watch the State of the Union proceedings at his official residence at the Washington Navy Yard when he the whole place shook up. At first he thought that some nearby gas tank had exploded, and so did his security detail.

The house was still shaking when the heavily armed agents rushed into the room and took-almost carried-Greco to the built-in safe room in the CNO residence. By the time the detail secured the steel lined door, they were already getting reports of multiple explosions at the White House and the Capitol. The detail established communications with the Pentagon offices of the Joint Chiefs as Greco stepped out of his robe and into his resplendent Admiral's uniform. Within minutes he was inside a helicopter flying to the Pentagon.

Arriving at the National Military Command Center there, he assumed the title of Acting Chairman of the Joint Chiefs of Staff. The reports of Principal casualties poured in, revealing the scariest scenario imaginable. Everybody was MIA, including the President and the entire succession team. Even Vice President Biden was gone. In a typical display of his usual poor judgment Biden had not gone to a 'safe undisclosed location' but had decided to preside over the Senate during the President's address.

Speculation was rampant. No one knew how the two sites had been so completely obliterated. No one even suspected it to be an act of terrorism. After all, the President himself had been playing down the changing nature of terror organizations for the preceding two years.

The first thing that occurred to the military was an undetected missile attack. The source of a possible missile attack was unknown, but Greco raised the defense posture of the Armed Forces to DEFCON 1.

As the most senior military leader alive, Joe Greco was flown to Camp David, where Air Force One took him up in the air. From Air Force One, Joe Greco made the only call he could have made in those circumstances. He informed the nation that he was in control until relieved by proper civilian authorities much like then Secretary of State and former general Alex Haig had done during an attempted assassination of President Reagan in the 1980s.

The next few calls went to key political players in both parties, the same people he had been courting for a post-military political career. He told them he needed their help to restore normal government operations as soon as possible. They all pledged to help him with his difficult task. He promised to call them again in the next few days with details of his plan.

The Army of God

Within the first 48 hours of America's collapse the Army of God that American mullahs had put together began to disrupt what little law and order was left in the country. They avoided large cities with sizeable police forces, concentrating initially on small population centers with large Moslem minorities. Although they met with law enforcement resistance, they were soon firmly established in local governments around large cities.

Greco could do little to help the local governments under siege. They would have to wait. As far as he knew the attack on America had been carried out by a foreign nation with missiles. He had to deal with that real possibility first. The Posse Comitatus Act prohibited the use of the US Armed Forces to carry out civilian police functions; and Greco's DEFCON 1 order had federalized all National Guard and reserve units.

Federal civilian law enforcement agencies could not help the small locales. They were busy carrying out the Acting President's immediate orders to prevent civilian unrest by confiscating privately owned firearms and explosive materials.

So the Army of God was free to continue its advance.

By the time he received the offer of cooperation from Army of God's leadership, Greco was more than ready to take it. He had little choice. Here was an armed group causing disturbances, who suddenly offered to help him 'until the emergency was over'. They told Greco that they had come out to defend American Moslems from popular retaliation for the Moslem-inspired attack.

Up until that point, Greco had disregarded the idea of a terrorist attack. It had been too massive, too powerful. But it occurred to him that dealing with a terror attack would have been much easier than dealing with a foreign attack. Maybe the Army of God knew something he didn't?

China

Just when he was getting comfortable with the idea of a terror attack, Chinese strategic aircraft and ballistic missiles began to make mincemeat of Provo air assets on the ground nationwide. So there he was, caught between a rock and a hard place. He took the Army of God's offer so that he could concentrate on the external threat.

The problem with defending against a Chinese external threat was that the missiles with which he could have retaliated were on lock down. The codes which he had needed to enable the activation of America's missile defense were under the rubble at the White House and at the Capitol. The National Military Command Center did not have a full set. So he had to sit there and take the Chinese attack.

When the Chinese contacted him and told him that they only intended to protect their investment and not take over America, Greco breathed a sigh of relief and got ready to negotiate with them to buy time.

NATO

Logically, he should have turned to NATO. But at the time of the attack the forces of the North Atlantic Treaty Organization were under cyclical American military command. That would have been great, but the American commander in place was not only under the organization's jurisdiction, but was also one of the many personal enemies Greco had collected over the years.

General Bill Maier was not the least bit personally inclined to help Greco out of the mess he was in; even if the fate of his country hung in the balance. General Maier's responsibility was to NATO, and the NATO civilian structure voted to delay the implementation of the mutual defense clause until the situation in America was clarified. The clause would have brought NATO forces to America's defense in cases of attack or terror; but it allowed members to opt-out of military action.

To really piss off Greco, Maier convinced NATO to integrate the overseas American forces into its own command until the USA had a proper civilian command structure to call them back home.

NATO was also intimidated by the Chinese attack. None of the members favored getting into a shooting war with China. So, by the time they would have had to make a decision to come to America's assistance, Greco had made his deal with both the Army of God and with China. He decided that NATO assistance would only complicate matters, and told them so. By that time, Greco had decided that he would have a better chance at the American presidency if he proved himself to be the man who had saved America during the present emergency.

The Committee for National Salvation

As he had promised them, Greco called his political patrons and drafted them into a temporary governmental structure, the Committee of National Salvation (CNS). He told them the CNS would help return the country to civilian rule as soon as the emergency was over. Of course, including the deeply divided Democrats and Republicans in the same governing body was hardly a recipe for success. When he also included the Commander of the Army of God, now denominated the Islamic Militia, the Militia's Chaplain and a Chinese observer from their embassy into the CNS, the committee became as useful as teats on a bull.

A bird in hand

Greco changed his mind about running for President. He had the presidency now. He was the Acting Commander in Chief. He controlled the CNS. Putting himself at the beck and call of some political party hack to run for a presidency he might lose in an election was very unappetizing. He was in the right place, at the right time. He currently had more power in his hands than if he were the real, elected president. If he played his card rights he could be in power far longer than the Constitution permitted an elected president. So he set himself to the task of running the country and recuperating the parts that were in the hands of the advancing Rebels, the Islamic Militia, and the Chinese. He knew he was smart enough to find a way.

Besides the CNS, he managed to give key military appointments to people he hadn't made enemies along the way, and who were power hungry enough to do his bidding. He gave temporary promotions to 'yes men'. He was the boss in a time of crisis. He didn't have to cater to women; but he was careful to keep his command racially and culturally diverse, with the sprinkle of women he had inherited. It wasn't wise to buck the *whole* system until he had consolidated his power.

He had to keep the CIA in place. The Director had managed to get himself uninvited from the State of the Union speech to attend to a crisis he had created. He had never really cared for Obama. So, he was alive and firmly in control of whatever the Director of National Intelligence let him do. Greco kept both men out of the CNS. He had enough headaches. Besides, he was toying with the idea of using the Agency's paramilitary units to weaken the Islamic Militia, for which he needed to keep the spooks under his thumb at all times.

Greco decided that the next steps were to stop the Rebels with whatever military units were left in CONUS then decrease Militia numbers by using it as cannon fodder against superior forces, and then by demoralizing the Militia by giving it only menial tasks. Joe Greco knew how to bide his time and maximize his power.

CHAPTER 9 — Making them Dance to his Tune

"The commander must decide how he will fight the battle before it begins. He must then decide how he will use the military effort at his disposal to force the battle to swing the way he wishes it to go; he must make the enemy dance to his tune from the beginning and not vice versa." Field Marshall Bernard Montgomery, 1st Viscount Montgomery of Alamein

1800 hours, January 15, 2015

Steve and Jude had driven south and then west toward Skyline Drive after crossing circuitously into Virginia over the US 15 Bridge. By that time, any potential surveillance would have been confused and defeated.

They arrived at the parking lot of the famous Luray Caverns, where some friends would be joining them. The tourist attraction had been closed since the fall of 2014, when a terrorist bomb made the ancient cave system collapse. Neither the FBI nor ATF had been able to identify the explosive used in the Chechen-style pressure cooker bomb because the collapsing rock walls had buried the forensic evidence. Since there was no one in the caverns when the bomb went off, the investigators had just closed down the site. Years later they would learn that Al Qaeda had used that attack to test the power of the octanonitrocubane they intended to use to bring America to its knees. The test had been successful.

The Luray parking lot was soon filled with the vehicles that brought together one of the first contingents of American Rebels. They formed a small caravan and headed further west. Past Interstate 81 they cut south to Harrisonburg and then west-north-west to Canaan Valley. At the Canaan Valley ski resort they picked up more Rebels and then took Route 219 into 72, which led directly into Kingwood, right across from a West Virginia National Guard reservation. They took the circuitous route on purpose, so that they could get the lay of the land. The word was that people were organizing at Camp Dawson to resist the illegal Greco government.

When they pulled into Camp Dawson they found what Steve colorfully described as an organized clusterfuck. The resistance forces were just groups of people equipped with civilian weapons and not much more. The lucky ones who got there first were able to get into the empty Army barracks.

Camp Dawson was different from most National Guard bases in that it had held the selection process for the legendary Delta Force. But even that process had immediately come to a halt under Greco. His military reorganization disbanded most special forces and reintegrated their members into regular units. So, when Jude, Steve and their friends arrived at Dawson, the Delta facilities were not being used. However, the base's tightly secured arms rooms contained pretty sophisticated weaponry which would later serve the Appalachian Command well.

0600 hours, January 17, 2015

Two days after their arrival, they woke up to the sound of aircraft landing on the base's airstrip. Six C-130s spit out about 500 Kentucky National Guardsmen and their equipment. The West Virginia guardsmen at the camp went out to the airstrip in force. The light colonel commanding them had led a West Virginia National Guard infantry battalion. He approached the lead Hercules and saluted a tall trooper who appeared to be in charge of the arriving troops. The Kentuckian wore no rank insignia, but all around him seemed to acknowledge him as someone of importance.

Jude and Steve grabbed their weapons and high-tailed it to the runway to see what the commotion was all about, and defend the base if it turned out that it was being attacked. Half of the rag tag army that had made Camp Dawson their home was out by the landing strip taking in the show. The Kentuckian surrounded by the camp's welcoming committee started to walk away from the plane towards the camp headquarters building cluster, when he suddenly stopped near Jude and Steve.

He turned right and headed directly towards Jude, leaving the greeting party in mid-stride. Steve looked at Jude and saw a strange smile on his friend's face, sort of between surprised and smug. He then looked at the Kentuckian and saw that he too was holding a smile hostage; a smile that was swallowed by his booming voice. "Look at what the cat dragged in, Colonel," he said turning to the head of the greeting party.

And then he said to both Jude and the West Virginian "Do you know what's up, Colonel?" when no answer was forthcoming he went on "Never mind, I'll tell you what's up" and then in chorus with Jude *the sky, the clouds, bird shit and Airborne Rangers.*" The crowd broke into a hearty laugh at the old Army disparaging remark. The Kentuckian's grin became ferociously wider as he grabbed Jude in a bear hug and lifted him bodily.

Jude could dish it out too. "Hey, Steve," said Jude in words powered by the air being forced out of his lungs by the Kentuckian grip "They sure can pile it high in Kentucky."

"Lookie here, Judeman. You all are out of uniform," said the Kentuckian to Jude as he released him from his hug and put him back down on the ground.

Jude looked up at his friend and told him in a more serious voice, "How ya doing, Ed?"

"Come along with me to wherever these mountaineers are dragging me, Jude. I'm sure they'll have a beer or two to help us catch up." Ed Sumter was a legendary consumer of the brew, with an unjust Army wide reputation for consuming too much.

"Sure. Can my buddy Steve come too?" said Jude pointing to his friend.

Ed stopped and pushed a massive hand at Steve, gripping his proffered hand and saying with a smile "Any friend of Jude's…" stopping in mid-sentence and getting Steve's response of "Good to meet you, sir."

The creation

Jude and Steve fell in step with Ed Sumter as they walked into the camp's headquarters building. The West Virginia guardsmen had a 'dog and pony show' prepared, with even a PowerPoint presentation. Lieutenant Colonel Stu Harrington briefed Sumter on the availability and disposition of two infantry battalions from the West Virginia guard, the extra weaponry left at post by the Delta Force guys, and the fact that he was the highest ranking guardsman since the two-star and his crew had gone over to Washington to kiss Greco's ass. He closed the presentation by telling Sumter that what was left of the Guard in the Mountaineer State was at Sumter's orders and disposition.

Sumter got up next and thanked the Lieutenant Colonel for his hospitality. He turned to the group, lifted his can of Bud, and told them "In the name of the National Rebel Command, I hereby accept the incorporation of the West Virginia Guard into the Appalachian Command." His pronouncement was followed by loud hooting and hollering, but mainly Army 'Hooahs', especially from the crowd that had gathered outside the building. The Kentuckian knew how to play an audience and continued, "The purpose of this here Command is to bring pain and consternation to one Mr. Joseph Greco, usurper of power in the country we all love and which we promise to bring back in all its glory. May God bless the United States of America" which was again followed by much hooting, hollering and stomping of boots.

The two Kentucky infantry battalions, one which arrived in the C-130s and another on the way by land, together with the West Virginia contingent had the combined strength of a reinforced brigade. This minuscule contingent would have to fight an enemy which was ostensibly superior in number and equipment, but lacking in legitimacy.

He then turned to the West Virginian Lieutenant Colonel and said, "We haven't yet figured out a rank structure for the Appalachian Command, except that those of us in charge of something are called 'Commander'. We do this for several very practical reasons. For one thing, it's been my experience that the enemy, any enemy, just loves to shoot those in command.

Personally, I don't relish getting shot, and I'd like to confuse them as long as I can to prevent chain of command losses.

Secondly, many of our civilians-turned-soldiers wouldn't know how to tell apart a sergeant from a general, and we have precious little time to train on military courtesy. I'd rather spend that time teaching our troops how to kill the enemy.

Finally, we need to ensure that our leadership inspires the troops. That doesn't mean that we are not going to have a rank structure in the Rebel Armed Forces." This was the first time that Jude and Steve heard the name of the anti-Greco force. "All it means is that we are going to take care of important business first, and worry about saluting later. For the time being, I'm just handing out commands. When the National Rebel Command in Colorado finishes the organization of the troops loyal to the real United States of America, we'll have a chance to transform ourselves into full-fledged armed forces.

They told me yesterday that they would like me to lead the Appalachian Command for now, and that I should make whatever operational appointments I need to take the fight to Greco with some sort of cohesion. Colonel Harrington" said Sumter turning to the West Virginian "with the authority vested in my by National Rebel Headquarters I appoint you Commander of the West Virginian contingent. Please do what you need to do to get them ready to move by land towards Washington the day after tomorrow at 0600.

I will make my temporary headquarters right here in this room. I would appreciate meeting with you and your staff tomorrow at 0800 hours to talk about our upcoming campaign. That's all. Dismissed... Jude and Steve, you all stay behind. We have to talk." The group and the outside crowd sounded off a simultaneous "Yes, Sir" that got Sumter to look at them funny.

0825 hours, January 17, 2015

Ed Sumter was very good at putting the right people in the right places. Within two hours of the organizational briefing, he had asked Jude to go around the camp identifying Ranger or other special operations personnel and putting together a Commando Unit to operate behind enemy lines, interdicting and harassing Greco's troops. He gave Jude proxy authority to detach from their current units the personnel he selected.

He also told Jude that he intended to use the C-130s and the Delta Force parachutes to drop him and his team behind enemy lines where they could add to Greco's confusion. Since there was no time to train together, Jude should use his best judgment on the selection of the targets they were going to hit.

Learning that Steve had been a Diplomatic Security Special Agent, in addition to an MP officer in the Army, and that he had spent the last two years as a State security liaison with the Central Intelligence Agency, Ed Sumter asked him to put together a "spook" team which could provide paramilitary support for his S-2 military intelligence staff. Steve's unit could infiltrate Greco urban areas, recruit intelligence assets, and carry out para-military intelligence operations in the heart of Greco territory. He wanted Steve's team to travel by land into Greco territory after putting together a plan to establish a spy network in the capital area.

Steve's and Jude's commands were almost interchangeable, except for the combat intelligence mission assigned to Steve's team, and the Ranger warfare operations capability in Jude's unit.

0600 hours, January 20, 2015

At 0600 on January 20, 2015 the Appalachian Command (AC) began its advance towards Washington, DC. At first, there was precious little resistance to the brigade-size force advance. As it went through townships and small cities its S-5 civilian operations unit organized city halls, police and fire departments into part of the Rebel forces. They left most civilian government organizations untouched except for the appointment of a Civil Forces Commander (CFC), a sort of liaison officer with the Appalachian Command. CFCs were trusted military members who had orders to let the civilians govern themselves as they saw fit, and whose main duty was to tell the AC if the town was still loyal, and coordinate their contribution to the war effort.

The CFC was also responsible for organizing the local government into the supply chain that would sustain the AC's operations with whatever the urban entity produced that was of use to the advancing Rebs, paying for the supplies initially with script and later with currency "liberated" from federal accounts.

The West Virginia countryside was not able to contribute much to the supply chain, except for the flesh and blood of its brave young men and women who had joined the advancing the Rebels.

CHAPTER 10 — Off to Battle

"Another woman handed her son his shield, and exhorted him: 'Son, either with this or on this.'" Sayings of Spartan Women, Plutarch's Moralia

1800 hours, January 28, 2015

When the AC crossed into Virginia, resistance from commands loyal to Greco increased. The toughest battle took place at Staunton, where the Virginia National Guard had been federalized into its parent unit at Fort Belvoir, the 29th Infantry Division.

It happened that federal units from Belvoir had joined the 116th Virginia Guard Brigade Combat Team (Stonewall) for exercises that had been scheduled a year before. In the midst of the reigning chaos, Greco had gotten reports of the AC's advance from West Virginia. He took advantage of the scheduled training maneuvers to intercept the attacking Rebs between Staunton and the Charlottesville National Guard armory.

Both Greco and the National Rebel headquarters had made a conscious decision to avoid using heavy air and missile fire power. The hearts and minds of the civilian population were an important concern for both sides. Non-combatant casualties were highly counterproductive. So, what air assets were available were limited to transport troops and supplies and other support functions.

Armor was a different story. What tanks and other combat vehicles were available stateside were put into service from day one. Tankers on both sides were presumed to exercise better damage control than guided missiles. As it turned out, as combat operations increased so did civilian casualties. Except for the areas where Rebel or Provo control was well established, America's normal life had come to a standstill. Civilians either hunkered down in place or left in throngs for safer areas.

The Virginia Area of Operations

Virginia was disputed territory due to its proximity to the nation's capital. So was the land west of the Mississippi. Maryland, with its liberal and docile population, quickly submitted to Greco forces. As its reward, it continued to have a relatively normal social and economic life along with the rest of the East Coast. Minimizing Provo-controlled civilian casualties in this modern day civil war was merely a theoretical concept, interrupted by military operations from time to time. The excesses of Greco government repressive organizations, such as the federal law enforcement agencies, also took its toll in terms of civilian collateral damage.

The Virginia 116th Brigade Combat Team (Stonewall) was the successor to the Civil War's 19th Virginia Regiment, which had been decimated by Union forces at Gettysburg. But that was ancient history now. The Stonewall Brigade was one of the most effective fighting forces in CONUS. Its training was impeccable and the quality of its troops superb. That said, the unit was made up of Virginians; soldiers who were mindful of their pride for their state and its traditions. Stonewall soldiers were painfully aware that the unit's federalization had put it on the side of the usurpers of American power.

Ed Sumter's advance on Staunton took into consideration the Stonewall Brigade's state of mind. Except for Jude's commandos, which quickly jumped into and began to operate in Provo controlled Maryland anyway, the Appalachian Command held its operations against the Stonewall Brigade to the highest standards of traditional military warfare. Civilian targets were scrupulously avoided. Expediency and timing gave way to humane considerations. Stonewall prisoners were treated as brother fighters unfortunately caught up on the wrong side of the tracks.

By the second week of the AC engaging the Stonewall Brigade, its fighters rose against the Greco government and switched their personnel and armament to the Rebel side. The AC welcomed them with open arms and so did the civilian population of Virginia. By the end of March, 2015, the combined forces had advanced to and captured Richmond, turning eyes toward the Washington DC objective. The 111th Field Artillery Battalion set up shop at Charlottesville and used its considerably effective firepower to help the Rebels take and hold the western shore of the Potomac River.

Regular army troops from the Carolinas, Georgia and the Deep South reinforced the Greco forces. Texas, with its large contingent of regular troops and National Guard remained aloof along with the other Southwestern states, refusing to join either side. By December 23, 2017, the war had come to a standstill. The Provos held the largest portion of the East Coast, curving west into Illinois. The Rebs stopped at the Potomac River, south of the Maryland border, hoping to receive material assistance from National Rebel Headquarters in Colorado. The Colorado headquarters was busy fighting the Chinese, who had controlled that area of operations since April, 2016.

As for the rest of the world, the United Nations in New York produced its ubiquitous useless resolutions stating that the Americans should stop their war. NATO had appropriated the overseas American forces, integrating them into their European command with the relieved consent and collaboration of its commanders, preventing them from returning to CONUS and taking sides. And the rest of the world just looked up from their religious perches to see which side would emerge victorious.

Israel and Kosovo

There were two notable exceptions: Israel and Kosovo. In the early days of the American conflict, Israel had announced for the first time that it possessed nuclear weapons, and brought them out to convince its enemies that they would not hesitate to use them. Immediately after the January attack on America, Israel leveled the Iranian nuclear plants, rendering Iran unable to nuke anyone. The Islamic Republic retained the ability of shelling out money and religious influence, but little else.

Israel also sent an Israeli Defense Forces (IDF) battalion to fight alongside Rebel forces, flying them to Dulles International Airport, where they took over the facilities previously held by the German Bundeswehr. The Israeli contingent held its ground, denying German air assets to the Greco government. By the time the Appalachian Command began its attack on the Greco controlled territories, the Israelis stood ready to train Rebel contingents at their facilities, fielding mobile training teams as their initial contribution to the fighting.

The Republic of Kosovo, along with other Western Balkan volunteers sent 300 Albanian fighters to help the Rebs. The help was substantial and the Kosovars gave a good account of themselves. They had always been grateful for the American help they had received when

Serbian extremists were trying to exterminate them through carefully orchestrated genocide.

The 300 fighters the Kosovars provided were also valuable in a symbolic sense: Kosovo was predominantly Islamic, with small Christian minorities. The Kosovars were also known for having saved Jews fleeing the Nazis in WWII. So there was a natural sympathetic compatibility between the international forces in the Rebel camp. Their presence on the side of the Rebels also gave food for thought to those in America who thought about the conflict in religious terms.

In practical terms, the Kosovo contingent messed up the Islamic cohesiveness sought by the Army of God/Islamic Militia members, sapping their effectiveness as a pro-Greco fighting force. The Kosovo contingent was stationed at Dulles with the Israelis until the Appalachian Command began its advance. It then joined the Rebel command in Northern Virginia.

CHAPTER 11 — All Hell's Breaking Loose

"I would like you to remember that no bastard, ever, won a war by dying for his country. He won it, by making the other poor, dumb bastard die for his country."
General George S. Patton, 1944

1830 hours, January 8, 2018

So he had felled the point man. Jude knew what that meant. The standard military response to an ambush was to hug the ground and return massive fire in the direction of the enemy, as the fire teams covered each other's counterattack. The poorly trained Militia would be unpredictable.

Finishing this thought at the end of a nanosecond, Jude embraced his sniper rifle and slipped out from under the Ghillie blanket, rolling silently and slowly down the slope toward the C & O Canal. This was a route he had pre-smoothed and tested for his exfiltration. Prior to setting up on his sniping position the night before last he had carefully walked the exit chute to ensure it was clear of stumps, jagged rocks, and rustling vegetation that could draw attention to his downward roll. More importantly, he made sure that the route would get him down to the canal fast.

It took a few seconds more than normal for the patrol to try to touch base with the dead point man. Then, all Hell broke loose. The patrol let out massive fire, but since they could not pinpoint the source of the silenced shot that killed their advance man their shots went wildly all around, and its fire teams remained glued to the ground instead of advancing by fire and maneuver. Greco's line units had given the Army of God only three hasty weeks of the most basic military training, so he didn't expect them to return fire effectively. But the patrol was only about 150 yards from Jude. It was only a matter of time before its leader guessed where the sniper had been and directed their fire upon the knoll, first from their own small arms and then from on-call mortars, artillery or even close-support aircraft.

Jude felt and smelled the mud as he rolled into the canal's murky, shallow water. Once immersed, he grappled blindly with the familiar bottom slime immersed under three feet of green, frigid water. He made his way in the general direction of a clump of bushes on the other side of the canal. That clump of bushes would hide his climb up the far bank onto the narrow dirt trail at the leafless tree line.

Unseen and unheard, Jude came up the other side, flanked by the hardy evergreen vegetation. He crawled over the bicycle path and rappelled down the rocky ledge of the Billy Goat Trail to the Potomac cove where he had hidden his Klepper kayak.

The kayak bore its gray skirt to cover the brilliant blue exterior. He put the sniper rifle into the cockpit, retrieving from its depths his more manageable M-4, which he hung around his neck. In one practiced move he pushed the Klepper into the water, sliding smoothly into the cockpit. He pushed away from the shore bushes with his right hand, retrieving the paddle from its holder with his left. In no time he was paddling into the treacherous but welcoming rapids that would carry him to the relative safety of the Virginia bank of the Potomac.

He had chosen this route because the rapids to the north would mask paddling noise, and the current would take him behind a big boulder on the Virginia side where he could stow the kayak for future use. Jude had often come kayaking in these rapids with a bunch of friends from Rockville, even though Angie hated it.

As he paddled across, the Militia patrol on shore was reacting just as furiously and ineffectively as Jude had predicted, creating a gap north of the ambush site. The way was clear for the Sibley snatch team.

With well-rehearsed dexterity he landed, hid the Klepper and began to negotiate the uphill riverside into the Virginia woods just as Provo 81 mm and 4.2 inch mortars began hitting the ambush site, and who knows what else, killing all kinds of trees, but not a single Reb.

CHAPTER 12 — The Ghost Walks

"Ghost - My hour is almost come,
When I to sulphurous and tormenting flames
Must render up myself"
Act I, Scene V, Hamlet, William Shakespeare

1858 hours, January 8, 2018

Climbing the steep embankment Jude's mischievous spirit emerged. It was time to test the security of the Appalachian Command Headquarters (forward) that is, the headquarters element actually in the field. He had agreed with Ed to so from time-to-time. Unlike the credibly defensible headquarters complex at Woodbridge, Virginia, AC (forward) was merely a collection of reinforced trenches from which Commander Ed Sumter could push his advance into the Capital Region.

Following traditional infantry doctrine the trenches would get improved daily until it was time to continue the attack or begin a retrograde action. The initial two-man foxholes would first be widened, then given a grenade sump and drier wooden floors to prevent foot rot. Time and enemy fire permitting, the holes would be dug deeper and covered with timber, red Virginia clay, and natural vegetation to minimize the effect of artillery or mortar proximity fuses and precipitation, all in that order.

When additional support troops could get there, the forward headquarters could get fancier. At this stage, listening posts (LPs) had been added a distance from the main bunker cluster to give early warning of approaching enemy recon patrols. This was followed by stringing field telephone commo wire between the main trench cluster and the listening posts to make communications more secure than by radio. Really fancy forward headquarters would even have cooking facilities for hot meals and, bathrooms, showers and infirmaries.

Ed had decided against getting too fancy because he believed that too many comforts made fighters soft and complacent and reduced their drive to attack and advance. So forward Appalachian Command (AC) personnel ate field rations and went to the bathroom in cat holes dug in the bush. The misery was attenuated by periodically scheduled rotations to and from Woodridge and closer troop areas. Returning forward elements would be replaced by fresh troops from the rear. Ed and his close staff would stay put for the duration.

Listening posts were simple affairs with a fighter in a Ghillie suit lying in a shallow trench with a field telephone, rotated every few hours. Initially, everyone pulled listening post duty except essential staff personnel. As the AC advance consolidated on the west bank of the Potomac a perimeter security element was brought up from Woodridge to allow fighters to return to duty and beef up patrols.

AC (forward) was not at a secret location. It had long been located through satellite imagery and side-looking radar. But it was so close to Northern Virginia population centers that the Provos were reluctant to use heavy weapons to destroy it. They'd rather use that against the Woodridge rear elements; but were again constrained by the potential for collateral civilian damage. The new American Civil War had its challenges.

1905 hours, January 8, 2018

Jude approached the headquarters area with as much stealth as if he were infiltrating enemy territory. After a while observing the LP relief pattern (patterns of any kind were against doctrine but where there nevertheless), he determined which LP had been out the longest and began his infiltration through that area, banking on the principle that alertness diminished towards the end of the watch. He sidestepped around the chosen LP, and went by the location not three yards from the prone Ghillie-suited fighter.

The next perimeter security obstacle was the line of outward bunkers, which he found following the commo wires, and whose foxhole buddies would rotate watch hours among themselves. Jude noted that the same alertness principle applied. Since these bunkers knew where the LPs where, its fighters would focus on other possible approaches. So Jude approached using the LP direction until getting almost on top of the outward bunker he had selected. He then circled around it unnoticed to continue his infiltration.

Once beyond the outward perimeter he felt sufficiently confident to 'ghost walk' upright and unchallenged right up to the headquarters sentry, who was enjoying a cigarette cupped in his hands. Ghost walking was a difficult technique that took patience, extreme care on foot placing, taking advantage of night shadows and natural lighting, and exploiting the human weaknesses of the opposing force.

Materializing behind the unlucky fellow he placed the business end of his Fairbairn-Sykes fighting knife against the sentry's neck. The sentry choked briefly on the smoke and surrendered his weapon when Jude whispered the order from behind his right ear. He then shoved the sentry into the headquarters bunker startling Ed and his staff momentarily. When the staff went for their weapons, he threw the sentry at them and pointed his carbine at the commander. "Drop the weapons or this fucking hillbilly gets creamed!" Jude whispered hoarsely.

Ed broke into a smile and told his staff to "do as the man says."

Jude was hardly a familiar face to AC (forward) command post personnel, except for Ed. He had been a lone-wolf operative since the terrible mission when his commandos were decimated. He received instructions directly from Ed, who kept him away from regular troops for very sound tactical reasons, including contributing to the myth the Provos had built around the man they called the Ghost. Ed had even assigned Jude the radio call sign 'Casper', as in 'Casper the Friendly Ghost' cartoons; a bit of hillbilly humor.

Jude had a non-descript hutch near the CP at AC (forward), but he was seldom there. Neighboring hutch tenants would sometimes see dispersed smoke from its built-in Dakota pit, but seldom its occupant. They knew the hutch belonged to the Ghost. But Jude preferred to be in the field, making Greco's life difficult all by himself. The times that he pulled his surprise infiltration tests coincided with new staff arrivals from the Woodbridge headquarters.

Turning into Jude, the Kentuckian said, "One of these days you are going to get hurt fucking around like that, Judeman."

With normalcy returning to the headquarters bunker, the embarrassed headquarters sentry recovered his weapon and returned to his post, swearing under his breath. Ed looked around and introduced Jude to the new officers in his Command Post staff. He also told the Ranger that prior to his rude arrival they had been following the Sibley snatch team's progress.

1910 hours, January 8, 2018

Commander Ed Sumter's tall and lanky figure bent over the large topographical paper map with his operations and intelligence officers. The signals man sat at another corner table manning the Single Channel Ground and Airborne Radio System (SINCGARS) radio. Jude had seen the antenna protruding through the camouflage and made a mental note to have the security detachment restring that tell-tale antenna properly.

The S-2 intelligence guy was making grease pencil notes on the map's transparent acetate cover. The radio was silent. Ed had imposed radio silence except in the case of the most essential transmissions, because 'the enemy can't intercept what they can't hear.' On the other hand the field phones kept the radioman busy screeching like a band of drunken crickets, even at this time of night.

The staccato of Provo artillery and mortars across the river punctuated the night as Ed hovered over the annotated map. He said to Jude, "From the sounds of it, Judeman, you made them Provos real mad at you."

Jude flopped down on the damp bunker's wood pallet floor and helped himself to a cup of hot coffee, which was the only luxury that his old friend allowed in the Command Post. He swallowed the first gulp enjoyably, feeling it roll down his esophagus, before answering his friend with a question:

"The snatch team made it across MacArthur?" asked the Ranger.

Ed turned slowly and sat on the floor next to Jude with his own cup of coffee answering in his usual chopped style. "Last transmission, they had arrived at the objective."

Jude suddenly got a rascally look on his face and raised his voice to attract the attention of the bunker's staff he had just met. "Speaking of transmissions, did you guys ever hear about when the Commander and I were stationed in the same infantry battalion in Germany during an annual maneuver?" At this, Ed groaned and rolled his eyes, but smiled anyway.

Without waiting for an answer Jude told them how the unit had failed to find the night's objective and got a call from the Division two-star general asking them where the battalion was. He described how Ed, who was then the battalion S-3 operations officer, and into his second case of beer, grabbed the handset from his radioman and, breaking radio discipline, told the General: "General, I want you to look at your map. I'm gonna shake this here pine tree, and when you see it moving on your map, that's where the fuck we are!"

The AC (forward) headquarters bunker went up in laughter and knee-slapping, defying the silence parameters. The laughter was so contagious that the fighters in nearby bunkers began to chuckle inwardly to themselves, drawing from the sounds coming out of headquarters that things were going well.

CHAPTER 13 — Command Decision

Even if you are on the right track, you will get run over if you just sit there. Will Rogers

1916 hours, January 8, 2018

In fact, things were going very well. The snatch team was able to profit from the distraction that Jude had created to cross from the C&O Canal into the swanky neighborhoods along McArthur Boulevard. They would mask their approach to Sibley Hospital by going through the partially abandoned housing developments.

One of the many Rebel sympathizers in the capital area who Steve had recruited had come up with actionable intelligence that the Provisional Council's Intelligence Coordinator (or G-2) was to undergo hand surgery there. The sympathizer was a scrub nurse at Sibley.

Provo G-2 Jeffery Byers was in charge of all intelligence gathering, reporting and coordination for the Provisional Military Government, a function once carried out by the Director of National Intelligence (DNI), who had died at the Capitol bombing. Byers was considered by many to be one of Greco's closest and most trusted associates. This was a rumor probably spread by the G-2 himself who was just another of the dilettantes and ass-kissers in Greco's inner circle.

Despite the critical state of the war, Byers had decided to remove a bone spur from the base of his right thumb that had been affecting his golf game. Sibley's hand surgeon was reputed to be among the best in the world.

The G-2 was very untalented himself, but knew how to surround himself with talented, experienced professionals. Unlike many of his co-religionists he had proven to be highly effective at his task. He provided Provo troops reliable, well-coordinated intelligence, much of it collected by Provo sympathizers in Rebel-controlled areas handled by the CIA. If only they had known what to do with it. Greco had asked him to travel to the West Coast soon after the surgery to liaise with the Chinese forces and coordinate a nationwide attack on Rebel units.

National Rebel Command headquarters knew that kidnapping the head Provo spook would be a significant blow to Greco, and had approved Appalachian Command's plan within minutes of its proposal. Ed and Jude had put together the plan, and Jude had volunteered to carry out the diversion himself, leaving the snatch to three Rebel intelligence operatives who were led by Jude's old friend from Diplomatic Security, Steve O'Neal.

Just as the laughter on the shaking pine tree story died down the snatch team broke radio silence. "Green Giant this is Lover Boy, over."

Ed lifted his large frame to the map table and responded gruffly: "Lover Boy, this is Green Giant, and it better be good, go."

Ed had warned Steve personally not to break radio silence and give only coded progress reports unless they had a damn good reason.

"We have a situation, over." Steve's baritone came through the airwaves clearly.

"Like I said, Lover Boy, it better be good. Go." Ed's eyes reflected his exasperation.

"Brass Ring (the assigned code name for Byers) had a visitor who was too good to be left behind. So we snatched her too. But since we have a long trek ahead of us, we would appreciate your picking her up at Midpoint to lighten our load. What to do with her is way above our pay grade. You might want to talk it over with Snow Cap, over."

Snow Cap was the call sign for the national headquarters in the Rockies, which was on another channel altogether.

The snatch plan called for taking Byers to an air strip near in Pennsylvania north of Cumberland, Maryland, from where a National Rebel Command aircraft would take him to a secure location in the Rockies. There, he would undergo debriefing and propaganda exploitation. However, the surprise second hostage was evidently someone of higher value.

Apparently she was of such high value that the snatch team hesitated to dispose of her in place in accordance with tradecraft. Steve had evidently determined that a bullet in the head would probably not be appropriate in her case. Ed always gave his field commanders the benefit of the doubt. After all, they were there and he wasn't. The Kentuckian was not about to second-guess the troops he trusted with a mission.

"Roger, Lover Boy", transmitted Ed looking at Jude, who nodded. "Casper will come up and take her off your hands. So, stay put at Midpoint until he gets there, and stay off the fucking air, out", admonished Ed.

After ending the transmission Ed told Jude, "It's gotta be worthwhile Judeman. Steve is not one to go off the reservation for no good reason. He knew that Colorado thinks the Sibley snatch is a critical operation."

"OK. I'll go pick her up," said Jude as he leaned his weapon and hydration bag against the bunker's earthen wall, on his way to the map table. Without breaking stride he told his boss: "I'll need a female fighter to come with me to bring the woman back."

Jude walked over to the map table to do a paper recon of Midpoint and possible routes there and back. Ed was silent for a moment as his eyes followed Jude.

"OK Judeman; what's the punch line?" Ed's eyes were mocking and open just a tad too wide. "Why would you need a female fighter to help you out? You afraid of women now?" mocked Ed as he looked at his staff officers. Two of them were women and broke into smiles at the joke.

Returning a grin of his own, but keeping his eyes on the map table, Jude admonished the staff officers pointedly. "You guys, be careful you don't go REMF on us spending too much time here at the comfy headquarters CP."

Calling Ed a Rear Echelon Mother Fucker was a risky affair, but it got everyone's attention.

Jude looked at Ed and continued pushing his luck. "Dealing with a woman hostage is not the same as handling a male hostage, Oh Great One. If she is as important as the Irishman said, then you would probably want her here in one piece. If she's got no nuts to squeeze, a gentleman of the old school like me is not equipped to deal with female behavior. A woman fighter can."

"What's this I hear? You gone soft on me?" Ed Sumter shot back while looking at his smiling S-3 (operations) officer. "The old Jude would not hesitate to put a bullet in her head if she as much as farted funny. And then the old Jude would have dragged her cadaver and dumped her at my feet like a pooch retrieving a dead duck."

Jude's retort came back sharply and quickly. "Well now, I'd be happy to do just that. But it might just piss off the Irishman. As big as you are, you don't want to piss off Steve. I've seen him tumble ten Harley-Davison hogs with their riders on it when he found a scratch on his Spyder. He and his spooks didn't go to the trouble of snatching the second hostage just so that the Ghost could waste her. You know who else might object at the notion? Colorado might object at the notion if she is as valuable as the Irishman says. That's why I need a woman to come along." There was that smile again, and it was all said in an unconcerned tone of voice. Pissing off Steve was not a good thing; but neither was pissing off Ed. Jude was walking a tightrope. The look on Ed's face told Jude that he had won this round, for now.

"OK, Judeman, let's do it your way," capitulated Ed with a groan knowing that it was time to leave well enough alone. Jude was the commander on the field, and Ed was experienced enough to abide by Teddy Roosevelt's counsel[1]. Turning to the sentry he said, "Son, go get me Hartmann, would you?"

---

[1] *"It is not the critic who counts: not the man who points out how the strong man stumbles or where the doer of deeds could have done better. The credit belongs to the man who is actually in the arena, whose face is marred by dust and sweat and blood, who strives valiantly, who errs and comes up short again and again, because there is no effort without error or shortcoming, but who knows the great enthusiasms, the great devotions, who spends*

CHAPTER 14 — The Trophy Wife

"Signor Hortensio, 'twixt such friends as we
Few words suffice; and therefore, if thou know
One rich enough to be Petruchio's wife—
As wealth is burden of my wooing dance—
Be she as foul as was Florentius' love,
As old as Sibyl, and as curst and shrewd
As Socrates' Xanthippe or a worse,
She moves me not—or not removes at least
Affection's edge in me, were she as rough
As are the swelling Adriatic seas.
I come to wive it wealthily in Padua;
If wealthily, then happily in Padua."
William Shakespeare, "The Taming of the Shrew",
(I.ii.62–73)

1805 hours, January 8, 2018

The Snatch Team's staging position had been plotted on the situation map at coordinates 38.970354,-77.181702, a point just north of the Legion Bridge ruins and about a mile south from the Billy Goat Trail. Steve O'Neal, Max Moore, Craig Stubs and Rob Mlynarski were waiting there for the diversion that Jude would create. They had come across the Potomac undetected on

---

himself for a worthy cause; who, at the best, knows, in the end, the triumph of high achievement, and who, at the worst, if he fails, at least he fails while daring greatly, so that his place shall never be with those cold and timid souls who knew neither victory nor defeat." Theodore Roosevelt ,"Citizenship in a Republic" Speech at the Sorbonne, Paris, April 23, 1910

a black Zodiac, a few hundred meters from what used to be the Legion Bridge slipping into the position under the very noses of Provo vigilance.

Greco forces had blown up the bridge only two months before to halt the advance of Rebel troops into the Capital region. The stump that remained on its Maryland access point on Interstate 495 was heavily guarded by a regular Army unit. It was too important to be left in the hands of the Militia.

In fact, the Provos anticipated that the next Rebel attack would come through the area. The zone between the destroyed bridge and what used to be the Carderock Naval Surface Warfare Center was the most logical route, if you considered the widening Potomac further south. It was heavily guarded. Despite the heavy Provo security, it remained the most direct route for the Snatch Team to approach Sibley Hospital. The route's unexpected directness might also contribute to the mission's stealth factor.

The plan was to infiltrate through the wooded area to the development around River Rock Terrace, which remained inhabited by important Greco personnel, boost a minivan or something large enough to hold all of them, and then proceeded down MacArthur Boulevard to Sibley Hospital.

There, they would dump the initial stolen vehicle past Sibley, somewhere along Loughboro, and change into the hospital scrubs that they were carrying in their rucksacks. They would then approach the hospital on foot from the parking lot. It was a simple plan and easy to implement. These were the two factors that might contribute to its success.

Steve's asset, the nurse, had stashed genuine hospital ID badges under a refuse container next to a bench on the south side of the parking lot, and left the ignition key in a minivan belonging to Sibley's security chief in the visitor's parking lot. She had also cached weapons on the way to the objective.

The security chief was an insufferable prick who would not miss his minivan at all for a long time, as he preferred to be transported around in an official car provided by the hospital. Along with the IDs, she had also left in the minivan a detailed floor plan of the VIP section, marking the room where the hostage would be.

Max and Craig would eliminate Byers' security detail and establish perimeter security. Then, Rob and Steve would carry the guy to the parking lot and get him into the minivan. With Max at the wheel, they would drive north over an extraction route which had been laid out to avoid as much contact with Provo checkpoints as possible. The cynical Steve would probably call it 'a piece of cake' and roll his eyes.

1832 hours, January 8, 2018

The start of the Provo artillery and mortar barrage on Jude's ambush position was the signal the snatch team was waiting for. They negotiated quickly what was left of the wooded area leading to the Canal, the Clara Barton Parkway and MacArthur Boulevard. They crouched on the west side of the boulevard waiting for the end of the Provo fire mission that Jude's hit had provoked.

As soon as the fire mission stopped what seemed like hundreds of Militia vehicles headed north on MacArthur. The armored vehicles of the Capital Area Rapid

Response Team heading to the ambush site went by first, followed by heavier vehicles bearing regular troops, and lastly the ubiquitous military square ambulances. The ambulances bore both the Red Cross and the Green Crescent, a very politically correct response.

Steve and his team rushed across immediately after the last ambulance had gone by, and before other traffic could resume. The swanky area neighborhoods were still there, but many of the houses were empty, the owners evacuated to safer zones. The hold-outs were mainly Provo government personnel, with a sprinkle of hard-backed diplomats whose countries were friendly to the Provisional Government.

Within a few minutes, the team reached the YMCA on 75th Street. Steve spotted a blue station wagon that had carelessly been left running on a nearby driveway. Max was relieved that she didn't have to break into a vehicle and hotwire it. Even though she was also a former State Special Agent, she had learned how to boost cars in her youth in Brooklyn, and the team relied on this useful side of her past experience. Max was so good at hotwiring that Steve and the others were willing to humorously overlook her predilection for the New York Jets over the Giants. In any case, the collapse of the Republic had also meant the end of organized sports.

1847 hours, January 8, 2018

It took them about 15 minutes to get to Sibley using the back roads. Once on Loughboro, they rolled past the hospital to assess the situation around it. Incredibly, there was little action there. There was a Metropolitan police car at the entrance, and that was about it. Steve guessed that the Provos did not want to advertise the presence of their VIP. As planned, they parked on Loughboro about 100 meters from the parking lot, past Dalecarlia Parkway. They put on the loose fitting scrubs and walked towards the parking lot as if they were a group of hospital workers returning from a coffee break.

The team entered the parking lot from the west, stopped by the getaway minivan to stash their pistols, and walked on to the covered hospital side entrance, where they were met by Steve's nurse, who told them loudly, within earshot of the Provo soldiers at the door that they were late and their boss was looking for them. Max began cursing loudly in her New York accent about their pretend boss' little dick. This drew a sympathetic smile from the guards, who gave only a cursory glance at their laminated passes.

Once inside the hospital, their nurse friend left them on their own and scurried to the west parking lot to get the Hell out of Dodge. She knew that her display of familiarity with the kidnappers would burn her. Later, she would join the Rebel fighting forces leaving behind all her earthly possessions. Such were the sacrifices that many Americans were making for their country.

1850 hours, January 8, 2018

In the meantime, the team followed highly polished corridors past the Gift Shop and up the staircase to the second floor. They stopped briefly to pick up four silenced AR-15s with folding stocks that had been stashed by the nurse under a cardiac crash cart. How she got them past the hospital security measures was a mystery to Steve and his colleagues. They checked the magazines, tightened the silencers, locked and loaded and donned balaclavas before they entered the second floor corridor. That was where the going got hairy.

Not 20 yards to the right of the staircase exit there was a clusterfuck of Provo guards, "smoking and joking", anything but doing security stuff.

They never knew what hit them.

Within seconds Max and Craig disarmed them before they could raise the alarm. Steve and Rob slid past them into the room.

Their abrupt entrance caught the guy on the bed in mid-smile, evidently a flirtatious smile aimed at the woman who sat on the edge of his bed. Seeing the smile disappear, the woman turned toward the masked armed men rushing into the room and was paralyzed with something between surprise and fear.

Steve held his weapon on the man and the woman while Rob went to the patient closet and threw a terrycloth robe at the Provo Intel chief. Neither Steve nor Rob said anything, but the gesture was enough to propel the guy to put on the robe in silence. By this time the woman had recovered from her initial surprise and said, "Do you know who I am? I'm Mrs. Greco. Put down those guns before my detail shoves them up your ass."

Steve's smile said it all. He looked at Rob half turning his head and said, "I told you it was always good to carry extra plastic ties." That was all Rob needed to hear to slap the woman's head. It made a calming impression on Mrs. Greco. He bound her wrists behind her back.

The head spook took in rather quickly, and in petrified silence, that these people meant business. He voluntarily turned around and offered his own wrists, one of which was heavily bandaged, but Rob slapped him for good measure just prior to securing his hands with the plastic handcuffs.

They put black hoods without eye holes on the hostages, pushing them out the door to where they saw Max and Craig and the trussed up and gagged security detail. Their friend's waists were bristling with the additional guns and radios. They re-entered the staircase, where they took their hoods off. They could function better unencumbered by balaclavas as they half-carried their charges down to the second floor hallway. Max looked out the door and gave the go ahead signal.

The snatch team rushed their prey past the Gift Shop, turning into the hallway that would lead them to the parking lot. One of the guards at the entrance was paying attention and lifted his weapon to confront the strange armed phalanx. Craig had taken the point and squeezed off two silenced shots, felling the two guards. He took their weapons and radios and held the door open for the team and the two hostages.

They ran to the minivan, loaded the two Provos and Max took the wheel. They were doing 50 mph as they ran through the pay barrier on to Loughboro.

CHAPTER 15 – Another Man's Treasure

"If I be waspish, best beware my sting." William
Shakespeare, *The Taming of the Shrew*

1900 hours, January 8, 2018

The radios were silent for the longest time, until a
Provo got alerted that something was up and issued
instructions over the air, not realizing yet that the snatch
team had taken radios from the security personnel. Some
Provo mental giant must have suspected a potential
compromise and had the net switch to crypto, which
Steve also did almost immediately. They heard the
Provos say that they knew the hostages had been taken
by rebel terrorists, but they did not yet have a description
of the vehicle or the direction it took when it sped away.

The snatch team had a few extra minutes. Max eased
off on the speed so as not to attract attention.

When they crossed into the Maryland suburbs, Steve
was able to raise Appalachian Command on the radio to
request that someone take the second hostage off their
hands. He couldn't tell Ed in the clear that they had
accidently bagged Greco's wife. But he was able to
convince the Kentuckian to take her off his hands so he
could deliver Byers to the airstrip without having to
worry about her also.

Steve knew that she was a much bigger prize than the
intelligence dickhead, and he was glad that Ed was
sending Jude to take her off his hands. She was too
valuable to trust her handling to anyone else.

They took Little Falls Parkway, turning left into River Road at the Mobil station and heading north. At this time of night traffic was light, but heavy enough to not let the minivan stand out. They drove over the I-495 Beltway overpass and Max turned left into the unsecured and unguarded gate at Congressional Country Club. Rob asked her, "What the fuck you doing?"

"We are going to change vehicles," answered Max in an unconcerned tone; as if she was just going to stop at a 7/11 to get a pack of smokes.

"At a golf club in the middle of the night?" Rob said incredulously.

Max explained that "some members leave their cars at the club when they go out of town; better than leaving them at the airport. The airport limos know where to pick them up and bring them back to when they return from their trips, and the cars get looked after by club staff."

The team was aware that Max knew her stuff, so no one asked how she would know something as random as that. Had someone asked, she would have told them how she had moonlighted at the club during major tournaments. She had been certain that the club was still working, despite the collapse, and that the new members would be the elite of the Provisional Government.

Passing the driving range on the right and the tennis courts on the left Max spotted a black Toyota Sienna as she entered the huge parking lot. She drove by it checking the area first, and then headed to the valet stand. The keys to the stored vehicles were kept in a locked but flimsy case there.

Max jumped out at the valet stand, and as luck would have it, some idiot had left the key case unlocked. She found the Sienna's keys right away and took them out without disturbing the other sets of keys. With any luck, it would be sometime until someone noticed the absence of the eight passenger van; hopefully way after it had served its purpose. She jumped back on the minivan and drove it to the Sienna, where everyone dismounted.

While they transferred their equipment and hostages, Craig drove the minivan to the parking spaces behind the tennis courts, to avoid telegraphing which car they had 'borrowed'. Max picked him up on the way out of the club, turning left into River Road at the front entrance.

2025 hours, January 8, 2018

Max kept to five miles under the speed limit so as not to attract unwanted attention. She took River north turning right at the T into Seneca. After around 6 miles heading east, Max made a sharp left into US 28 at the Shell gas station. US 28 would take them north through Dickerson, over the Monocacy River to Tuscarora Road past the Rocky Point Creamery, to the safe house, short of Point of Rocks.

Everything had happened so fast that by the time she drove the Sienna into the barn to the right of the safe house the Provos had yet to fully mobilize to find and try to rescue Mrs. Greco.

Steve, Rob and Max led the hostages into the wood frame house through the kitchen door. Craig stayed behind cooling down the Sienna with a water hose to reduce its potential thermal footprint. Craig was the only one of the three who had not been a Special Agent for State. Instead, he had worked counter intelligence for Langley and had an arsenal full of deception techniques. When he finished cooling down the Sienna he jumped on a mountain bike that was kept in the barn and rode to the point where they had turned into Tuscarora. He retraced their route examining the road for telltale signs of the Sienna's tire tracks. So many times fresh oil drops, or a cigarette butt had betrayed otherwise adequate procedures.

2055 hours, January 8, 2018

Once in the house and again wearing hoods, Steve and Max hogtied the hostages in separate bedrooms. They took off the hostages' hoods and adjusted the gags so they could breathe normally, providing a measure of relative comfort. As soon as Craig and Rob secured the safe house, they would quench the detainee's thirst, feed them and give them a bathroom break. These people were valuable to the Rebs.

Max handled the woman and Steve handled the man. It was a federal law enforcement truism that women agents could handle female "perps" better than guys, and this particular woman had shown her talons early on at the hospital, when she tried to scare the team with her attitude. Stick our rifles up our asses, "dontcha know", thought Steve imitating Rob's North Dakota accent in his mind. Boy, what a surprise package he had for Jude.

2255 hours, January 9, 2018

The team had secured the safe house and been working two hour watches for the past twenty six hours when Max alerted them that someone had just clicked the radio three times, the signal from the relief team that they were about a kilometer from the house. Craig and Rob geared up and left through the patio door. From the patio they entered the tree line and headed south, toward an orchard that would give them an unobstructed view of the area.

Within four minutes they heard the radio click twice and then a transmission in the clear asking for permission to approach. Steve gave it. Seconds later, they saw two figures break out of the tree line. They relief team was good. Neither Craig nor Rob saw them until they let themselves be seen.

Despite their admiration for flawless tradecraft, they approached from behind and disarmed the figures, who had evidently been expecting it and posed no resistance; a man and a woman, despite the camouflage. They walked them into the house where Steve hugged the guy.

CHAPTER 16 — Kate

"...Toto, I've a feeling we are not in Kansas anymore." Dorothy, The Wizard of Oz, Lyman Frank Baum

2015 hours, January 8, 2018

The snatch team's extraction route had been designed to sacrifice speed to deception, and to deliver Greco's intelligence chief to the Hager Airstrip in Pennsylvania, across the Maryland border from Cumberland, Maryland. From there, a C-12A executive military aircraft staffed by the National Headquarters would fly him to Colorado.

The small community of Point of Rocks had been designated and code named "Midpoint", not because of the distance to the airstrip, but because there was an available last ditch crossing to Virginia, should things go south.

Ed and Jude were bent over the map looking at crossings back into Virginia from the safe house when the blackout cloth opened and a woman in ACUs came in, adjusted her digitalized camouflage combat uniform and said, "Did you call for me, Ed?"

Both men turned at once and looked at the woman. It took Ed a second or so to regain his focus and then he said, "Oh hi Kate, this is Jude Winthrop."

The expression on her face betrayed pleasant surprise. "It's sure an honor, Commander. My crew thinks highly of you." Jude received the flattery with a flat expression on his face, even mildly annoyed, and answered her flattery with a question. "What crew is that?" which was not precisely what Kate expected to hear.

Ed answered for her, "Commander Kate Hartmann, formerly Captain Kate Hartmann of the US Army's Military Police is in charge of our perimeter security. She..." Ed turned to her, "But you can brief him, Kate."

Kate was visibly discomfited and with her Irish (or rather German) up because of the tone in which Jude asked about her troops, even after she had gone out of her way to be nice. She switched her gaze from Ed to Jude and explained a little too sharply, "I lead 40 battle-tested MPs and civilian law enforcement personnel in this command, Commander. We have never had a breach."

"Until tonight, Commander Hartmann, when I broke into your perimeter unnoticed and got into this bunker and surprised the living heck out of our boss." For Jude there was no excuse for half-assed performances and his tone reflected it.

"I was going to say until tonight myself, Commander, if you had only let me finish. You'll agree with me that it's no dishonor to be beaten by The Ghost," said Kate in a last ditch attempt to win Jude over through flattery. "However, we all learn our lessons. Don't try the same thing tomorrow night."

The words were a little too quick, a little too much of a dare, and she spit them out a little too fast.

Ed broke in to lessen the tension. "The reason I called you, Kate, is that we need your help. We just heard that the Sibley snatch team picked up an extra hostage who was visiting the Provo G-2 when the snatch took place. They couldn't tell us the name over the radio, but they did say that the extra person had a higher collateral value than the G-2 himself. So Jude volunteered to go take her off the snatch team's hands at Point of Rocks. And he made a good case to have a female fighter help him bring her in. That's where you come in."

"I'll be happy to provide a top notch trooper to accompany the Commander," said Kate to Ed while looking at Jude out of the corner of her eye.

"Actually Kate, I would like *you* to go with him. I'm sure all your fighters are top-notch, but if we are dealing with a high value target I don't want to take any chances. You are well briefed on everything that happens in this command. This is a sensitive situation that requires your experience and seniority," Ed told her seriously without betraying his amusement at the obvious discomfort of his two subordinates.

Jude broke in "Ed, I trust the Commander's judgment. If she thinks the person she has in mind can do the job, so be it." It was an obvious maneuver to avoid taking Kate along. He had enough to worry about as it was. The last thing he needed was a belligerent partner.

"Good try, Jude." said Ed and turning to Kate "And good try to you too, Kate."

Ed broke into the crocodile smile he reserved for when someone was trying to put something over him. "I would appreciate *both* of you taking this up for me," he half snapped at them.

End of discussion.

Ed had asserted his authority. Structure and rank were serious problems in the Rebel forces. Some Rebs had held positions of high responsibility and authority prior to joining the fight. Some had earned their positions while fighting the Provos.

In Jude's case, because he had been an Infantry officer in the Army Rangers, Ed had initially put him in charge of an elite commando unit which was decimated in an attack on a Provo target near Gettysburg, PA. He himself was captured, wounded but alive, and held at Carderock Prisoner of War facility for two days. He escaped while being transported to Provo HQ for a more thorough questioning than the Militia interrogator could provide.

He retained the Rebel rank of Commander despite having no one to command because the Provos were scared shitless of his exploits, and Ed knew how to manage the enemy's perceptions. After his commandos were killed, Jude used his sniping talent and pent up hatred to put away close to two hundred Provos and Militiamen. The Provos called him "The Ghost" and Ed was more than happy to capitalize on their fears. Besides, both Ed and Colorado wanted to resurrect Jude's elite unit under his command for upcoming operations against the Chinese. So Jude kept the rank of Commander.

Ed Sumter had been the S-3 in a mechanized infantry battalion where he and Jude had served while they were stationed in Germany, awaiting deployment to South West Asia. Ed had stayed in the Army, getting rapidly promoted during the 5 years in which Jude had whiled away his time in the Foreign Service.

Being from Kentucky, National Rebel Headquarters in Colorado identified Ed Sumter early on for a regional command centered in Appalachia. He had performed brilliantly, driving the Provos to the east bank of the Potomac River and keeping them there. Jude and Ed went way back, but Jude always acknowledged Ed's authority in front of others, despite feeling free to let him know a thing or two when they were alone.

As Ed had left no room for further discussion Jude was sort of sore at his friend for making him lose the upper hand. Taking command, he turned to Kate and spit out his orders, "We leave in an hour. Draw rations for three days for yourself and the prisoner, and 200 rounds of ammo. Also bring a set of ACUs and Gore-Tex winter boots, including a field jacket with liner and long underwear for the hostage. She's probably not dressed to hike the woods in January. Your size will do. If she is not in shape she will just have to squeeze into them. I'll split the weight of the prisoner food and gear with you later."

"200 rounds seem a lot to me, Commander", bit back the fiery redhead.

"Well, Commander, there is usually a lot of shooting when I'm around," Jude told her with unmistakable finality.

Kate acknowledged his orders dryly, but she was somewhat mollified because he had noticed that she was in shape. She was as susceptible to vanity as the next person.

2130 January 8, 2018

Kate joined Jude at the patrol jump-off point on the headquarters' eastern perimeter. Jude had decided to go up to Point of Rocks using the Maryland side of the Potomac, which provided better operational security than the overly built-up Northern Virginia riverside. They would cross at Olmstead Island and follow the sides of the Olmstead Trail to the C&O Canal, then take the canal's surrounding wooded area north to the rendezvous point.

Fifty yards after the last perimeter listening post they stopped in a well-concealed orchard and did a buddy check. Weapons, ammo, rations, accessories all checked out. The rattle check went well too. Their equipment was as silent for night operations as they could make it.

Preparing for the infiltration, they began to camo-grease each other's face, but Jude stopped as his hand reached Kate's nose suddenly. She felt his eyes burning through her.

"And what do you call the perfume you have on, Commander, Ho Number Five?" He could actually feel her face redden and heard her tight reply come through obviously bared teeth, "I don't have perfume on, Commander. It's just plain soap. You would have known it if you ever used it yourself."

"Don't get your panties in a knot, Kate. A trained soldier can smell your 'just plain soap' 500 yards away. In fact, that's how I bagged tonight's kill. So, get behind that brush and rub some dirt on your skin to kill the scent before it gets us killed."

His using her name took some of the sting off his censure. But once her German was up, it was up. She was so angry at the guy that she barely took two paces toward the brush cover he had pointed out, fell on her knees, unbuckled her equipment and took off her ACUs and underwear down to the skin. Grabbing fistfuls of rich Virginia dirt, she rubbed the scent off her skin ferociously, as if she wanted to wash Jude's censure away along with the scent. Her modesty was buried so really deep in her anger that she didn't even notice she had taken her clothes off in front of the man.

Jude was so shocked by her nearly nude figure that he averted his eyes, but not before taking in the fact that she was really in shape, as he had implied in his earlier instructions. He was not only embarrassed by her nudity, but he also felt weird. It was the first time he had seen an undressed woman since Angie. He felt as if he had betrayed her memory. So now he added anger to his initial low assessment of the woman's professionalism.

So when a dressed Kate moved back toward him, he resumed slapping the camo grease paint on her face with more force that the waxy consistency required. For her part, each grease streak he applied she returned just as forcefully on his face, until the last one was nothing but a slap.

He grabbed her hand as it hit his face and held it with a steel fist, giving her the same look he would have given a Provo about to die. His other hand had gone for his British fighting knife, and it was halfway out of the scabbard when he stopped himself. To Kate's credit her look was just as vicious, and she had also gone for her K-bar when she sensed him freeze in his mistake.

Reaching an obvious stand-off, he turned and picked up his M-4 carbine, moving back to the trail without a word. Kate followed silently.

2330 hours, January 8, 2018

Two hours of negotiating the bush without a word between them got them to the Virginia shore inlet that sits across from Olmstead Island. The river had created many such formations with the dragged sediment it had built up through the eons. Olmstead Island was an exception; the Potomac carved it out of the rocks that would then become the rapids between Great Falls and Little Falls.

Just south of the rapids, to avoid possible Provo outposts and with well-rehearsed economy of movement, they tethered the backpacks to their waist as they stepped into the frigid river water fully clothed. On the Virginia side of the Potomac the current they stepped into was strong and the water smelled of ice melt, although it was still technically fall for another two weeks. The winter ACUs and long underwear provided a degree of comfort which rapidly disappeared when they emerged on dry land.

He swam ahead without looking back even once until they reached the island's shore. He then turned around and extended an arm to help Kate out of the water. She brushed away his hand.

Jude knew that the Olmstead Island Trail was linked with the C&O canal route by small foot bridges further ahead. He had chosen to risk using the footbridges. If the Provos had any security around the bridges, they would be distracted by the sounds of Militia artillery fire erupting periodically to the north. They were still reacting to his hit from two nights before.

Beginning to negotiate the brush he thought she had really given a good account of her infantry skills coming across to the island. No big deal. There was never a question in his mind that she wouldn't be a capable partner on this mission. He had just been annoyed that the REMF had forgotten basic patrolling and infiltration techniques, such as getting rid of smells and rattles.

Soaked to the bone from their Potomac swim in the cold moonless night they walked east on the Olmstead trail; she about two meters into the bush on the right side, and he the same distance on the left. They waited about 10 minutes to look out for an enemy presence before crossing each of the foot bridges that connected the trail.

With the current state of Provo training, enemy guards would have betrayed themselves in less time than that, but Jude preferred the overkill. The final and most dangerous crossing was on the C&O canal itself, a few hundred yards south of the boarded up Great Falls Tavern and Visitor Center. The fact that they did not find a single enemy sentry along the way confirmed the state of Provo training: pathetic.

Still wet, cold and miserable, they made relatively good time through the Maryland woods until the breaking dawn caught them at Blockhouse Point Park. They holed up there to spend the morning hours. They found a ground depression in a clearing beneath high tension wires where they could build a drying fire without betraying their position. The trees would diffuse the smoke.

Jude dug a Dakota fire hole, which is, in fact, two holes connected from below. One hole was for air intake to keep the fire fed, and the other hole was for the actual fire.

Keeping their fast drying underwear on, they spread their soaked garments on fallen branches around the fire hole and wrapped themselves in camo thermal blankets, while embracing their carbines. The heat of the thermal blankets would dry their underwear. Jude took the first watch over Kate's objections.

Kate didn't argue. She was that tired.

CHAPTER 17 — Introspection

"This above all: to thine ownself be true,
And it must follow, as the night the day,
Thou canst not then be false to any man."
Polonius to Laertes, Act I, Scene III, Hamlet, William
Shakespeare

1150 hours, January 9, 2018

Towards noon, Kate stirred and saw Jude's blanketed figure sitting by the embers, already dressed. When he saw her move, he filled his canteen cup with water and placed it on the fire hole's still hot embers to warm it for instant coffee.

"You shouldn't have let me sleep so long," she rebuked him. "Watches are supposed to be two hours each." She was still hostile towards him.

Jude just threw the almost dry clothes at her and continued warming the coffee water. She dressed quickly and inexplicably under the blanket. After all, he had already seen her nearly naked. Kate blushed at the thought and wished she could have taken back all of last night. She had seen the look of hurt in his eyes through the entire paint-slapping episode and guessed that there was something there, some history that she should know.

She didn't know how to follow his silence without weakening her pride. For his part, Jude didn't know how to explain Angie and his feelings to her, so he just clammed up while he rummaged through his bag for food. She did the same and brought out a long range patrol ration (LRRP) which she was about to heat with the enclosed heat tablet when he spoke.

"Read the ingredients and don't eat anything that has garlic or onion," he said. "They carry for a long distance and the smells are not native to the region. If we were in a garlic or onion producing region it wouldn't matter. But here it does."

And he added, trying to cut the tension a little with a half-smile. "The onion and garlic warning is not because I'd like to kiss you, Kate. The Militia eats a lot of that and my first reaction is to shoot at garlic and onion."

She looked at him for a moment that was longer than she intended, and then said in an almost normal tone, "And what do you eat, hotshot? Just so you don't shoot yourself accidentally, I mean."

This brought up his real smile for the first time, and she noticed that he was almost handsome in a rough kind of way. His light blue eyes and white teeth literally sparkled on the chiseled features, and she wondered how he hid those from the enemy. And then she immediately answered herself that he probably didn't smile as he was squinting before shooting at his prey. But the end result was that the tension was almost gone. What remained was necessary for the fighting.

He rummaged a little more in his bag and threw a baggie of dried figs and walnuts at her. "Here. You owe me."

She caught it in midair and looked at it mockingly horrified, "And this is what keeps you going?"

"Oh, sometimes I eat a worm or two for protein", he added totally serious, as he chewed. "No, really."

And there was that half smile again, and after a small pause he told her, "I'm not really as much of an asshole as I sound, you know?"

"I wish I could start last night over again," said Kate in a low voice. It was a whispered semi-apology of her own.

"Life doesn't give second chances, Kate," said Jude gravely and almost withdrawn. "But this ain't life. It's just two grunts stepping all over their own crap." And then he gazed into her eyes. "Yeah, I started it. I get pissed off like that when I kill someone. I guess I get angry at their being stupid enough to let themselves be killed. I got nothing against your crew, and if truth be told I'm a pretty good infiltrator. Your sentries didn't have a chance; did a lot of that in the sandbox."

"Iraq or Afghanistan?" Kate asked. She was amazed that the slug across from her could put two introspective sentences together. He was not only handsome, but he even sounded half smart.

"Both. And Waziristan in Pak country too. Look, let's worry about this gig now, and maybe we can have a beer later and be friends and tell war stories. I just called you a grunt, and to me that's a compliment, so don't get pissed again. I know that MP Officers have to pass Infantry Officer Training at Ft. Benning with the rest of us ground-pounders. Last night I could have sworn your red hair had caught on fire and your green eyes were a mountain lion about to pounce on me. So, peace out, OK?"

He ended with a two finger V.

That really floored her. She didn't know what to say next. And what was with him noticing the color of her hair and the color of her eyes? How had he looked at her that closely? In which way did he look her over, as a buddy or as a woman? She was so confused that the only thing she could come up with was a low voiced response: "Deal."

They ate in silence and he fell asleep within seconds and without another word, for he was afraid that he had said too much. It had been a long time since he had said so much personal stuff to another person, especially a strange woman. She looked at him in the camo blanket. Not a sound, not even heavy breathing marred his sleep. She thought he looked tense even when he rested.

She tried to pay him back by letting him oversleep, but he was up like an alarm clock in two hours time. He then told her to get her gear so they could resume the trek to the safe house.

CHAPTER 18 – The Safe House

"Neither dead nor alive, the hostage is suspended by an incalculable outcome. It is not his destiny that awaits for him, nor his own death, but anonymous chance, which can only seem to him something absolutely arbitrary. He is in a state of radical emergency, of virtual extermination." Jean Baudrillard, "Figures of the Transpolitical", Fatal Strategies (1983, trans. 1990).

1420 hours, January 9, 2018

Their pace was unbearably fast in the brush, but slow and cautious at the dangerous crossings. They had to assume that Provo troops would be out in force over the two choke points at White's Ferry and the Monocacy River feeder. White's Ferry was the only Potomac commercial crossing between Virginia and Maryland in the 50 walking miles from the Chain Bridge to the US 15 bridge at Point of Rocks.

The Provos had closed down White's Ferry when the Reb Appalachian Command began to operate in Northern Virginia. They didn't really believe that the Rebs would try to cross on the ferry boat. But the ferry boat was tethered to an underwater steel cable to prevent it from being carried away by the currents. It was this cable that the Provos thought that Rebs might use to guide them during an underwater infiltration.

The Monocacy River fed into the Potomac a little way up from White's Ferry. It wasn't really navigable, but it could serve as an infiltration route for amphibious teams to carry out sabotage at the many strategic points it crossed all the way up into Gettysburg, Pennsylvania.

Upriver was where Greco had commandeered the old Ike Eisenhower farm house near Gettysburg as his own Camp David and the Monocacy infiltration route threatened it across from US 15. He remembered that all too well. He lost his commandos attacking that target.

So Jude decided to move further inland around both of these choke points. That forced them to cross the open farmland around Poolesville and Dickerson, while hugging the edge of whatever tree lines they found. Approaching Point of Rocks they used what cover was available on either side of US 28. The safe house where they would pick up the hostage was located before getting to Point of Rocks, at the intersection of US 28 and Old Licksville Road.

2255 hours, January 9, 2018

When Jude guessed they were about a mile away from the safe house, he clicked the radio's transmit button twice. It would warn Steve's team of their approach. Arriving at the tree line about 200 yards from the house, they sat for a while in a clump of trees to do some visual recon before making a voice transmission alerting the snatch team.

Kate was glad to drop to a prone position after the fast pace the Ranger had set on their trek from Blockhouse Point Park. Her legs were on fire and her back ached.

After 20 minutes of no movement inside or around the safe house Jude made a brief radio call to the Snatch team. "Lover Boy, this is Casper. We are at the objective and walking. Out."

They had not walked 20 paces when from out of nowhere in the surrounding woods two black-clad figures in ski masks surrounded and disarmed them.

Their escorts took them inside the wood frame ranch house where a hooded Steve greeted Jude with a fake gut punch. He nodded at Kate. At that point, their escorts returned their weapons and everyone shook hands all around.

This ritual took place in total silence. Tradecraft demanded silence in hostage taking situations. People who are trussed up with nothing to do tend to remember the words of their captors: a chance the Rebs did not want to take should things go south.

2330 hours, January 9, 2018

Stepping out on the porch and dragging Jude and Kate with him, Steve offered hoods to both of them. Jude shook his head declining the hoods. "She's going to see our ugly mugs even through the face paint the whole trip back to headquarters. Who the fuck is this golden goose anyway?"

Steve paused briefly for dramatic effect then said in a low voice heavily laced with relish and mirth: "Mrs. Amanda Greco."

Jude and Kate were startled and shared a fleeting look. Amanda Greco was the Admiral's 27 year-old trophy wife. Greco had dumped his wife of 30 years for the sweet young thing with a pageant title in the other room. That was a good measure of his character.

Amanda Wellington had been Miss Pennsylvania in 2010, and was still a knock-out blonde with everything in the right places, as Steve would put it. Her value was not only symbolic. The old sea dog was head over heels in lust with the woman. To her credit she appeared to reciprocate when they were seen together in public. Stranger things had happened, thought Jude, because Greco looked as good as a shriveled prune in Navy garb.

Jude tugged Steve out of Kate's earshot and said, "What the fuck, Steve? When you found out who she was, why didn't you just drop everything and take her back to headquarters? She's worth a whole lot more than the fucking spook, my man. Ed's gonna be furious."

"No, he won't" retorted Steve calmly. "Think, Judeman. Colorado wants the spook to debrief him of whatever intelligence he may have. He is of no personal value to Greco other than as the repository of intelligence information. He's probably already been replaced and the information he had scrubbed. On the other hand, this chick has personal value to Greco. The faster we can trade her back to him in exchange for whatever we want, the better. It's be a pisser if she is taken to Colorado and we then have to get her back from National for a trade-off to benefit the AC. Never happen."

Jude knew better than to interrupt Steve while he was putting together an argument. So he bided his time. "It will take national headquarters forever to decide to hand her back to us, if at all. Then there's the question of what her price should be. You know that Ed would want to swap her for some of our captured buddies. Colorado doesn't have as much of a stake as we do in bringing back our own. They are too busy with the Chinese."

"That stint at Langley made you think like one of their pirates, eh knuckle dragger?" said Jude jokingly. Knuckle-dragger was the in-house slur diplomatic officers at State had for their special agent colleagues in Diplomatic Security.

Looking thoughtfully at Steve's eyes Jude added, more gravely: "Did it cross your mind that Colorado has a better strategic view than we do in our hillbilly headquarters? And, what about the sound military principle of letting the Boss Headquarters make the fucking brilliant decisions?" Jude was almost whisper-shouting at his friend.

"Precisely my point, buddy," shot back Steve in a low harangue. "Ed is our boss, not Colorado. Remember your old friend Ed? He is the leader who should make this particular decision. Besides, you knew our team didn't have secure voice and this is not the type of stuff that you transmit in the clear. Ed would have a shit fit."

"We have to let Ed make the decision. For all I know he will decide to send her to Colorado. But it should be *his* decision. So, you and your girlfriend have to walk the woman back to headquarters? Good training, troop! Maybe that will help you snap out of your funk, good buddy" and then Steve said softer, with a hand on his friend's shoulder "Ya gots to start thinking straight again. Time to get over it, dip weenie."

'Dip weenie' was the slight special agents used for diplomatic officers, especially when they were being dip-weenies, like Jude was being right then.

He hated to admit it, but Jude knew Steve was right. What the hell was the matter with him? Ever since Angie got killed his mind was a jumble. How the Hell was he functioning at all? The same with the Kate business. He just had to get on the ball and not dump his personal grief on the people he worked with.

He looked at Steve and knew that the guy had actually been too fucking gentle with him; a true friend. Steve had trusted Jude to come back to the world of the living at some point when his buddy was ready. But it was time already. The look he exchanged with Steve said it all. He grabbed the Irishman's shoulder and squeezed it in acknowledgement as they rejoined the others inside the house.

CHAPTER 19 – Jude's Rangers

"C-130 running down the strip
Airborne daddy gonna take a little dip
Stand up, hook up, shuffle to the door
'Chute's gonna open on the count of four…"
Traditional Ranger running "Jodi"

2015 hours, January 20, 2017

The C-130 from the Kentucky National Guard carrying Jude's Rangers was flying at 10,000 feet over the Maryland countryside. Up next was a High Altitude Low Opening (HALO) jump. Flying so low was a way to avoid having to follow the usual pure oxygen protocol at a higher altitude. A major risk of HALO is hypoxia, which happens when you fly in an unpressurized cabin, which is a requirement for the jump, without following the accepted oxygen protocol. No jumper ever yearns for hypoxia.

The Greco armed forces had not changed IFF (Identification Friend of Foe) transponder settings for aircraft in Rebel hands. It was almost impossible to determine which aircraft the Chinese had destroyed, and changing the IFF could impact on surviving Greco-friendly aircraft from Pope Air Force Base in North Carolina, and Wright Army Airfield in Georgia. Both bases were still loyal to the Provos. So, the Ranger's C-130 flew over Greco controlled territory unchallenged.

Jude put together his team in record time on January 17, the same day Ed ordered him to do so. He knew some of the team members from his deployments to Iraq and

Afghanistan. In fact, some had joined him at the Luray Caverns parking lot after getting his call to action. He identified the rest from the Camp Dawson fighters. There were 19 Rangers in the team, counting himself.

He armed the team from the Delta force armory at Camp Dawson with the same type of organic Ranger weapons they had used before. To a man, they had nixed the Carl Gustav antitank recoilless rifles in the armory in favor of the older, but more reliable M-72 Light Antitank Weapon (LAW). The LAW was lighter: each fighter could carry two of them, and they were disposable. They didn't worry about having to break the casing to deny its use to the enemy. Greco forces would not reuse them like the Iraqi and Afghani terrorists did.

Each Ranger carried an M-4 carbine with 200 rounds of ammunition; Glock 17 pistols, instead of the laughable Berettas; several M-67 fragmentation grenades; and, an Integrated, Intra-Squad Radio (IISR), originally designed for the USMC but used by Delta. Two of the Rangers carried M-249 SAW light machineguns instead of M-4s, with extra ammo distributed among team members.

For the HALO jump the Rangers would be using MC-4 Ram Air Parachute systems that had been stocked at the Camp Dawson Delta armory. One of the team selection criteria Jude used in picking his team was graduation from Military Free Fall (MFF) School; because of the flexibility HALO jumping would give the team. Even though the warehouse had Military Free Fall Advanced Ram Air Parachute Systems (MFF ARAPS), most of the team members were more familiar with the MC-4.

In addition to the parachute system, each Ranger carried an altimeter; a Yarborough Reeve GB 5.5 knife (except for Jude, who kept his Fairbairn-Sykes); helmet, over-gloves, polypropylene thermal underwear and free fall boots. Their combat packs were light on sustenance gear and rations since they intended to live off the land. Not a difficult task in a built up area like Maryland.

2016 hours, January 20, 2017

The Rangers felt the aircraft slowdown considerably just before the Jumpmaster walked through them for a final look-see. The rear ramp had dropped seconds after the Jumpmaster strapped himself to the steel line. As soon as the green light came on, they shuffled to the rear of the C-130 and threw themselves into the dark winter night without hesitation.

2018 hours, January 20, 2017

The C-130's navigator had dropped them right over the DZ, drop zone, an elongated 100 x 400 meter clearing in the Frederick Municipal Forrest, about a kilometer from Hamburg Road. Their NAVAIDs guided them into the clearing with minimal steering after chute deployment. All 19 of them landed without difficulty, and walked silently on the Maryland frozen ground cover as they collected their parachutes. The Drop Zone was not active, or hot as they say, so they took their sweet time to collect and hide their parachutes.

Rallying around Jude after hiding the 'chutes the Rangers headed off in a south-south-east direction. The terrain in the Frederick Municipal Park was wooded, mainly evergreens east of Gambrill Park Road. A little over three miles following that azimuth they arrived at a dry creek bed, which they had marked as point B in their map recon. Crossing the creek bed they hugged the tree line in an east-south east direction until shortly before Edgewood Church Road. There, the terrain changed from woods to suburban. They still kept to the thin tree line but the pace slowed down to avoid detection from the houses they passed.

In less than a mile, they went by a group of wooden buildings near a frozen pond; a farm they had marked as point C on their map.

Then came the hairy part: crossing plowed farm fields. Despite a cloudy winter night, crossing open farmland is very risky in an infiltration. It's not only that your silhouette can be framed against what light may be filtering through the clouds, but there is a good chance that people in the ubiquitous farmhouse could spot you. Plowed, frosty land also retains footprints easily; not a good thing for a group of special operations types who are trying to go undetected. The dry creek bed they were following kept them going in the right direction, but gave scant cover.

When the point man spotted the Rocky Spring Cemetery on the left, they knew that they were about a mile from the target: Fort Detrick. They scurried north to wait at a wooded grove behind a building they had identified as a veterinary hospital.

0130 hours, January 21, 2017

The Rangers established perimeter security and ate the only field ration they had brought with them. They just rested. The adrenaline was pumping too intensely to take a nap.

The war had not yet touched this part of Maryland, and the Walnut Ridge Shopping Center in blocking the Ranger's way had costumers until about 2100 hours that Saturday. A school building next to the shopping center was totally dark.

At 0130 Jude silently gave the 'get ready' signal. Each of the Rangers turned to his buddy and checked for rattles and camo; they held on to the slides for a quiet 'lock and load'. The breaching team checked its wire cutters. The machine gunners identified the extra ammo bearers, and, they all did a radio click-check.

Fort Detrick

Fort Detrick had been the center of chemical and bacteriological warfare sporadically since World War II. A couple of workers died in the 1950s from exposure to the bugs they were working with at the facility. When that happened, the Army claimed to have stopped the experiments and lethal agent production. It opened the US Army Center for the Environment, a Scientific Library, and a personnel data center, and loaned several of its building to the National Cancer Institute's HIV Drug Resistance Program. This last function remained controversial. Conspiracy theorists insisted that HIV had been invented at Fort Detrick.

The current rumor was that the Greco government had reopened the biological warfare research and development facilities after the terrorist attack in 2015. True or not, Ed Sumter had chosen it for the Rangers' first operation. At the very least, an attack on Fort

Detrick, the City of Frederick's largest employer, would bring the war to a large population center in Maryland and ruin Greco's beauty sleep for a few days while people argued about whether the attack had released dangerous contaminants so close to the nation's capital.

The plan was brilliant in its simplicity. Breach the fence across from the Walnut Ridge Shopping Center. Shoot up Building 459, which sported a maze of PVC tubing on its roof and around it. Blow up the base's water tower. Break into the Sultan Street motor pool, steal the getaway vehicles, and shoot up the main gate at Rosemont on the way out.

The team would then proceed north on US 15 to the second target: the Eisenhower farmhouse at Gettysburg PA, the one that Greco had converted into his personal Camp David. From that location, the Rangers would exfiltrate cross-country into Virginia to rejoin the advancing Appalachian Command, hitting targets of opportunity along the return route.

All plans go to Hell at the execution phase.

0200 hours, January 21, 2017

The two-man breaching team cut the bottom of the wire fence at precisely 0200, bending the flaps open while the rest of the Rangers entered the compound. The main body of Jude's Rangers headed south-east, leaving a three-Ranger fire team at the Sultan Street motor pool and a two-Ranger demolition team at the water tower. The other fourteen soldiers ran southwest toward Building 459.

At 0205, the Building 459 attackers opened up with everything they had. An M-72 LAW round disintegrated the main door, followed immediately by a pair of frag grenades. A pair of Rangers went to the west side of the building and shot up what appeared to be three large butane tanks. The tanks contained instead some sort of flammable liquid, which blew up into a large and loud fire tongue.

At the same time, the demolition team brought down the water tower with pre-packed C-4 charges they had drawn from the Delta Force armory. The demolition team joined the motor pool team to increase the number of getaway drivers to five. As the water tower's supports bent and crashed the tank into the main building, the Center for the Environment, the five stolen vehicles, four Humvees and a two-and-a-half ton truck sped south on Miller Drive to pick up the Building 459 attackers. Heading north on Beasley, the deuce-and-a-half took the lead as the machine gunners poked their instruments of death through the canvas top over the cabin and obliterated the guard shack at the main gate and the personnel within.

With the way clear, the escaping Rangers drove south on Rosemont Avenue and then north on US 15.

0300 hours, January 21, 2017

In less than an hour, the Ranger's convoy reached the Eisenhower National Historic Site at Baltimore Pike, in Gettysburg, PA. The attack on Fort Detrick had been so swift and unexpected that the Provos had not been able to react to it in time, or to notice the direction the stolen vehicles had taken.

The Provos were following the SOP for incidents at Detrick. Any news release written on the attack would have to get cleared by the highest military authorities. As it was, everyone did in fact think that the facility was still being used for biological and chemical warfare R&D. Catching the culprits would have to be weighed against raising the level of paranoia in the area surrounding Detrick. So, any follow-up action against the Rangers would have to wait.

0305 hours, January 21, 2017

The Provos didn't even alert other area facilities that a band of bad guys was running amuck in the countryside. Jude and his Rangers arrived unnoticed at the wooded area across from what used to be the Eisenhower Farm, and was now Joseph Greco's private retreat.

They left the vehicles right on SW Confederate Avenue, and followed the tree line until just before the skeet range, where a new wrought iron fence, constructed to Secret Service specifications, blocked their way. The tools that the breach team brought would have been useful for a chain link fence, but not for the inch thick wrought iron bars. There were probably ground sensors to worry about, too.

The Secret Service had made a deal with Google Maps to block publication of visual security details on the site. As a result, Jude's Rangers had gone into the second objective blind and unprepared. They had had no time to do surveillance or any type of useful recon. Jude and Ed decided that none was needed, because they knew that Greco would probably not be on-site. The objective had been to shake him up, not to kill him or to deny him his little pleasures.

Jude had the Rangers bring the two light machineguns and four M-72s up to the fence. They waited until the Secret Service agents on duty scrambled to investigate the disruption that the ground sensors had almost certainly reported. The skeleton staff left behind when Greco was not home was substantial and well-armed, but they could not compete with trained, battle-tested Rangers.

0306 hours, January 21, 2017.

As the agents rushed to their observation points the house's east wall caved in under the impact of two M-72 rockets. The big building was also hit by two rockets, but the structure was more substantial than the old farm house. Immediately after the rocket impact the light machineguns raked the target with fire.

A four-man insertion team jumped the security fence and ran towards the site, following the tree line that ran past the skeet range. As they passed a small building next to the skeet range the Rangers lobbed two fragmentation grenades at it. The frags caused a gigantic explosion that shook the ground. Greco's men had been storing ammunition and explosives in the small building.

The light machineguns ceased fire when the small building exploded and another four-man team jumped the fence, and stormed the site under cover fire from the fire team nearer to the skeet range. The LAWs had done a 'job' on the structures and their occupants. The team in the open only drew pistol fire from the big building; an uncharacteristic response for Secret Service agents trained to return fire with their ever present FN P-90 sub machineguns. The actual farmhouse was silently engulfed by a growing fire that the M-72 rockets had started.

The Rangers that were in the open, led by Jude, threw themselves on the ground and laid cover fire so that the team from the skeet range could move ahead. As the maneuvering fire team advanced, Jude spotted a man with a square box on his shoulder appearing on the south side of the big building. He aimed the box toward the Rangers on his right. It was a Stinger anti-aircraft missile and he was about to launch it at the rushing Rangers!

Jude drew a bead on the man with the Stinger and fired a short burst with his M-4 that hit the man in the suit center mass, but not before he could squeeze the missile's trigger. The missile flew towards the maneuvering Rangers as the Secret Service agent fell to the ground. The missile streaked, hovered, and redirected itself toward the burning building by the skeet range, which blew up in a cloud of exploding embers.

The Stinger is a heat-seeking missile. Jude couldn't guess what possessed the USSS agent to try to use an anti-aircraft weapon against troops in the open.

When the maneuvering team hit the ground to lay cover fire for Jude's team, the four men rushed the big building. Jude knelt by the missile man whose body was crumpled upon the Stinger's casing. He noticed that the man had not been wearing body armor and the 5.56mm rounds had torn his chest open. Jude also recovered the radio the USSS man had dropped when he fell. No one fired at the Rangers from the buildings.

0312 hours, January 21, 2017

The Rangers were mopping up when Jude spotted three armored Suburbans parked on the quadrilateral, north of the big building. He radioed his Rangers to close in on the SUVs. As they got near them, two doors were thrown open and three men stepped out with their hands up.

Jude yelled at them, "Get on the ground. Get on the ground." They complied quickly.

The Rangers rushed at the prone men keeping them in their carbines' sights. One of the men had prayer beads wrapped around his left hand. The nearest Ranger grabbed him by the hair and lifted his head from the ground telling him, "Salam alekum, motherfucker!"

The man responded by spitting at the Ranger. The man missed, but the Ranger's boot didn't. It hit the prone spitter squarely on the left ribcage.

The Ranger yelled at Jude keeping the man's head in his grip. "Boss, I don't think these guys are Secret Service."

Jude rushed over and squatted by the man, searching his pockets. He found a laminated card printed in Arabic credentialing the man as an officer in the Army of God.

By this time, the Rangers had finished searching the site for bodies and survivors and established perimeter security around the Suburbans, where Jude and the other Rangers were binding the prisoners' hands with plastic ties. Jude called over one of his Rangers. "Fared, come over here."

The Ranger rushed over and knelt by Jude pointing his weapon towards the outside sector of the perimeter he had been guarding. Jude aimed his own carbine in the same direction, assuming the man's duties as he told him,

"Find out why these guys are here instead of the Secret Service".

Fared turned to the Militiaman and was about to ask him in Arabic what Jude had said in English when the prisoner turned at Fared, spit in his face–this time not missing–and said in perfect English with a southern twang, "I don't need no fuckin' 'kafir' to question me. I speak your fuckin' language. But not for long. That's one of the things that's gonna go when we take over."

Fared wiped the spit off his face, returning a glob of his own that caught the Militiaman square on the left eye. He laughed at the prisoner and told him, "Of course I'm a freaking 'apostate', asshole. I'm a Lebanese-American Christian. But, you see the guy by the fence? He's a Lebanese-American Moslem. He'll be happy to squeeze your nuts. Your buddies in Chicago got a hold of his little sister last month. He's not squeamish at the sight of a bloody scrotum. So your choice is this: Either you talk to me or to him."

"Or to me," said Jude, with his eyes still on the perimeter he was guarding. "Now that I know y'all fohm Georgiah," he continued in a bad imitation of a Georgia accent. "I wanna heah y'all's last wohds telling me WHADDA FUCK YOU DOING HERE!"

This last phrase Jude changed into an exaggerated intonation of his native Brooklyn accent. The Ranger drew his knife and placed the point right on the man's jugular.

"OK. OK", capitulated the Militiaman when the sharp point of the commando knife lightly pierced the skin on his neck. "We are training on VIP protection. They let us guard the place when Greco's not around."

The prisoner on his right shouted at his colleague, "Shut up. Shut up. Don't tell them anything."

Jude looked at Fared while still covering the perimeter with his M-4 "Fared. That's all we need to know. Bind his legs." To the other Rangers Jude said, "And you guys tie up those other two. Strict silence as of right now. These guys talk 'kafir'."

He hadn't used that line since Afghanistan, and the other Rangers chuckled at the memories it evoked.

Jude pointed at the Suburbans. They all mounted up and sped toward Red Rock Road in the west to make their getaway, leaving the three Militiamen trussed up like chickens at the parking lot.

0330 hours, January 21, 2017.

None of the Rangers saw the helicopter gunships as their rockets struck the Suburbans near Warfield Ridge Observation Tower. The last thing Jude felt was his SUV rolling onto the ancient battlefield, communing with the Gettysburg dead.

CHAPTER 20 – Prisoner of War

"Army Code of Conduct

I - I am an American, fighting in the forces which guard my country and our way of life. I am prepared to give my life in their defense.

II - I will never surrender of my own free will. If in command, I will never surrender the members of my command while they still have the means to resist.

III - If I am captured I will continue to resist by all means available. I will make every effort to escape and to aid others to escape. I will accept neither parole nor special favors from the enemy.

IV - If I become a prisoner of war, I will keep faith with my fellow prisoners. I will give no information or take part in any action which might be harmful to my comrades. If I am senior, I will take command. If not, I will obey the lawful orders of those appointed over me and will back them up in every way.

V - When questioned, should I become a prisoner of war, I am required to give name, rank, service number, and date of birth. I will evade answering further questions to the utmost of my ability. I will make no oral or written statements disloyal to my country and its allies or harmful to their cause.

VI - I will never forget that I am an American, fighting for freedom, responsible for my actions, and dedicated to the principles which made my country free. I will trust in my God and in the United States of America."

1235 hours, January 21, 2017

Jude hurt all over. He opened his eyes, but he couldn't see. There was a hood over his head. His hands and feet were tied. He was lying face down in the rear foot well of an SUV. The vehicle was rolling, and every bump found another part of his body that hurt.

Part of his ACU top was wet; with blood, he supposed. But the wet part didn't hurt. He took stock of his condition. His left leg was numb, but that could be because the plastic bindings at his ankles were so tight they cut into the flesh through his thick wool socks. His head throbbed as if an elephant had reluctantly gotten up after sitting on it for an hour. Another bump, another stab of pain. There it was, the left shoulder.

The bumps gradually diminished as he felt the SUV go up an incline. It felt like a ramp to a highway. The SUV began rolling smoothly, just as he felt another stab on his neck. Dark sleep.

1345 hours, January 21, 2017

There were hands holding his arms and hands holding his legs. The rest of his body was up in the air. He was being carried. Carried and quickly thrown on something soft…a bed? No, the soft part was thin over a hard surface.

It was a gurney. The gurney rolled on in silence. The people pushing it were professionals. They didn't talk. They didn't receive directions from anyone else. Or, maybe they had done this so often that there was no need to talk.

Doors clicked open and the gurney emerged into a warmer place. He was somewhere where there was heat, out of the punishing winter.

"Put him in number 4," said a voice, the first he had heard. A little more rolling then a door opened. Hands clutched his hands and other hands grabbed his legs.

Up in the air, then smashing into a hard surface. He had been thrown on a floor, still trussed up.

It hurt.

Sleep came.

1405 hours, January 21, 2017

A door clicked and a rush of warm air finished the process of waking, which had begun seconds…no, minutes before. Steps from leather soled boots with leather heels smacked against the cold concrete. Who the hell wore leather boots anymore? The point of one of them buried itself in his left side, sending an electric pulse up to his left shoulder. Other boots stomped in, but those were the sound of rubber soles.

A pair of hands tugged at his black hood, ripping it from his head. Jude's head flopped down hard onto the concrete floor. This time when the pain hit him, his eyes saw flashes of light, a bare bulb on the ceiling, a smirking face looking down at him, and the backs of two camo uniforms leaving through the open door, shutting it firmly behind them.

"Welcome to my world, kafir" mocked the thin falsetto voice. Another kick. "Let's establish the rules from the outset, kafir. I ask. You talk. Clear?"

Another kick.

"Let's start with something easy, like your name," screeched the voice as the next kick landed in the soft void below his left ribcage.

Jude heard himself moan, but he grabbed the moan with tight lips and just exhaled to relieve the pain. Leather boots. Leather riding boots, that's what they were. The man squatted next to his face. He hadn't bathed or brushed his teeth recently.

The hand pinched his left ear and lifted Jude's head a little, only to drop it where it smacked the concrete again. "Let's hear a name, kafir. I want to hear words out of your mouth, not moans".

Jude went into the disembodied mode they taught him at…was it Bragg? Benning? Fort Benning. In the hut they called 'the hole'.

He began to recite to himself the Code of Conduct, interrupted by ear pulls and head smacks. Minutes went by. The pain in the back of his head was getting worse. He waited as long as he could, as they'd taught him. And then he exhaled: "Winthrop."

A smile brightened the man's face.

"Ah, Winthrop. Yes, Winthrop. I don't suppose there's something more to that name, is there?" screeched 'Boots' in a rising crescendo.

More ear grabs, more head smacks. It seemed like hours, but Jude knew it had only been minutes until his captor got the word "Jude" out of him.

"A Jew!" howled his captor "A fucking Zionist dog!" Jude didn't know whether he should laugh or cry at the man's asinine assumption. Another kick to his side, then the door opened. Someone whispered at 'Boots'.

His captor stood up and turned to leave, but not before burrowing another foot into Jude's side, twisting it and pushing it further in. Jude's cloudy mind came up with a comedy line he had once heard from a standup comic: "Fellow, you really know how to hurt a guy!"

He surprised himself at this humorous thought just before he passed out from the pain.

1645 hours, January 21, 2017

Jude could tell it was dark outside because the light bulb over his head shone brighter. It was the only source of light. He turned his head awkwardly around and spotted the window from where the darkness filtered into the room. The floors were bare now, but they had once held either carpeting or linoleum tiles.

Linoleum tiles. He could see their square shapes outlined in the dried adhesive that checkered the floor.

The door creaked open. Jude saw that it was a plain wooden door with a reinforced translucent window. This must have been sort of an office at one point. Random thoughts to keep away the pain, he told himself.

Two guys came in. One wore a suit with a bulge on the right. The other wore ACUs with a Velcro rank-a black oak leaf: a lieutenant colonel.

'Suit' lowered a digital camera to Jude's face and captured several frames. He also shot the bloodied ACUs. 'Uniform' just stared at him. Jude thought he saw a smile.

'Suit' pulled out a knife and cut the plastic bindings around Jude's hands and ankles. The wave of pain shooting through his liberated limbs almost made Jude faint again.

A private with a side arm walked in. He carried a paper bag and a plastic bottle of water, which he placed next to Jude.

"Lock the door and stand outside, and don't let any of these guys in," said 'Uniform'. Then more whispered words were passed between them as 'Suit' and 'Uniform' stepped outside.

It took Jude a long while to stand up. He examined his body, gingerly touching the sore parts, which were many. There was a bad, seared cut on his left shoulder, sort of like a bullet scrape, but wider. He guessed it might have been a large caliber projectile. The caked blood must have been from it. The pain in his head was atrocious.

He sat down against wall, slowly unscrewing the cap on the water bottle. He took a sip that turned into gulps that emptied the entire container. He slid back against the wall clutching the paper bag. In the bag he saw there was some sort of white bread sandwich. He wolfed it down. It had been hours since he last ate anything. Then it hit him: his men! Where were they?

Jude hobbled to his feet and banged on the door. "Hey, private! Hey, private!"

He saw the silhouette of the Provo through the translucent glass turn toward the room…and turn away again. "Hey man. I just want to know where my guys are. Are they in the next room? Are they OK?"

The silhouette turned once again and barked through the door, "Ain't nobody here but you. Now shut the fuck up."

Jude slid down the wall to the floor again. Thoughts assailed his subconscious: They're dead. They're wounded in the hospital wing of whatever this place is.

What is this place? He peered at the superimposed bars through more reinforced translucent glass. It was a makeshift cell. Something else must have been here before. A gigantic wave of nausea wrapped up around him.

He vomited, soiled himself, and fainted.

0645 hours, January 22, 2017

Jude woke inside something soft and white. He felt bandages around his head with his left hand. He had tried to touch them first with his right hand, but it was handcuffed to a bed rail. He had woken up to the scrape of a portable x-ray machine being rolled up next to his bed. When it was over his head a guy in scrubs said, "Don't move" as if he could have with the searing pain. There was a whirring sound.

As 'Scrubs' wheeled the machine out he said to the armed uniform with him, "For sure a concussion. I don't need the picture to tell."

Yeah, it made sense. He looked at himself lifting the bed covers with his left hand. He was naked. Someone had scrubbed him clean. Then he remembered he had thrown up and everything had gone black. Just then a guy came in with the private. He was also wearing ACUs, but of a different camo pattern.

The man threw a hospital gown at Jude's bed and ordered him to put it on. He slid into it the moment his right hand came out of the handcuffs, but he had neither the strength nor the modesty to tie the back strings. The private did that before he helped him walk out of the room. Jude took a chance "Hey, Private…Private."

The young man turned around and looked at Jude. "I just wanna know about my buddies." There was pleading in his voice. Jude's beseeching got to the private.

"I ain't supposed to talk witchya, man," the private said in almost a whisper.

"Wait, please. I just need to know," said Jude.

"Ain't nobody here but you, man. Just shut up. You gonna get us both in trouble." The private walked him into another room with another hospital bed in it. His guard left and closed the door behind him.

Hours went by. Jude saw Provos pass through the window ten feet from his hospital bed. Another armed guard entered the room with a male nurse who sculpted him, took his blood pressure, gauged his temperature with a digital thermometer, and looked at his injured left shoulder. Not a word was said.

0800 hours, January 25, 2018

Jude could tell it was 0800 because the 24-hour clock over the passageway door said so, and because it had been about an hour since they had brought him coffee and a plate of chipped cream beef or 'shit-on-a-shingle,' as it was traditionally called in the Army.

His left arm was in the guard's grip; the same private as the first night. They were walking down the hallway again. And they would stop at the MI captain's office again. The intelligence insignia, the dagger through the heraldic sun, was all over his face but nothing on his uniform. The captain would ask his questions again and Jude would remain quiet again.

This time, the captain did not end by calling the private to take him back to his cell. This time the captain said, "Well old buddy, tomorrow you are going to wish you had talked to me. The civilians at Langley are taking over this evening. I can tell you were one of us before you turned, so I really feel for you."

And the Captain got up and with his hands behind his back walked around the seated Jude. "Look. I've told you about me…West Point grad…bottom of my class…that's why they wouldn't give me a combat arms commission and I wound up in MI."

Nothing from Jude. "I told you about my wife and son staying back home in Connecticut."

The Captain saw the cloud pass by Jude's blank stare. "I hit a nerve, didn't I? Look, Jude, tell me where your family is, and I'll let them know you're OK. Promise."

"You know, I've got your 201 File. You were a Ranger officer, and a good one. You would have made Major in record time with the fruit salad that was on your chest. Especially the Silver Star you got in the Sandbox."

Jude's eyes kept the straight-ahead stare. "Given time, you would have talked to me." his interrogator intoned remorsefully, "We could have been best buddies at another place and time."

And a few seconds after, "We checked on your DD-214 home of record and couldn't find Angie. A neighbor told us you had moved out of state, but she didn't know where to," said the man using the information he had to get the prisoner to talk. Strict tradecraft.

Silence.

"Come on. You owe it to Angie. I can let her know where you are. Maybe she can even visit you later on."

Jude turned his eyes at the Captain; if looks could kill...

"They're gonna make you talk, buddy." The Captain was dry and serious now.

"Any chance you would spill your guts to me, now? …Last time." Jude fleetingly thought the guy was honestly trying to help; just like an alligator helps a duck sitting on the swamp's surface, his alter ego told him.

The look on Jude's eyes told the Military Intelligence Captain that it was useless. "Private, do your thing." The interrogator had used his 'outside voice'.

The guard came into the room, held the door open and walked Jude back to his cell.

1915 hours, January 25, 2017

No lunch at 1130. No dinner at 1800. They were softening him up. It was dark when they came for him.

Two black clad paramilitaries from the Agency rushed into the cell and threw him forcefully against the wall. One pressed his face against the wall's cold surface, while the other plastic-tied his hands.

What, no handcuffs? These guys were definitely not MPs, nor law enforcement. They hauled him out of the cell and shoved him down the hallway, and then out of the building into the freezing winter evening, all while still wearing his backless hospital gown.

Jude got his first look outside and immediately recognized the place. He had driven almost daily by the Carderock Naval Surface Warfare Center, and passed the arched roof of its main structure, which loomed above him now. Another shove propelled him to the truck with the black tinted-glass side windows, where another black-clad figure, probably the driver, was holding the rear door open for Jude. One of the two guards climbed inside with Jude firmly in his grip. The other got into the cabin with the driver.

The truck lurched forward with a jolt that made the guard and his M-4 jump on his seat. The jolt lit up Jude's consciousness. Another bump knocked the guard sideways on his metal bench.

They were probably coming out of the security gate, thought Jude. He mentally ran through the flaws in the transportation operation. They should have never put an armed guard inside with him. They should have metal 'cuffed him to the seat instead of relying on plastic ties.

The transport took a huge round ramp over Clara Barton, heading south. He could tell from the facility now being on his left. If only the vehicle veered right at the fork, then they were going to take him to Langley over the Chain Bridge. That would be excellent.

They veered right at the fork.

Jude's mental computer was working overtime. There was a traffic light at Chain Bridge where they would have to stop, if it were red, before they turned right on to the bridge itself. Past the bridge, there was an upgrade that was difficult to negotiate on a very bumpy road. He made his decision.

Turning right after the traffic light the truck's gears strained in advance of the coming rise. The vehicle jerked up at the end of the bridge, as it turned right on to Chain Bridge Road.

Jude swung his head to the left into his guard's face, knocking him down from the metal bench, the M-4 clanking on the metal floor. He swung his right knee at the guard's sternum, propelling its bone spikes into the heart and killing him instantly. The jolt at the end of the bridge had masked the confrontation between the two men in the back.

Writhing on the truck's floor, Jude worked his butt and then his legs through the well formed by his tied hands, reversing the plastic tie to the front. Jude felt for a pulse at the guard's neck to make sure he was dead. He then rummaged with his bound hands through the dead guard's pockets until he found something sharp: a fingernail clipper. He turned the clipper towards him, put the plastic tie between its jaws, and then snapped it.

He was free.

Taking a chance that the cabin he was riding in was not armored-and why would it be? - he lifted the dead guard's M-4, turned the selector switch from 'Semi' to 'Auto' and emptied the magazine in it against the bulkhead behind the driver and the other guard.

He felt the van slow down on the upgrade and start to roll backward down Chain Bridge Road. He had hit at least the driver.

Before the van came to a rolling stop, Jude relieved the dead guard of another magazine, locked and loaded the M-4 and pulverized one of the tinted side windows. He then dove out head first and landed on the asphalt.

His right shoulder hit the pavement below, but he was hurting so much all over by now that he almost didn't feel it. He got up and ran into the brush and down the embankment under the Chain Bridge.

Jude spotted a trail on his right as he went down the embankment. It was the Potomac Heritage Trail, where he and Angie had often hiked on weekends. He turned around and headed north on the empty trail and ran until it turned into Pimmit Run. In less than a mile he had crossed under the George Washington Parkway and soon an unlit McMansion loomed before him.

Jude waited in the brush for a few minutes, taking time to see if there was any movement inside the house. He was shivering, still in his open-back hospital gown, and he hoped the house could prove a source of food and clothing.

2035 hours, January 25, 2017

Jude cautiously circled the house to spot not only movement but the tell-tale alarm signs. Yep, there they were: the blue octagonal ADT lawn signs. Now he knew he had to be quick because the house was sure to be monitored. He spotted the piano room's door to the terrace and decided it would be his entry point. He looked through the glass without touching it, and spotted the staircase to the second floor. His plan was to get whatever clothing he could find in the second floor bedroom closets, and then run out of the house through the kitchen and pantry, grabbing food and drink. He was starving.

Then he had a bad thought. What if there was a dog? He knew he couldn't kill a dog if his life depended on it. Well, maybe if his life really depended on it. Focus, he told himself. Cross that bridge when you get to it!

Putting his fear aside, he turned his head to avoid glass chards and smashed a glass panel with the M-4. There was no apparent reaction to the glass breaking, but he was barefoot and had to tread lightly so as not to cut his feet, the infantryman's prize possession. He reached through the broken pane and unlocked the door.

He rushed hell bent up to the second floor, hoping for the best. He found the master bedroom and a gigantic closet. No people, no dog, yet. He grabbed hiking shoes, woolen socks, jeans and a warm shirt; and then a black North Face ski jacket. The shoes and clothes were a little big on him, but at least he could wear them. As he was leaving the closet he saw a cell phone on a table and pocketed it. Time was of the essence. He estimated five minutes to an alarm response, knowing that it would probably take a little more.

He ran back down to the kitchen and found the pantry. He filled a plastic grocery bag he found on the granite counter with as much portable food he could carry. As he stuffed in several Hershey bars left on top of the kitchen table, he spotted the lights coming up the driveway. The car did not have police lights, not even yellow security guard lights. It stopped by the front door. A man and a woman got out laughing and joking and walked towards the door, leaving the car running.

Jude knelt behind the kitchen's center island and held the M-4 at the ready as the couple ran up to the second floor, laughing playfully at having left the tickets on the night table. As soon as they were out of sight, Jude went out the front door, got into the running car and sped out into the night. He changed cars as often as he could, stealing first a blue Camaro and then a black Mini. He drove west into the Virginia country side where he knew the Appalachian Command would be advancing.

CHAPTER 21 — Hell Has No Fury

"Heaven has no rage like love to hatred turned, Nor hell a fury like a woman scorned," spoken by Zara in Act III, Scene VIII, The Mourning Bride, William Congreve, 1697

2335 hours, January 9, 2018

When Kate and Jude walked into the bedroom where the Greco woman was hogtied and gagged, the hostage's face went bright and then quickly somber again. They were the only two Rebs whose face she had been able to see up to now. She was no dummy. She understood what it meant to be able to see the faces of the kidnappers. For sure they were going to kill her. What was left of her composure hit a new low.

Jude abruptly turned to Kate and said, "Do your thing, Kate."

Amanda's face turned a whiter shade of pale. Kate understood the psychological importance of the moment and cocked her carbine while looking at Amanda intently. At the sound of the chambering round, Amanda lost both her composure and her bladder control.

Kate laughed at the woman's terror and handed her carbine to Jude. Jude hung her carbine from his left shoulder by kept his own M-4 trained on Amanda while Kate went into her rucksack to fish out the ACUs she had brought for the hostage.

Kate turned to Jude and Steve, who had walked into the room, and told them, "I've got this. You jocks step out while I dress and cater to her humid majesty. This is not a peep show."

Kate's words both confused and calmed Amanda, adding to her embarrassment for having soiled herself in fear. Jude turned to Steve, adding a compliment to his nemesis of the last two days. "Let's go. If she says she's got it, she's got it."

Minutes later Kate dragged a drier and ACU attired Amanda through the bedroom's doorway into the living room. She had replaced the plastic hand restraints and the gag, but left her legs free so that the woman could walk on newly booted feet. Steve took this as his cue, nodded good-bye at Jude and disappeared into the spare bedroom where they kept the other hostage.

What happened next did so with tremendous economy of movement and words. Once Kate gave the all clear from the window, Jude threw Amanda over his right shoulder in a fireman's carry and slid effortlessly out the door to the front porch and into the night.

Both teams left the house simultaneously, the snatch team through the rear entrance with their Provo G-2 and Jude and Kate and the Greco woman through the front.

As Jude's little team disappeared into the woods surrounding the safe house, they heard the Sienna's motor turn-over and pull away to continue its journey toward Cumberland.

Silence returned to the empty frame house.

2350 hours, January 9, 2018

Once in the woods, Jude realized that they had to cross as soon as possible into the relative safety of the Northern Virginia no man's land. Through sheer combat exhaustion both fighting factions had remained on each side of the Potomac River. It was a temporary stalemate. But by now the Greco forces would all be out searching for Mrs. Boss.

In fact, her value to both sides was understandably high. Really, thought Jude, the snatch team should have changed plans altogether and taken both hostages to AC (forward) and fuck Colorado. Precious time had been lost. When Jude and Ed had been pouring over the map for the return route, they had agreed that it would probably be best to cross back into Virginia as soon as they got the hostage in custody. Now, Jude was certain.

They had tentatively agreed on using the old Noland Ferry landing. Despite the name there was no ferry boat, but there was a landing where recreational craft had been available for rent in pre-Greco America. The Provos had closed up Noland and boarded it up, but the chances were good they had not removed all the rentals. In the worst case scenario, if there were no boats, it was only a short swim to Heater's Island in the middle of the Potomac River.

The other factor for using the landing was that the Provos were concerned about the Rebs landing in Maryland, not leaving from Maryland. With Heater's Island to its immediate west and open fields to its east, Noland Ferry Landing was not the optimal location for a Rebel push from Virginia. So its security in that respect should be minimal. Jude handed Amanda to Kate and took the lead.

0120 hours, January 10, 2018

Kate was disgusted at the sight of the shouldered hot chick rubbing herself all over Jude; or at his hand firmly on her butt. All at once she stifled that thought and got angry at herself for thinking that way. After all, Jude was nothing to her. But it came down to the old 'I saw him first' complex which has plagued womankind since cave dwelling times. So she gave Amanda Greco a good shove just for the hell of it so as to get her moving and let her know who was boss.

In the meantime Jude led them in a westerly direction using the thickest cover he could find up until they got to the clearing where the high tension wires ran by the MARC train tracks. Having no other choice, they rushed across the open terrain with their prisoner.

They were soon at the C&O Canal. Up this way, at this time of the year, it was just mud. So they crossed it at a run and spent a good 10 minutes afterwards cleaning the sticky mud from their boots. Through all of this, Kate bumped and pushed and hurried Amanda along despite her tied hands and gagged mouth.

Whenever Jude looked back he would find Amanda's eyes looking at him in a silent prayer for salvation from the mad redhead who was driving her like an obstinate cow. Jude took it all in stride with a smile, understanding fully what was really going on. The woods thinned and their pace slowed near the landing.

There was a road that ran parallel to the canal, ending in a concrete platform that descended into the water. They spotted a Provo Humvee parked at the edge and froze in their tracks. As far as they could see, there was only a driver inside it. He looked to be either asleep or bored to death, texting his friends or listening to music through ear buds. Whatever the case, the Provo was just looking down into the steering wheel, not watching out for the enemy.

Kate pushed Amanda to the ground and held her there with the left hand while her right pointed the M-4 carbine toward the enemy vehicle. After a few minutes of observation to determine that the driver was in fact alone, Jude got Kate's attention, pointed at his chest and ran his right index finger across his neck, signaling that he would take care of the Provo.

The Ranger approached the vehicle at a crouch. As he reached the driver's door he unsheathed his Fairbairn-Sykes knife silently and transferred it to his left hand.

From a distance Kate saw him slither up to the truck's window in total silence, slowly examine the position of the guard's head using the Humvee's left hand rear view mirror, and strike with the speed of a cobra.

No fancy stuff like in the movies. The stiletto just went up into the guard's ear and its point was stopped at the inside top of the man's skull. He took the knife out in the same motion: no sounds, lots of spurting blood. Jude went still after the kill. His eyes scanned all around and his ears listened for sounds from inside the landing's house. Nothing. He replaced the dagger in the leather scabbard after wiping it on the dead man's sleeve and disappeared into the bushes around the house, carrying his M-4 carbine diagonally across his chest, what the Army calls 'at port arms.

He was gone for what seemed to Kate like an eternity but was in fact only minutes. She thought Jude was probably OK because she didn't hear shouts or shots from inside the house.

In time, Jude reappeared at the front door. He was calmly drying his hands with a kitchen towel, and signaling for Kate to approach. She lifted Amanda up and pushed her towards the house. The women had not reached the door where Jude was still drying his hands when they heard the growl of an approaching vehicle.

With all the shoving and pushing Amanda's gag had come loose and she managed a weak shout for help. Kate hit her with an upper cut and Amanda fell to the ground like a sack of potatoes. Jude lifted her up, throwing her once again on his shoulder as Kate secured the rear. They ran towards the landing. Jude reached a grounded canoe into which he threw the unconscious Amanda Greco, while he and Kate heaved it into the water.

They both jumped into the canoe forward and aft of the motionless Amanda and took hold of the paddles. Right about then the truck's headlights lit the Humvee and honked.

Two Provos dismounted quickly and walked toward the Humvee when the second honk drew no reaction from the driver. As they reached the driver's door, the truck's headlights illuminated the figure of their comrade slumped behind the wheel. They locked and loaded their M-16s simultaneously and crouched as they looked all around. One of them climbed briefly to check that their buddy was really dead, and confirmed it to his colleague. They then moved cautiously toward the house.

They went in the house in a bad imitation of TV cops clearing a suspect premise. After a few moments they exited through a door that opened towards the concrete platform and spotted the canoe pulling away in the shadowy river water. While Jude paddled towards Heater's Island, Kate was covering the rear. When the

Provos appeared in her sight she squeezed off two shots, dropping them both with an economy of lead that would have pleased a Chinese executioner[2]: two rounds, two men.

She then calmly turned towards the front, grabbed her paddle and fell into Jude's rhythm towards Heater's Island as if nothing had happened. Time was of the essence because dawn was creeping in around them and other Provos had to have heard the shots. They reached the island quickly. Kate disembarked, dragging Amanda to the shore while Jude pushed the canoe back into the water, to be carried away by the current.

---

[2] Chinese PLA executioners were known to spend only one bullet per victim, and then sending a bill to the victim's family for the cost of the bullet.

CHAPTER 22 – Heater's Island

"[warning Billy over the radio] Billy? Get outta there! Come about! Let it- let it carry you out of there! What the hell are you doing? Billy! For Christ sake! You're steaming into a bomb! Turn around for Christ sake! Billy, can ya hear me? You're headed right for the middle of the monster! Billy?... [starts crying]" The Perfect Storm (2000) directed by Wolfgang Petersen

0155 hours, January 10, 2018

Heater's Island had been a wildlife sanctuary back in the day; a place for anglers, hunters and bird watchers. It was no longer so. Jude had made an educated guess that there would be no Provos there since their doctrine was to contain the Rebs on the Virginia side of the Potomac from the safe Maryland shore, not from some island in the middle of the river. But he was hyper vigilant anyway, and as quiet as the thorn bushes, the now re-gagged and awoken hostage and an angry Kate would allow. It took only a few careful minutes to get to the island's western shore. With any luck they would be able to cross and be well into the Virginia side before sun up.

In escape and evasion situations Rangers prefer to move at night and hole up during the daylight.

Jude pointed Kate and Amanda into a natural hole in the brush, under the umbrella cover of a thorny bush close to the ground. He moved on into the woods to recon their immediate area. Kate literally sat on the prone Amanda while Jude spent the next hour or so going over their tip of the island and choosing a crossing point to Virginia.

The island was about a mile long by half a mile wide in its widest part. There were all kinds of birds, ranging from herons to mallards to wild turkeys. And there were deer. But not a creature stirred in the path of the Ranger.

Jude had found a hunting stand right on a tree adjacent to the bush where he had left the women. He decided to keep watch from there after returning to theme.

Close by their improvised lair there was the wreck of an old car, obviously carried there by a flood. Further out there were the ruins of a wooden farmhouse and its barn. But there was no other sign of life.

Jude walked back down along the shore to where the women were. He chose a point to wade across the Potomac, and marked it with a cairn so that he could find it later. He also noted that the current was kind of rough; something strange for this stage of the river and the time of the year.

When he got back, he saw how tired Kate looked and decided to take a couple of hours rest, sacrificing half the operational time before dawn. He took into consideration that the enemy did not seem to be in hot pursuit, and that resting a bit would increase their effectiveness, especially during a river crossing.

Jude unraveled his paracord bracelet and used the nylon cord to help Kate tether Amanda to the base of the bush, to give Kate time to sleep while he kept watch from above.

No sooner had he climbed the tree, and Kate had begun to relax when the gagged Amanda kicked her leg. Kate's predictable reaction found her K-bar tickling the hostage's neck in a lighting move. With wide eyes Amanda signaled Kate that she was thirsty. To Kate, the Greco woman was quickly becoming a royal pain in the ass.

Jude was having a fun time watching Kate deal with the beauty queen. Kate looked up and, noticing his smile, signaled her displeasure with her middle finger. She then whispered at Jude that if he found it so funny he should come down and take care of the bitch. When Jude made the motion to go down to do so, Kate dismissed him with a gesture and untied Amanda so she could hold the canteen.

Kate was passing her canteen to the woman when the hostage swung it against Kate's jaw. The unexpected blow knocked Kate down. In a surprisingly fast move, Amanda grabbed the K-bar from Kate's boot with her bound hands, slicing quickly through the plastic ties. She turned towards the stunned Kate, the business end of the knife moving to strike the downed fighter, when the barrel of Jude's carbine pressed against her neck and froze her in place. There was hatred on her face as she reluctantly dropped the knife.

Jude retied her hands with fresh plastic ties, secured the gag and tended to Kate, who was getting up. As he helped Kate stand up, the former MP Captain connected a lightning fast side kick at Amanda Greco, catching her in the stomach; the hostage doubling over in pain. It was all Jude could do to keep Kate from retrieving the K-bar and scalping the bitch. Kate was strong, and as he held her he felt the hidden power of her muscles against his grip.

Wrapping his arms around his partner's, he whispered hoarsely in her ear to stop and remember their mission was to take the Greco woman back to headquarters.

Kate looked at him with clenched teeth and fierce eyes that were dripping tears of rage. Jude held her close to his chest and her anger appeared to subside into angry, silent convulsions. In a sudden move, Kate loosened his grip on her and lunged once more at the prone Amanda, stopping short under the steel vise of the Ranger's arms.

"Am I gonna have to knock you out to make you stop?" Jude told her in a low voice. She exhaled and gave up with finality, sheathing her knife. But her eyes were locked with Amanda's, who knew at that point that Kate had declared open season on her.

Jude asked Kate to take up the watch on the deer stand since her anger was not going to allow her to sleep anyway. He hog-tied Amanda Greco with his paracord, tethering her again to the bush, and fell asleep next to the hostage within seconds in an impressive display of equanimity. Up on her perch, Kate thought about the man and the way he did things. And she thought that she was thinking much too much about him. She then put her entire focus on the watch.

0400 hours, January 10, 2018

Towards 0400 Kate broke out the rations for her and the Greco woman. She refused to release her hands and had to feed her, taking special delight in trying to choke her with each mouthful. Jude watched the operation from above with a smile. This would be the last watch before they swam across to the Northern Virginia shore. Meantime, Jude noticed that it was getting cooler and windier really fast.

Storms that hit the area usually come from the west at breakneck speed. This one was no exception. The rare thing was that it was happening in winter, but then, the weather had been acting crazy for a bunch of years.

The worst part was that they had not counted on having to deal with a storm. The wind blew softly at first and increased its force exponentially within minutes. The island was being buffeted by 20 to 30 miles per hour gusts that bent trees and bushes toward the east. Jude thought he spotted a squall line on the northwest and kept an apprehensive lookout for twisters, tornadoes or water spouts. He wasn't sure which version could hit the Potomac.

A sudden crack of light–winter lightning, wouldn't you know it?-illuminated the brush around them. Jude didn't need the additional concern of being hit by lightning or have a tree fall on them. It was clear that they would have to seek better shelter and postpone the crossing until the storm subsided.

Amanda Greco was terrified of thunder and lightning and bent twisted into the bush as her bindings allowed. Her body jumped each time a bolt of lightning cracked nearby. It shuddered at the menacing rumble of thunder. Kate might have been slightly concerned about the storm herself if only she weren't enjoying so much its effect on 'the bitch'.

Jude had originally decided against staying in the farm house because the abandoned wooden buildings would have been too obvious for Provo searchers. But he didn't think the Provos even knew that they and Mrs. Boss were on the island, and the storm was getting too strong and too wet for operational effectiveness. He grabbed Kate's arm and signaled to follow him, which began another round of pushing the Greco woman around. So off they went in the direction of the wooden structures. They got to the buildings within minutes and quickly dropped to their knees.

He and the women waited a while in the tree line to ensure there was no movement in the empty buildings. When they saw no signs of danger in or around the wooden structures Jude signaled Kate to stay put so that he could go clear the buildings. Just then, a humongous tree fell down only 10 yards in front of them.

That did it. They both ran for the barn dragging Amanda, diving on the way behind the fallen tree.

Jude looked at Kate, pointed at his chest and resumed his sprint to the barn while Kate covered him from the fallen tree. He led into the wooden structure with his carbine turning its barrel from side to side, and up and down, checking every inch of the dilapidated frame. He crouched behind a half wall, and signaled the prone Kate and her prisoner to run across while he covered their approach.

The wind was howling, the water was coming down by the bucketful and the structure groaned at each gust of air. But they found a corner that was fairly dry and took protective positions there. Jude was covering the rear and Kate the front, with Amanda Greco between them, tethered this time to Kate's waist.

After a while they dropped their guard a little along with their rucksacks. Jude used a microfiber towel from his bag to dry his carbine and inspect its magazine. Kate followed suit. Amanda just coughed into her gag from the exertion and the cold. The storm did not show any sign of slowing down. Large trees bent dangerously around them. Once in a while one fell in the wood line.

The Potomac roared past them as if telling them it was not the time to think about swimming across.

The rush to the barn through the woods and thorn bushes had gashed their skins and ripped their ACUs. The Greco woman looked fairly unscathed but Kate's face and shirt were bloody. Jude crawled up to her and shined his tactical LED light over the bloody spots, much to Kate's embarrassment. He spotted a gash below the collar and pushed her shirt aside to inspect it. The thorn bushes had done a job on her skin despite the strong ACU material.

He went into his bag and produced a small first aid kit, and from it the tweezers he reserved for thorns and ticks. He ran the light over her skin, removing thorns and treating the deep scratches with disinfectant. He turned his head away and had her inspect her breasts herself because the bra was also bloodied, but the blood turned out to be from the deep scratches below her neck. As he turned to protect her modesty he couldn't help but catch a glimpse of perfectly round and firm breasts. He blushed beneath the camo face paint.

All through this, Amanda kept her eyes on how Jude touched Kate and cared for her wounds. He even caught the look on Jude's face and saw his face turn away when he accidentally saw too much. She also noted Kate's submission to Jude's touch. A woman knew those signs instinctively. She pondered how she could profit from the situation.

CHAPTER 23 — Carry Me Back to Ole Virginny

"An' I'll dream for ever more, Dat you're carrying me
back to ole Virginny,
To ole Virginny shore"
Traditional Folk Song (1840's version)

0630 hours, January 10, 2018

The storm raged on for the rest of the hours of darkness. Towards dawn, the trio was still wet and miserable despite the barn's protection. Sheets of rain drove into the structure and roof leaks made Jude wonder if it was worth it to risk discovery for the small comfort they derived from the shelter. The dawn came in unnoticed in the black clouds, except that they became grey instead of black, and less threatening. The thunder and lightning could be heard, but at a distance. The rain became an annoyingly fine spray.

With the advent of daylight Jude risked another Dakota fire pit dug into the barn's earthen floor. Its purpose was coffee, not warmth or dryness. But they held their canteen cups in their hands thankful for the warmth. Taking pity on the Greco woman Jude took the gag off and let her sip from his cup, all under Kate's weary gaze. "You try anything bitch and I'll cap you." Kate told her, marking her words with the business end of her carbine touching the woman's forehead.

Amanda was able to speak for the first time between sips. "I need to pee. Please untie me. I swear I won't try anything."

"What are you, a piss machine?" Kate spit out with all the venom she could muster.

"Do you want me to take her?" Jude asked Kate semi-jokingly.

"You know?" Kate looked at the woman "Sure. You take her. I know I wouldn't be able to piss a drop if a man was looking at me."

"No, please" pleaded Amanda "I don't think I could do it either."

"Yeah, Jude, you take her. You don't need to go behind a shrub either since you're going to be watching anyway. In fact, take her to the middle of the clearing in plain sight of the forest critters." Kate baited the woman.

Jude strolled up to her and replaced the gag. He helped her up and was leading her outside the barn when Kate got up and swiped Jude's hand off the woman's shoulder. She then gave the Amanda a hearty shove toward a large tree that had fallen right beside the dilapidated house. She also gave Jude a scalding look. Jude just crouched there smiling. He kept his finger on the trigger guard and his eyes on the tree line. He was tired of surprises.

The women had not walked ten yards out of the barn when Jude heard the familiar sibilant whoosh. In a split second he reached them and threw himself over both of the women as the first mortar struck the ground.

The 'thump' of the shells told him they were 4.2 inch mortars. But their pattern told him that the Provos didn't 'have eyes' on them. They were saturating the island just in case the Noland boat landing attackers were on the island. Had they had a forward observer, the shells would have been bracketed closer and closer until they hit the target. A second grouping confirmed his suspicion that the Provos were just firing-for-effect because the shells fell on almost the same places.

The third grouping didn't come in. The fire mission stopped.

Mortar doctrine called for three groupings before 'firing for effect'. He bet someone had stopped the fire mission when alerted that there might be a chance that Mrs. Boss could be hit. There would be hell to pay if she got hurt. There would be hell to pay for whoever authorized the blind fire mission anyway.

However, that also told Jude that the suspicion that the Greco kidnappers might be on the island could force the Provos to send troops to check it out. They had to get out now; and the only way out was to swim the Potomac across to the Virginia side, no matter the weather, the current or the time of day.

0650 hours, January 10, 2018

Jude ran to the barn and retrieved the rucksacks. He passed Kate's rucksack to her like a relay racer passing a baton. Kate was already on the move towards the island's shore shoving the Greco woman in front of her. She caught the rucksack and put it on the hostage to keep her hands free to work her carbine. 'The bitch' ought to bear the load too.

At the shoreline they caught a break. There was a lot of vegetation floating down the river that could provide cover for their crossing.

Jude spotted an approaching clump of bushes that was almost made to order. As it floated by he entered the frigid water and pushed Amanda in. The Greco woman was again loosely tethered to Kate's waist. Entering the water after Amanda, Kate hung her carbine behind her back and concentrated on keeping the Greco woman afloat on the debris.

They moved into the center of the floating mini island to get some cover from the Provos who would certainly be watching the river after their fire mission. While Kate kept a hold on Amanda, Jude was steering the floating platform with strong scissor kicks, guiding it towards the Virginia side. Jude remembered from his map recon that there was an inlet about half a mile downstream which might allow them to come ashore unobserved.

Their ACUs provided little protection against the frigid water, though. Hypothermia was a real danger. The cold water's one saving grace was that it numbed the cuts and scratches, and relieved muscles still sore from last evening's exertions.

The current was swift and Jude saw the inlet after a few minutes. He struggled to keep their floating refuge moving in the right direction. Twenty feet into the waterway the second island's vegetation already offered sufficient cover to redirect their natural raft towards the Virginia shore. Nothing was ever more welcome to Jude's feet than the riverside mud that suddenly sucked up his boots.

He submerged and helped Kate extricate Amanda Greco from the floating bushes. The trio then began the wading toward the Virginia shore.

0700 hours, January 10, 2018

The water in the inlet was surprisingly shallow, allowing the trio to stand up and slush toward higher ground yards away from the actual shore. Jude was walking backwards keeping the rear as Kate pushed Amanda ahead. That's why he was able to spot in the distance the Zodiacs departing from the Maryland shore toward Heater's Island.

As a rule, the Provos defending the Washington DC area did not venture into Rebel held territory. Rebel fire was accurate and brutal. But from time to time elite Provo units probed the Rebel lines to find a way to harass them and staunch their advance toward Washington DC.

The way the soldiers worked the Zodiacs told Jude that these guys were regular Army, not Militia. It wouldn't be long before they covered the length and width of Heaters' Island and determined that Jude's group had been there. For one thing, they had not covered the Dakota hole in the barn in their rush to get out.

There were three Zodiacs moving to the island using a special ops spear formation. Jude knew that the situation was serious. Provo doctrine called for special ops troops to take the lead of recon-in-force battalion-sized elements. So they could be facing an unexpected Provo advance into Reb controlled Northern Virginia. Jude added the Greco kidnapping factor and decided his next course of action instantly.

He knew that a Rebel 155mm self-propelled howitzer battery had moved into the outskirts of Leesburg only days before. He didn't know if they were ready to take a fire mission but he had to try. He took a quick GPS reading and "trans-guessed" it to Heater's Island. Taking his tactical radio out of its plastic protective bag he transmitted "Great Balls of Fire, this is Casper, fire mission, over."

Seconds went by before a cautious voice came over the airwaves, "Casper, this is Great Balls. Authenticate, over."

"Shit," muttered Jude as he fished inside his front pocket for his plasticized authentication card. "Ready to authenticate, over," he shot back fully understanding that while he did that, the artillery battery would be in touch with Appalachian Headquarters to find out if this 'Casper' was authorized to call fire missions. The battery had no knowledge of any ongoing operation involving him.

"Authenticate Kilo Juliet, over", radioed the artilleryman.

"I authenticate Yankee, over," said Jude after checking and rechecking the letter groupings on the card.

The 155 battery came back on the air requiring a second authentication for good measure "Authenticate Quebec Papa, over."

"I authenticate X-Ray," responded Jude.

Five long seconds passed, and then a business-like voice came over the air "Send your mission, over."

A breath of relief came from Jude's lungs. Ed had authorized the battery to take his mission.

"Coordinates 392664-775319. I say again coordinates 392664-775319. Troops in the trees. Mixed HE and Willie Pete fire for effect. I'm getting the hell out of Dodge and don't have eyes to bracket, over" Jude told the battery as he and the women increased their pace into Virginia.

Jude and the women were already on drier land when he heard "Roger. Coordinates 392664-775319. 3 rounds HE. 3 rounds Willie Pete. Troops in the trees. Fire for effect. Good luck to you. Fire mission out.

An instant after the words "fire mission out" he heard the whistling of the 155 shells followed by a scary rumble and the trembling of the entire river basin. It was much too close for his liking. The first was followed shortly by two more barrages. He had ordered high explosive and white phosphorous shells to start a fire that would deny the area to both the special ops Provos and any following regular troops.

The artillery battery understood that since Jude did not "have eyes" on the place upon which he called the fire mission they should not expect a call back from him with the results of the fire mission. The artillery hated this. The Alpha priority that the AC Commander had given Casper meant that the guy on the ground calling the mission knew what he was doing. Much later Intel would tell them that Casper's instincts were on the dot and that the mission had obliterated Heaters Island and stopped a battalion-size probe into Reb lines.

CHAPTER 24 — Got My Own Problems

"Half a league, half a league,
Half a league onward,
All in the valley of Death,
Rode the six hundred"
The Charge of the Light Brigade, Alfred, Lord
Tennyson

0745 hours, January 10, 2018

The earth was still trembling when Jude, Kate and Amanda broke into a fast trot out of the area. About a mile away, Jude stopped them and got "on the horn" with Ed.

"Green Giant actual, this is Casper, over." Since most radios at headquarters were handled by personnel other than the commander, when Jude called for 'Green Giant actual' he was telling the radio operator that he wanted to speak with Ed himself.

"Casper this is Green Giant, wait one" responded the radio operator to let Jude know he would go get Ed.

"Roger, Green Giant. I'll wait." shot back the Ranger. While he waited, Jude heard what sounded like intensive artillery fire further south. A moment later:

"Go, Casper," the deep Kentucky bass came on the air.

"I just entered the Alpha Oscar and request 'meet and greet', over." Jude asked for any nearby wheeled patrol to pick them up to take them to headquarters.

"No can do, Casper. We are busy on the Alpha Oscar" shot back the booming voice.

Busy on the area of operations, meant to Jude that his friend must have been knee deep in Provo shit. Later he would learn that the push his fire mission had stopped at Heater's Island was only a part of an all-out Provo attack on the Appalachian Command.

Greco had ordered an almost suicidal advance on the Rebels without preparatory artillery or air support to avoid hurting his wife. He even gave orders to not use the 60mm mortars light infantry units usually carried, crippling his troops' chances for success. Joe Greco had set up his own troops for defeat.

"Roger, Green Giant. We'll make our way to your 20. Request notification of security elements to grease our way in, over." asked Jude, muttering curses under his breath.

"Grease your own way in, Casper. Green Giant out" came back the disappointing response from his friend.

Pounding the ground was getting old, and he wanted to get rid of his baby-sitting duties to help the Command fix whatever was making the AO 'busy'. Meanwhile, the distant rumble of artillery increased.

0745 hours, January 10, 2018

The reinforced Provo division was dropped by Chinook helicopters along a line spanning the Virginia shore on the Potomac from Fairfax to what used to be Reagan National Airport. The light infantry troops augmented with Militia forces were just dumped on the ground without fire support, not even from gunships, owing to the possibility that Mrs. Boss might be in the area. The experienced officers on Greco's staff protested to the Navy man that he could be throwing away over 10,000 lives.

But the Navy man was impervious to good counsel. All he thought about was his fine piece of ass in the hands of the fucking Rebs, and it irked him.

The mobile Leesburg 155s and the two 105mm batteries on the ruins of what used to be the Pentagon sent fire missions controlled by Reb forward observers. The ferocious Reb artillery killed transport choppers in the air, and shredded Provo infantry and Militia on the ground.

Before noon, the Rebels had repelled the invaders, killing more than 800 Provos and wounding over 1,500; a carnage not seen in the area since the second American Civil War began. Many of the troops tried to swim back across the Potomac when it became clear that Greco had set them up for defeat and that fighting the Rebels was not going to be a 'cake walk'. About 2500 Provos surrendered 'en masse' to a Rebel counter attack put together on the spur of the moment.

The Rebs had trucked in a battalion sized unit from Woodridge to augment the reinforced brigade that held the AO. Towards 0900, National Headquarters sent a rare flight of three F-15s out of Morgantown, West Virginia, to mop up the Provo troops on the Rebel side of the Potomac. Less than 6,000 Provos made it back to their lines. Those who made it back did so by swimming back under heavy fire, and through the heroic efforts of a few Provo Chinook flyers who defied orders to take the valuable transport choppers out of harm's way.

Greco left his dead and wounded on the Virginia battlefield. Rebel troops and civilians had to dig graves and transport the wounded to safe locations to tend to them.

Greco's staff feared a Reb massive counter-attack and flew into the Capital region what regular forces they could fit into their few transports from Fort Bragg, North Carolina and even from Fort Benning, Georgia, which at that time were not yet under Rebel Control.

Greco's staff was not wrong on the counterattack. Ed and his Appalachian Command staff had begun to plan it from the moment the Provo attack started, and implement it as soon as they saw gaps in the Provo advance.

In the end, an effective counterattack didn't take place. Ed knew it was the tactically sound thing to do. But two things stopped him.

The first was an intelligence report about the troop movement from Bragg and Benning. Despite the small size of the contingents, those were battle-tested regular troops; they were sure to exact heavy Reb casualties per capita. More importantly, he would have had to fight troops that were not altogether committed to Greco. Ed had hoped to either keep them out of the fight, or get them to join the Rebel ranks when he was ready to continue his push to DC.

The second thing that stopped the counter attack was Colorado's refusal to send back the F-15s to soften Greco lines across the Potomac. According to the National Headquarters, its air assets were 'over-committed.' "Whatever the fuck that means to them spineless bastards in Colorado," muttered Ed.

0755 hours, January 10, 2018

When Ed told them about the AO being busy, Jude understood that they must have been under Provo attack. Jude and Kate decided to move north with their prize, and then reverse direction to AC (forward) to avoid getting into a hot AO. Changing the direction of their movement was the right thing to do. It not only masked their intended destination if anyone were keeping track of them, but bought them time to avoid a situation which might prove dangerous to the hostage.

Jude was confident that Ed could repel the attack, as he had in the past with several smaller incursions. But that was an assumption, and Jude disliked assumptions.

Deep into the area south of US 15, they found a working pickup at what used to be one of the Northern Virginia wineries that lined the route. The winery had been abandoned since the Provos retreated to the other side of the river. Its fields had been laid fallow by the Moslem Militia in the early days of the war because of religious intolerance for alcohol.

Jude spotted the pickup from the tree line and approached cautiously from behind a burned out vegetable stand. They were in a hurry, so he took a chance that the pickup was still in working condition and that there would be no bad guys around. He was lucky on both counts. The truck responded to Jude's first attempt to hotwire. It whined and growled, but its engine turned over.

Kate had been waiting in the shrubs by the abandoned stand and shoved Amanda into the truck when the engine started. She put her between Jude and her, warning the Greco woman that she would cut off her right tit if she tried anything funny. Amanda believed her.

It took them over three hours of stealth driving through back roads to arrive at the AC headquarters in Great Falls Park.

1005 hours, January 10, 2018

They left the truck at Old Dominion Drive where it met the aptly named Difficult Run Trail. Using the trail, Jude and Kate approached the bunkers and reinforced trenches of the field headquarters on foot to avoid getting zapped by Kate's newly sensitized and highly agitated security force, made even more so by the Provo attack.

Kate took the point hoping to be recognized by her troops more favorably than the Ranger whose comments she had used to chastise them before she had left on the hostage retrieval mission. She stopped short of the first listening post about 25 yards from Old Dominion Drive, dropped to her knees and raised her arms.

The LP immediately challenged her with sign and countersign. Kate was hoping that they had not changed the countersign schedule because of the Provo attack. They had. But the LP identified her anyway and called the watch leader. The watch leader dropped her recognition smile and raised her carbine instantaneously when Kate told Jude to advance with the prisoner.

Following impeccable tradecraft, the watch leader made the advancing Jude and his prisoner drop to their knees and put their hands up. She would have shot the non-complying Amanda unceremoniously if Kate hadn't told her that the prisoner's hands were bound and could not come up. The smile returned to the watch leader's camo-painted face, and her finger caressed the trigger guard the moment she recognized Jude. Kate empathized with her subordinate, but it was time to move.

Past the listening post, Kate and the others arrived at her hutch. She handed Jude her field telephone and cranked it for him. "This is Casper. Pass me to the CO, Operator."

"Wait one," responded the metallic voice. Jude knew that the operator would be testing the line for continuity to ensure that the caller wasn't an infiltrator who had tapped into the secure land-line.

"Speak to me. Watcha got?" resonated Ed's deep baritone.

"We are back with the bundle, boss. Request permission to approach the CP to brief you," answered Jude.

"I trust your judgment, Casper." It was a statement of trust as well as a warning. It simply was not done to bring an enemy non-combatant into the headquarters area, especially when the area was under attack. But Ed knew that Jude would never violate SOP without a damn good reason.

Kate put on a black hood on the Greco woman and shoved her out of her hutch.

CHAPTER 25 — The Goose that Laid the Golden Egg

"...As he grew rich he grew greedy; and thinking to get at once all the gold the Goose could give, he killed it and opened it only to find,—nothing." The Goose With the Golden Egg, Aesop.(Sixth century B.C.) Fables, The Harvard Classics, 1909–14

1010 hours, January 10, 2018

They negotiated three other challenge points on their way to Ed's Command Post. Jude was now sure that Kate had laid out a few effective four-letter words on those who let the Ghost fool them. That wasn't going to happen again in the near future, and this wasn't going to be a cakewalk. The security troops they met along the way acted uniformly 'by the book,' and were really sharp too. They all also gave Jude pointedly dirty looks. Two of them joined their boss to help guarding the prisoner.

Ed intercepted them about twenty yards from the CP bunker. The Appalachian Commander was wearing a helmet and body armor, with a carbine strapped to his chest, just like his security detail. Before anyone could say a word, he asked his detail to give them privacy and took Jude and Kate aside, leaving Amanda Greco with the guards.

Jude whispered to Ed, "If I knew for sure your jaw wouldn't drop I'd take her hood off and let you enjoy laying eyes on Amanda Greco."

Ed whispered back, taking in both of them and looking sideways at the hostage. "You have got to be kidding me! So Steve was right."

"He was more than right, Ed. The knuckle-dragger is in tune with your brain waves. He said that we could profit from her more here at the Command than they could in Colorado."

He laid out Steve's thinking on trading her for Appalachian Command POWs. "Do you want to pow-wow on a strategy?"

"That's the only way to go, Judeman. You guys did well and Steve is thinking right. Let's get together at 2000 hours. Got any place to keep the hostage? Far as I know we haven't yet built a brig on the grounds", mused the Kentuckian with an accent that sounded more like a Hollywood Daniel Boone each time he spoke.

"I'm not going to take any chances with her," said Kate. "She's quite a handful. I can't tell you how many times I wanted to waste her."

Jude interrupted, "What's going on, Ed?"

"Provos hit us all along the river. The S-2 estimates a reinforced division. But they came across without preparatory artillery, not even mortars. Our artillery made mincemeat out of them, and by the time our grunts closed in they surrendered in droves. They crossed at daybreak, and by 0900 they were in full retrograde. Colorado is sending a flight of F-15s from Morgantown to help mop them up.

Frankly, I wanted to use the air support to help us with a counter-attack, but Colorado nixed it. I guess they don't want to capitalize on our victory; bunch of fools.

I was on the way to the beachhead when you guys arrived. It looks like we have trouble processing the large number of surrenders.

By the way, it looks like the fire mission you called up north stopped a pincer envelopment. They had sent a battalion or so to hit our left flank. Good job!" smiled Ed.

"Save that for the 155s at Leesburg, Ed. No one is going to be hiking on Heater's Island for the next few years", interjected Kate.

"Well, they're no longer at Leesburg. They rolled down to Ashburn to be able to better support our counterattack" said Ed looking at his watch and heading out, followed by his security detail.

Getting back to Kate, Jude whispered in her ear: "Kate, I think we should sit on her ourselves as much as possible until we figure how to do what we have to do, no matter how 'strac' you troops are," said Jude, using the traditional Army term that meant 'Strong, Tough and Ready Around the Clock'. "You and I have a lot invested on this bitch to leave it up to anyone else. Where do you think we should keep her?"

"I say we use my hutch as a calaboose for the time being, and we go from there. And, Jude, my guys are going to do the guarding. It's their job and we just have to trust them to do it right." She spoke with finality and pointed the hostage to the two guards as she walked by them. The two guards lifted Amanda none too gently as they followed their leader. Jude had been silenced with common sense and superior leadership. Instead of resenting Kate, his admiration for her grew.

They walked back to Kate's hutch. The hostage had already seen it and it made a lot of sense to restrict her geographical knowledge to what she had seen and to where she had been, relatively far from the CP.

Also, Kate's hutch was a modest one, and would not be a suspect location to satellite imagery. Like other hutches, it was really just a hole in the ground with a grenade sump and a raised sleeping area, and some overhead muddied logs. It was perfectly adequate as a temporary jail.

1015 hours, January 10, 2018

She and Jude slid into the unpretentious quarters with their hostage. The ground was still damp from the storm that hit them at Heater's Island. But neither Jude nor Kate cared much about the Greco woman's physical comfort. They pushed around Kate's few private possessions making room for the three of them. When that wasn't enough, Jude asked one of Kate's troops to take a few of the items to Jude's hutch for the time being. The trooper looked at Kate and got her approval in the form of a nod prior to doing what the Ranger had asked.

They kept a collapsible camp stove and used it to heat coffee water and provide a meager source of heat for the three of them. Kate checked Amanda's plastic ties and threw her on the raised sleeping area. She wasn't about to take any chances with this bitch. She only hoped that she would ask to go pee, just so that she could say "no."

But it was not to be. The Greco woman was so tired from the events that she was snoring before she could even think about any other physical discomfort. Besides, Kate was sure that Amanda had emptied her bladder as they floated across the frigid Potomac.

Jude and Kate sat on the floor pallet as they waited for the water to boil. When the water reached the boiling point they caught themselves looking at each other. Jude smiled out of embarrassment. Kate smiled out of being caught.

"Nice digs," said Jude tongue in cheek with an exaggerated look around. Kate gave him a twisted grin in the manner that women have always let men know that they knew what they were thinking. But Jude really didn't have anything complicated in mind. He just felt awkwardly in need of saying something.

Kate was having an effect on him. He could not pinpoint what it was but his brain was all jumbled up. He felt comfortable around her, and would no doubt trust her with his life. But she was strangely disquieting. The Greco woman slept soundly, snoring away.

They added luxuriously scarce coffee grounds to the boiling water. He'd heard rumors that the coffee came from the well-stocked larder of former Vice President Dick Cheney, who had built a house on nearby Chain Bridge Road. No telling how this type of rumor spread, but he would not put it past Kate to raid for vittles.

While Jude was busy with these thoughts, Kate's consciousness was one third on the coffee, one third on the Greco bitch, and one third on what to think about this guy. He was distant, but he pushed himself near with his words and the way he looked at her. And then he climbed right back into outer space with just a word, or just a movement, or even with the way he did not smile. She knew he had baggage...the wife who died at the White House...the comrades he lost at the Gettysburg Greco house. But so did she.

CHAPTER 26 — The Fundamental Things Apply

"Of all the gin joints, in all the towns, in all the world, she walks into mine." Rick, Casablanca, 1942.

The Farmer's Daughter

Kate Hartmann grew up just like many other little girls did, in a farming community near Wichita, Kansas. Her dad was just a nice guy who had a chicken farm. Her mom was just a nice woman who taught her daughter about the usual things women learn in a farmhouse: the way to handle a husband and the uselessness of going beyond high school. After all, by the 12th grade she would have identified a good enough guy and aspire to an adequate life.

Luckily, she was an only child. She often joked about how thoughtful her parents had been not to saddle her with sisters and brothers. Being alone gave her plenty of time for introspection.

She did meet a boy in high school who, by all outward signs was "the one." By the time she graduated she had made love awkwardly with the pimply potential husband, tried her first and last cigarette, and downed her first and last shot of whiskey. She decided that she wasn't cut out for the life that awaited her. So the day after graduation she walked into an Army recruiting office and came out with a promise of a military police specialty and officer training.

Kate was somewhat of a loner during basic training at Fort Stewart, a hard thing to do among a whole bunch of rowdy girls in the female barracks. The memory brought a smile to her face. She clearly recalled how a drill instructor had yelled at them: "There are 51, 843 inches of cock on this base and none of you is getting any of that until you clean this fucking barrack!"

She didn't quite know what would become of her life in the Army, but she knew that she wasn't going back to the chicken farm in Kansas. And so she didn't.

She was first at OCS officer candidate school. First at Fort Benning's Infantry Officer Basic Course (even over the males). First at Airborne Training and first at Fort Leonard Wood Military Police school.

She made her bones in Iraq and Afghanistan with the 82 Military Police Company in support of the famous "All American" airborne infantry division. She was promoted to Captain in record time, and had been designated "promotable" to Major by the time the American Republic collapsed.

Confused, like every salt-of-the-earth service member in CONUS, she was locked down at post by Greco's Provisional Military Government until the Chinese forces bombed a Kansas chicken farm. She was granted a week's worth of 'compassionate' leave to go home and put the family affairs in order.

Searching through the rubble and finding what was left of the old couple who were her parents, the answer became clear. Within weeks, she had joined the Rebel Appalachian Command during the advance through Virginia. It didn't take long for Ed to recognize her talents and to put her in charge of headquarters security.

Oh yes. The pimply boy was run over by Greco's tanks while taking a rare stance on something besides rock-and-roll and whiskey. He had been a non-starter, but that had been as close to a "starter" as she had gotten.

1945 hours, January 10, 2018

About 15 minutes before they were due back at the CP, Jude came out of the fog of thought that followed a great cup of coffee. He motioned Kate to join him outside the hutch.

"I don't want to teach you how to suck eggs, but you do agree with me that it will take your best troops to guard this bitch while we are not in the hutch, don't you?"

Kate nodded smiling at the understatement, and ran her troop roster through her mind settling on four of her best people. She sent one of the guards for them and personally installed them at their new post. She put two inside with the hostage and two guarding the outside. Guns would remain outside the hutch, the prisoner would be tied up at all times, and no one except Kate and Jude would have access to Amanda. Kate did not reveal the hostage's identity to the guards, but she was sure that at some point the bitch would do so to impress her captors. When Kate departed the area she left them with the traditional security warning: 'What you see here, what you hear here, let it stay here, when you leave here'.

She and Jude headed out toward the CP and Kate said, "So how do you think this should go down?" In her experience, meetings required prior discussion with potential allies on the different options, and even preparing contingencies.

Jude said, "Ed has probably been working a plan all by his lonesome. He will tell us honestly what he thinks and ask us to shoot his plan full of holes. That will be our job."

"But what if…?" Kate started to say.

"No 'what-ifs', Kate. Just listen to what he has to say, and if you don't agree then shoot him down. Ed's a big boy, and he's been wrong before. And the best part is that he *knows* he's been wrong before. If he thinks you've got a point, he'll give it to you. Ed's no Machiavelli either. If he wants to go one way, he'll go that way no matter how sound you think your arguments are. Just be yourself and tell him what you really think."

That was the longest speech she'd heard from Jude.

Once again, Kate didn't know how to take this man. She knew he was smart, but he wasn't pushy. He seemed like an open book, but she had seen him act with stealth and cunning. One thing was for sure, he was loyal to his friends. Did that also include her?

Her reverie was interrupted by their arrival at the CP. Ed had returned from the beachhead and was sitting on the ground by his sleeping bag, nursing a cup of something hot. He was lost in thought. He gestured to them to sit on two wooden ammo boxes that served as furniture for company. He raised his eyes from the cup and said, "Speak to me".

Jude was first. "Steve was sure that you'd like to trade her for some of our POWs. He was also against passing the buck to Colorado; something about them taking too long to make a decision, and in the end a decision that wouldn't include our best interests. Does that sum it up, Kate?"

She nodded pensively.

"And what do you guys think?" Ed said looking at both of them.

"Bottom line" answered Jude "I agree with Steve. I had concerns about following the chain of command, but

Steve reminded me who was boss" adding a smile at this point that Ed acknowledged. "My initial reaction was that Colorado would be pissed if we bypass them. But then the Irishman made a good point about their being so far away and out of touch with Appalachian needs; worrying too much about the West Coast and theoretical crap. I think we should trade her for our guys and worry about Colorado later."

"And you, Kate?" Ed pierced her with his eyes.

"Jude suggested I listen to what you had in mind and then give you my opinion. I think you have learned that I speak my mind often and loudly. But Jude has a point."

She paused ever so briefly. "Look Ed, I'm a cop who thinks she's a grunt. I'm good at tactics, not strategy. I'd really like to hear how you think this should go down and contribute to it in any way I can. But don't worry, if I don't like what I'm hearing I'm going to tell you. And I'll also tell you how I think you should fix it."

Smiling in approval and nodding agreement Ed replied, "OK. Here's how I see it: the simpler the plan the better. I get Greco on the phone, tell him I have his wife and that I will trade her for all the Appalachian POWs he has in custody. How does that sound?" He delivered the last sentence in a cheap imitation of Fess Parker playing Daniel Boone.

"Needs work, boss," said Jude. "My experience in horse trading is not as extensive as yours but it seems to me that we should give the bastard a list of names, including locations where held if we know them, rather than just leave it up to him to go back and forth on who he has and who he's willing to trade. We should also make it real. 72 hours and I'll personally shoot the bitch."

"No way, Winthrop", interrupted Kate. "I've had dibs on the hoe since Heater's Island, and if someone's going to cap her it will be me," said Kate with a thin smile but so passionately that the two men just looked at her and were not sure whether to believe her.

"Forget it, Bonnie and Clyde," said Ed smiling. "We don't kill civilians just like that. Due process is the only way to go. Now, if it happens in the heat of battle while she's trying to stick a knife in you, that's different. But not in cold blood" and he followed up pointing at Jude, "I've known this guy longer than I care to admit. I'm sure he would never hurt a woman."

"Yeah, I know," said Ed stopping a possible objection with raised hands. "It's a macho thing, but that's the way it is. That's why I agreed to send you up with him."

Then he added with conviction: "That said, I don't wanna leave any doubts how we do things in my command. We can joke about many things, but we don't kill unarmed civilians, we don't rape and we don't pillage. That's not the American way." He exhaled when he got to this point.

"I like our plan," he said glancing back and forth at the two officers. "You two go work with the S-1 and the S-2 on what we know about the POWs. Get me a list. In the mean time I'll call Greco and tell him to stop his attack before his troops kill his wife accidentally. And I ain't kidding about that. It was sort of dicey while you guys were tiptoeing through the tulips and boosting cars."

"How'd the boys do, Boss?" This was a serious question from Jude.

"We took some casualties and they took a lot more than us. That Militia is in serious need of training and "cojones." After a while there were more of them swimming back in the Potomac than being mopped up by our guys and picked up by our cracker boxes. If I had you and your old team, Jude, I would have sent you in during the attack to do some serious damage in the rear."

Ed paused to drink. "By the way, when you get a chance take a look around the new troops and see if you can put together another commando unit. I need you deep across the river doing your thing before Greco can organize the troops he brought up from Bragg and Benning."

"On it, Boss," a sedate sounding response because it hurt just remembering that last mission. "But I thought Colorado had plans for a West Coast deployment?"

"They do. I will carefully consider their needs…after I've considered ours. Now, go talk to the One and the Two, and let's get this show on the road."

2350 hours, January 10, 2018

It was nearly midnight when they finished putting together all the intelligence the staff had on the POWs. It turned out that there were over 100 POWs in the capital region alone, many of them in the same Naval Warfare facility where Jude had been interned. There were rumors that the regulars and the Militia were vying for their custody; the Militia arguing that the regulars ought to run the camps, not the Militia. Being a jailer was demeaning to both groups, each arguing that it interfered with their fighting mission.

Jude did not believe that Greco would trade them all for his wife. So he and Kate started to prioritize the list. This was a difficult task both in emotional and in practical terms. Were the medics more important than the infantry? The women more at danger of being maltreated than the men? And what about the wounded?

Around 0300 they walked back to Kate's hutch exhausted. They both had to check on the hostage before flopping down to a well-deserved sleep. When they got there they found that Kate's security troops had set up an effective watch schedule, checking the binds every once in a while, and eliminating routine from the operation, which could be exploited by both the prisoner and any would be rescuers. The security troops had even improved the hutch's reinforcements with extra timber, to make it more like a real jail.

Even Jude was impressed.

The one flaw in the arrangement was that Kate had no place to sleep.

"Come and crash at my hutch for the time being," was the surprise invitation from Jude which Kate received with a combination of incredulity and suspicion. If they had been within earshot of her troops she would have had to turn down the invite to prevent rumors. As it was, it sounded like an appropriate suggestion from her comrade-in-arms, for a good reason and with no ulterior motive.

Even then she said, "I don't think so." She sounded firm. "I'll go back to the CP and grab a corner."

"OK" he capitulated in a matter-of-fact tone, but added, "You won't be able to sleep at all with the staff running around."

"Ed can," retorted Kate just for the sake of argument.

"Ed can sleep standing up on the back of a deuce and a half," added Jude with a smile, remembering the sight of the Kentuckian doing just that on a 2 ½ ton truck in

Germany, and casually adding, "It's not like I'm going to compromise your virtue, you know?"

"That has nothing to do with it. I can take care of myself." They had arrived at Jude's hutch by the time Jude said, "OK. You stay here and I'll go climb a tree or something. Your camp reputation will be safe. I need you rested to get on with the POW work in a few hours."

"I don't need you to protect my camp reputation, Winthrop. I can take care of myself. Get in the hutch. I'll take one side of the sleeping platform, you take the other."

And that was that.

CHAPTER 27 — The Message

"And Hades seized her and took her loudly crying in his chariot down to his realm of mist and gloom."
Persephone, Homer

0605 hours, January 11, 2018

Jude woke up under the weight of an arm and a leg in a tangle of thermal blankets; his and hers. The arm and the leg felt strangely comforting. He was tempted to leave them there and go back to sleep when he looked at his watch and noticed it was 0605. He brushed the arm and the leg aside, waking their owner, who became flustered, turning her angry back on him.

"We overslept, Hartmann. Let's get moving. Get yourself together while I go wash my face." He walked out of the hutch, noticing that a half-asleep Kate was following blindly, not having quite yet woken up. When he paused at a tree near a water bucket she almost bumped into his back. "Not so close Hartmann. I can do this by myself."

A fast turnaround with a quiet "Oh!" ended the problem, but resulted in even more embarrassment for Kate. Jude smiled at her discomfort all the way to the headquarters hutch.

He had taken to calling her by her last name immediately after she called him by his last name. She wondered if it was just payback or if he wanted to put more distance between them. How could that be after what they had been through? Was he again reacting to his loss?

When they got to the CP the Assistant S-1 was spelling his boss, so that 'the One actual' could sleep. But he had been briefed and had been doing some work on the POW list on his own. Within 20 minutes they were ready to meet with Ed again and finalize their position on the prisoner exchange.

"Good work," said Ed, while dialing the Greco headquarters internal number that his intelligence officer had given him. "This is Commander Sumter of the American Appalachian Command," he said into the phone.

Ed put the cell phone on speaker so everyone could hear what was said next, and they heard "Who, what?" from a confused Provo voice on the other end.

"I already told you, son. This is the big bad guy across the river. Put that half-baked sailor boss of yours on the line…and tell him we gonna talk about his wife," added Ed just in case Greco needed convincing.

Faster than he expected, a voice said, "This is Admiral Greco. Who is this?"

"You guys…either you don't talk with each other, or you have trouble understanding American. Which one is it?"

Ed spat out the words, hoping to throw his opponent off balance. "Listen well, 'cause I'm only gonna say this once. I need a fax number or an email address to send you a list of people we want in exchange for your trophy wife."

"I don't know what you are talking about. My wife is safe at home and I don't negotiate with terrorists," retorted the Admiral.

"Which is it? She's either safe at home or you don't negotiate with terrorists. Can't be both, Squid," said Ed, using the Army insult for a Navy man.

"Both. No, she's safe at home." By now Greco sounded not only confused, but pathetic.

"OK, Squid. Stop stepping all over your Richard. Don't do much for your image. And stop stalling, you can't trace this phone, and even if you could you would find out I'm calling from across the river, where your forces have been surrendering for the past 15 hours or so."

Ed said this with such satisfaction that Greco must have known it was true. "So I'm gonna hang up now and give you a chance for what I just told you to sink in. When one of my men calls back in ten minutes I want that fax number, or that email address." Ed hung up.

Jude had suggested this negotiating technique, including not calling him back for twenty minutes instead of ten. Keep them guessing and wanting a callback. It was all part of Jude's psychological operations training, by the book. That Fort Bragg psy-ops course had finally paid off.

Ed looked at Jude and Kate. "How did I do?"

Jude nodded and said, "It's shouldn't be a man calling back. Kate should call, then someone else. We have to keep him wobbly. And, let's not hand over the final details until tomorrow."

"Calling him tomorrow won't work, Judeman. We need to shoot our POW list to him the moment we have numbers and locations, or he's bound to think we don't have our shit in order…all our ducks in a row, I mean."

Ed looked directly at Kate when he caught himself using four letter words in front of a woman. He was that much of an old-fashioned gentleman.

Kate turned to him and said, "Shit in order is quite all right, Commander. Heard the fucking word before, you know?"

They all cracked up together, relieving some of the tension of the moment. Ed and Jude looked at each other, deciding just then that she was OK by them, and almost inducting her into their private camaraderie; almost being the operative term. There was a very special bond between those two.

CHAPTER 28 — The Plan

"Mas sabe el diablo por viejo que por diablo." "The devil is wise because he is old, not because he is the devil" Spanish proverb

0655 hours, January 11, 2018

Twenty minutes later it was Kate's turn to call. They expected Greco would have passed the onerous duty to one of his staff, but the Admiral himself answered. "Sumter, I have the fax number for you, but how am I gonna be sure that-"

Kate interrupted him. "It's not Commander Sumter, Admiral. I know he said one of his men would call you back. Instead, one of his women is doing it. He couldn't call you back, even if he wanted to. Good leaders prioritize. Between talking to you and taking a crap, the crap won. That's how much we think of you. Spit out the number or the email address."

"Who is this?" the stuck-up sailor was enraged. The freaking Reb really had a subordinate call him, instead of doing it himself. Not only that, it was a broad.

Kate added insult to injury, intoning sweetly "I was kidding about the crap, Admiral. The fact is that you are just not important enough for the Commander, sorry to say. I'm a member of his staff. I'm Amanda's jailer. I've had to put up with the bitch for over 48 hours, and if it had been up to me I would have shot the cunt. Now, stop wasting my time and give me the number."

Greco, chastised, replied: "You may fax your document to 202-456-2461. But, please, don't hurt her.

She's not a combatant." A flash of pity went through Kate's mind when she heard the desperate plea, but only momentarily.

"Like I said, taking pity on the bitch is above my pay grade. I guess there will be a correlation between how fast you move on this POW list and how well she makes out. If I had my druthers I would ship her back to you a little bit at a time; out now." She looked at Ed and Jude as she finished the conversation. They looked back at her with obvious approval. She had done well.

"So, have you worked on the exchange procedures, Jude?" He actually looked at both Jude and Kate as he asked the obviously unexpected question.

Jude glanced briefly at Kate and told Ed, "Yeah, we gave it some thought." he fibbed rather quickly; the 'we' giving Kate credit. "It's important that he returns the POWs in stages, so that we are sure to get at least some of them in case he gets tempted to renege and drops artillery on the group as soon as she is safe with him. We plan to break the prisoners into five groups, coming across the river on separate barges at the same time we float Amanda back to him. I say at the same time because he's never going to agree to send them across before he gets his wife back," said Jude.

"She gets to ride back to him with a ballsy escort who will waste her if Greco gets tricky. He will probably pack the POW barges full of explosive to detonate by remote control if *we* get tricky. So we tell him that she can leave the barge when the last of the POWs touches ground. In the meantime, we get the artillery pieces at Leesburg and at Woodbridge to lay some final protective fires and counter-battery preparations just in case the exchange goes south. So far so good, Ed?" asked Jude.

"What then?" pushed the Kentuckian with a twinkle in his eye.

"We have all five landing points covered with fire teams, until the prisoners get into the trucks and ambulances. We 'didi'-the army term for 'moving out quickly' in vogue since the Vietnam War-to five safe, separate points, where we will sort them out just in case he tries to infiltrate his people among the prisoners. In the best of all worlds we would wait releasing the woman until we have ascertained that the prisoners are OK. But there is no such thing as the best of all worlds. The plan is not perfect, but it's there for you to change it as you wish." Jude sat down cross-legged when he finished. He knew what to expect.

Ed said, "give me a minute" as Kate spoke up. "If you don't mind, Commander, Jude and I will step outside while you think about this," and she took Jude forcefully by the arm as they left.

Climbing out of the CP hutch's entrance she spoke at Jude with clenched teeth, "What the fuck, Winthrop? When did *we* come up with this plan?"

Still facing away from the hutch Jude asked her sarcastically: "You got something better, Hartmann? That's all I could pull out of my ass on the spur of the moment. We should have come here prepared with a plan all worked out among us, but he caught us with our pants down. Well, do you have a better plan?"

At that point he stopped and looked at her.

"Wasn't that what I told you before the initial meeting? But, Oh no! The Ed expert shot it down. 'We have to play it straight with Ed, my good buddy'. And all the time I bet you were concocting all of this shit in your head so I wouldn't get a chance to put in my five cents.

Well mister, I don't know if I could have made the plan better than it is. But this is the last time you pull this crap on me."

They glared at each other. He defused the tension, speaking calmly and in a low voice. "When I said to play it straight with him I meant that we should not concoct any plots to push our point of view. And that was for the initial meeting. He had given us his thoughts already and just asked us to fill in the details. We really should have talked about this, but I just didn't think about it. My response to Ed was the best I could come up with given the circumstances."

She responded with silence. She knew that he was right.

0700 hours, January 11, 2018

Greco was furious when Kate hung up. He picked up the phone and threw it at the nearest wall. Unfortunately for him, the phone striking the wall brought down many of his framed diplomas and awards. No matter, he would get some gofer to put them up again. The nerve of the fucking bitch talking to him like that! If it weren't that Amanda was in their hands he'd level all the suspected locations for the Appalachian Command headquarters.

Joe and Amanda Greco had an argument when she announced she was going to visit Byers at Sibley. The guy was only his head spook, eminently replaceable. He'd gotten the job because a former Secretary of the Navy had recommended him. But the guy didn't know his ass from a hole in the ground. He had copied the CYA style of national security reports, not once recommending what he should do, but giving bogus estimates and indecipherable options. He had to do everything around here. These people would turn on him on a dime. So there was no reason why his 'First Lady' should have wasted her time visiting him at Sibley. Unless there was something he didn't know.

Her argument was that, as First Lady, she had to show concern for the troops, especially his closest collaborators.

He had learned early on that the ship of State was a lot harder to control than any of the naval vessels he had previously commanded. At least his sea commands were self-contained, and everybody knew the rules. When an officer was in a passageway all the unimportant people in it hugged the bulkheads to let him by.

That's what he was talking about: immediate, unquestioning obedience. No backtalk by all the pseudo-intellectuals in the corridors of power. Sometimes he wished he had died along with all the others Joint Chiefs. Never mind! He would find a way to get this place shipshape.

And to get back talk from his own woman! It's a good thing that she knew enough not to talk back in public. What a guy had to put with to get a nice piece of ass! This whole episode would teach her he hadn't been kidding. What he said was serious stuff. Martha had understood the rules the first week of their marriage. Too bad she got old and ugly. He hoped that if Amanda ever left him for another man it wouldn't be for a geek like Byers.

His adjutant walked in interrupting his daydreaming. "Admiral, here is the list the Rebs faxed us. There are over 120 names in it. General Jackson said he'd get to work on it right away. Also, General Jackson wants to brief you on the operation across the river."

"That briefing will have to wait, Ernie. In any case, the fucking hillbilly across the river already gave me the report very succinctly. Our troops either swam back across the river or surrendered faster than they could haul them away. As for the list, tell Jackson that I expect his briefing at 1300 on how he's going to get Amanda back. Some hillbilly bitch was telling me on the phone just now how she would ship her back to me in little pieces; and that, my young friend is not going to happen in my presidency!"

This last part was a high pitched growl that carried through the walls in his improvised headquarters.

His adjutant knew enough to put some distance between him and his boss when Greco was ranting and raging. This was one of those times.

0715 hours, January 11, 2018

When they returned to the CP bunker Ed cast them a knowing look and mused with his eyes on the rafters. "Not too shabby for having pulled it out of your ass, Jude. See, Kate? That's one of the things you could learn from your boyfriend here. It's what we call in the Infantry 'thinking on your feet'."

Kate corrected him. "He's not my boyfriend, Ed"

Sumter cut her short to do what he did best in tense situations: tell a joke.

"Did you hear the one about the Italian Mama who comes to visit her son and finds that his roommate Maria is a very attractive woman? Mama immediately assumes that they are involved, but they both assure her that they are just friends, roommates.

A couple of days after Mama leaves his roommate Maria tells the son that she hasn't seen the sugar bowl since his mother visited, and that maybe Mama took it.

The son gets all defensive and tells Maria that he will email his mother and ask her. So he sits down and composes an email that says: 'Dear Mama, I'm not saying that you "did" take the sugar bowl from my house; I'm not saying that you "did not" take it. But the fact remains that it has been missing ever since you were here for dinner. Your Loving Son, Anthony.'

In response, Anthony gets an email from his Mama that says: 'Dear son, I'm not saying that you "do" sleep with Maria, and I'm not saying that you "don't" sleep with her. But the fact remains that if she was sleeping in her *own* bed, she would have found the sugar bowl by now. Your loving Mama.'

And the moral of the story is: 'Never bulla shitta your Mama'."

Jude and Kate cracked up at the joke. But all of a sudden Kate thought back at sleeping in Jude's hutch and blushed crimson. She had no idea how Ed could have known about that.

In fact, Ed didn't know about the sleeping arrangements. He had been making a reference at Jude's trying to put one over him with the plan they hadn't discussed. Kate's sudden blushing told the Kentuckian that he may have struck a nerve.

CHAPTER 29 — The Finger

"If your right hand makes you stumble, cut it off and throw it from you; for it is better for you to lose one of the parts of your body, than for your whole body to go into hell." Matthew, 5:30

1315 hours, January 11, 2018

Early that afternoon, while they were busy putting together the instructions that Ed would give Greco, the field switchboard operator rushed in and told Ed that Greco's aide was on the line waiting to connect him with Ed.

Ed looked at the others befuddled at how fast Greco had reacted to the list and grabbed the handset next to the map table.

"This is Commander Sumter," the staff heard him say, followed by a silence where they could almost hear the Provo President squeak at their boss. They did notice that Ed had grown serious and his demeanor darkened like when he was really angry.

The next moment Ed, seething with anger said, "I've got to say you have big brass ones, Greco. At 1800 hours we will deliver Amanda's left pinky to our end of the Legion Bridge. It will be in a tiny, dainty little box. My troops will allow your messenger to pick it up. One messenger. Bye, y'all."

The silence in the CP was sepulchral. Ed stood up, unable or unwilling to say a word. He hushed the switchboard operator to whom he had given the cellular phone with a sharp, "Don't answer the sumbitch until I tell you".

Jude and Kate had heard what Ed had told Greco. Were they really going to send the Provo Amanda's pinky? But they had heard it clearly enough. It was Jude who broke the silence. "Commander? A private word."

He wasn't about to let his friend turn into a monster.

Instead of answering Jude, Ed walked over to his corner of the CP and rummaged in his rucksack until he came up with a small cardboard box bearing the Lord & Taylor emblem. It was the type of little box in which cheap jewelry was sold, set on a bed of cotton padding. He removed something shiny out of it and put it in his pocket. And then he walked over to Kate and asked her to step out of the CP with him.

1315 hours, January 11, 2018

"I have Commander Sumter on the line, Mr. President," buzzed his aide.

Signaling General Jackson to wait, Greco picked up the phone much too fast, and made a mental note not to ever do that again, for it was a sign of weakness. "Sumter, I have your list. Now, before we talk about this, I want to talk with my wife. That's a sine qua non. No tickee, no laundly."

Jackson could not hear what the Rebel commander was saying, but he saw the color suddenly drain from Greco's face.

"No, wait…" The 'no' was high-pitched and desperate, but the Rebel commander had hung up.

Jackson took his cue from the Commander in Chief's unprofessional display of emotion and silently left

Greco's office. No telling how the martinet would react. Frankly, he was getting really tired of the man.

Four attempts to reestablish communications went unheeded on the Rebel side.

1315 hours, January 11, 2018

Outside the CP hutch Ed preempted Kate "I know whatcha gonna say, Kate. Just hear me out. I want you to take a good look at Amanda's left pinky. Take a picture of it if with your cell phone. Then, I want you to go to see Lieutenant O'Connor at the aid station back in Woodridge. He's a buddy of mine. He's set up a large aid station to deal with all these casualties in an emptied out, abandoned supermarket.

He uses the supermarket's meat locker as a makeshift Graves Registration cooling depository. That's where he is keeping the unidentified body parts his medics picked up on the battlefield. He will keep the body parts fresh until they can be identified and sent to the next of kin for burial.

Ask him to let you see the body parts, find a female fighter's detached left hand, match it as close as possible to the picture of Amanda's hand and ask him to chop off the pinky with a scalpel…something professional like. Then ask him to disfigure the finger print as if it had happened in the struggle, as if the finger was cut from a live person. Tell O'Connor that I will make him a eunuch if he so much as whispers a word to anyone about this. You personally stick the pinky into this here little box and bring it to the CP in a cooler. And not a word to anyone and that includes your boyfriend."

She protested weakly, but was relieved by the turn of events. "He's not my fucking boyfriend."

Ed shushed her. "Whatever. Not a word to him either. Let everyone in the CP think that I've lost it. It has to be believable for it to work. Do you read me?"

"Yes, Sir. Loud and clear, Sir," said Kate with a conspiratorial smile.

While Ed returned to the CP, Kate rushed to the improvised jail that held Amanda. She walked in asking the inside guards to step outside. The guards saw her pull her K-bar as they left.

She walked over to the blindfolded Amanda, who had heard the familiar unsheathing of the K-bar. Smiling to herself for the scare she was about to give the Greco woman, Kate unzipped Amanda's ACU shirt, sliced up the thermal undershirt and cut her bra open with the K-bar. She then removed the gag so the woman could scream for the benefit of the guards and whispered to the hostage: "I'm going to cut off you left nipple, cunt. Hold still."

In one swift motion she touched the breast with the cold blade and viciously pinched Amanda's nipple, extracting a piercing cry from the Greco woman who actually thought her nipple had been cut off. Amanda Greco fainted, as Kate had expected.

Kate then replaced the gag, straightened the thermal undershirt and the bra below it, and then zipped up the ACU shirt. The bitch would just have to be uncomfortable with the cut bra and underwear in the winter chill.

Kate pulled out her iPhone and took a close up of Amanda's limp left hand, which had been the real reason for the whole drama. The fact that she was passed out helped a lot.

Picking up the K-bar from the hutch's floor, she sheathed it and walked out smiling, holding the empty little box in her hand. She ordered the guards to stay out of the hutch for the next 12 hours, even if the bitch cried out through her gag.

The sentries, who had never seen that side of their boss, nodded with concerned expressions and followed Kate with their eyes as she departed camp.

1330 hours, January 11, 2018

Kate returned to the pickup truck they had abandoned at Old Dominion Drive and sped to meet with Lieutenant O'Connor at the aid station in Woodbridge. She had called him and told him on behalf of Commander Sumter to safeguard the unattached limbs he was guarding until she got there. O'Connor had worked for Ed for a long time and knew better than to question that kind of order from his boss, or even to wonder about it. As a fellow Kentuckian he just knew that the 'big sumbitch' boss of his was up to something.

Kate used the 40 minute drive to Woodbridge to think. For one thing, she was scared at the enjoyment she had derived from frightening Amanda. It worried her. She didn't think she was that type of person. In fact, during her time in 'the sandbox' she had never allowed the spooks to use torture on the prisoners her MP unit was guarding. It was against all she believed. She was aware that the spooks would 'waterboard' them when they got to their headquarters; but she'd be damned if they were going to do those things on her dime.

This last episode with Amanda scared her. She was scared of how easily she could deal with being mean. Killing a soldier in battle was no problem. But, this was an unarmed civilian in her custody.

Then, there was Jude. She still didn't know what to think about him. She had given up thinking she didn't like him. She did. But, what now? Was she ready to deal with all his baggage and all her baggage in the middle of a war? To what end? It's not as if either one of them was ready to hit the chapel, get themselves 2.5 kids and set up house in the suburbs. A hole in the ground was all she had; and all he had too. And what if he got hurt or killed?

It seemed to her that she had avoided entanglements for so long that she was not prepared to deal with Jude now. God, this morning she woke up embracing the guy! Talk about embarrassment! And to make matters worse he had not even made fun of her. He had just carefully moved her arm and her leg from his body. God forbid he would find out that she had been dreaming about making love with him under a thorn bush at Heater's Island; this thought held her as she arrived at the converted Woodbridge Giants supermarket with the Red Cross on the roof.

1415 hours, January 11, 2018

"Lieutenant O'Connor, I presume," she said with a wide smile, almost merrily jumping off the pickup when she spotted the guy in the bloodied overalls.

"The one and only, ma'am." The guy was just as tall as Ed, but really skinny. She wondered what the hell they ate in Kentucky to make them grow so tall. He continued with a twang "You must be Commander Hartmann. Ed just hung up the phone, but not before telling me that I was to do precisely what you told me, no matter how weird. Didn't want to tell him that I been doin' nothing but 'weird' for him since the day he hired me for the Guard in Louisville."

This brought a smile to Kate's face, and it sort of relieved her that the guy seemed to have a sense of humor. "Did he also tell you what your fate would be if you did not do as you were told?" said Kate, mischievously.

"Sure did, ma'am. But old Ed forgets that me and Julie already have six kids back in Louisville. Ain't gonna be needin' to sing bass no more," he chuckled.

Kate told him what she needed, and it made him pale. But he led her to a grisly collection of body parts in the meat locker which were waiting to be reunited with bodies they may find. There weren't very many women hands in stock, but Kate was able to match one closely to the picture in her phone.

He pulled out a scalpel from the medical kit and quickly sliced the pinky from the dead hand. The guy was so far beyond pale that he was light green. Kate took pity on the Lieutenant and disfigured the fingerprint area herself with a pair of pliers. There you go; something else she couldn't have done a short time ago.

She put the finger in the box, and the box in a small cooler filled with ice, thanked O'Connor and sped away towards the camp.

CHAPTER 30 — Ire's Catalyst

"The moment of truth, the sudden emergence of a new insight, is an act of intuition. Such intuitions give the appearance of miraculous flushes, or short-circuits of reasoning. In fact they may be likened to an immersed chain, of which only the beginning and the end are visible above the surface of consciousness. The diver vanishes at one end of the chain and comes up at the other end, guided by invisible links." The Act of Creation, Arthur Koestler, 1964

1735 hours, January 11, 2018

Kate and Jude made their way back to the ruins of the Legion Bridge, Virginia side, on the desolate and war-ravaged VA 193 and then across Scott's Run Nature Preserve, walking up to the bridge's carcass through a ritzy development below the former traffic artery. It was dark, and the lack of city lights made it even darker, covering their approach.

Carrying the cooler with his left hand, Jude asked Kate to stay behind with the Reb platoon that was guarding the bridge's approach. The platoon commander told him that there had been no movement on the Provo end. Jude then disappeared into the boulders on the right, doing what he did best and what had earned him the moniker "Ghost".

From his vantage point atop one of the bombed out boulders that used to be part of the bridge Jude kept a silent vigil for about 20 minutes. He had located the Provo contingent on the other side of the Potomac through his night scope. Greco had sent the varsity team. His experience and power of observation told him he was dealing with CIA paramilitary troops. They were waiting by their Zodiac for the signal to come across.

Jude slid to a lower boulder on the right and blinked his tactical LED flashlight three times precisely at 1800 hours. The Provos answered with the same signal from next to the Zodiac.

Leaving the cooler with the pinky on the boulder, next to his lit flashlight, Jude retreated to another high perch 50 yards to his left and wrapped the M-4 sling around his left arm, taking aim at the cooler from the shadows of the ruins. The guard platoon had a pre-set artillery fire mission on the area, just in case the Provos got tricky.

The CIA operatives sent to retrieve the finger were good, but Jude was better. His illuminated LED flashlight resting on the rock served as a point of reference to the Provos, but the war time dimmed city lights on the Maryland side enveloped the enemy in a deadly aura. At this distance Jude would not even need a sniper rifle.

The Zodiac touched the Virginia shore and its troops jumped out and hugged the earth; each operative covering a pre-arranged sector. One of them got up after a few seconds and walked toward the LED beam. Jude said a silent prayer that no one from the guard platoon got an itchy trigger finger. It was important to build trust for the upcoming exchange.

The way he moved, the operative was probably a former Seal who had been manning a Langley desk for a while. There was a certain over-confidence to his demeanor that came from relying too much on written assessments. An Army Ranger or Green Beanie, or an active duty SEAL would have moved with less bravado, trusting nothing in the silence of the night. All well and good, thought Jude, and kept his eye on the advancing Provo.

The operative arrived at the beam, took out a waterproof bag from his jacket and put the small cooler inside it without even opening it. His movements were careful, much too slow. His head was bent down knowing that someone was looking at him. He was probably scanning the dark with rapid eye movement.

The slowness of his movements was not normal. It made Jude take his eyes off the man and scan the beach once more, counting prone figures. Six had come across, counting the box gofer. There should have been five prone operatives next to the Zodiac. There were now four. One was missing.

Jude slid down and to the left of the boulder. He scanned the brush from the beach to the area where he knew the guard platoon was providing covering fire. He almost missed the subtle movement of a stick on the ground that shouldn't have moved on its own. There he was.

But wait, there were a number of leaves about 10 meters up from the infiltrator that should not have been moving either.

The lack of sound from either one of the disturbances was eerie. Jude assessed that someone from the guard platoon had spotted the Provo and correctly set out to intercept him, instead of firing on him. He moved his eyes back to the finger gofer and saw that he was still there, making a big deal out of securing the box. The Provos had evidently decided to use the pick-up to their as cover for an infiltration.

The infiltrator kept moving, more ground debris mysteriously displaced, but the interceptor remained still, meaning that the Provo was not aware that he had been made. The next movement showed a silhouette pointing a carbine at the infiltrator, who rose slowly, too slowly. Jude decided at that moment that the finger gofer was the lesser of his problems and began a fast, silent crawl towards what he knew would happen next.

He was only a few feet from the Reb with the carbine when he saw the infiltrator swiftly strike at the weapon, wrapping his hand over the breach to prevent it from firing. The operative still thought he'd have a chance if he dispatched his opponent.

In a seamless move the Provo released his hand from the carbine and sent an uppercut to the Rebel's jaw with his right hand while the left grasped his boot knife. It was a classic move to swing the blade up to the opponent's upturned neck and puncture the windpipe.

The Provo's knife was nearly at the Reb's neck when it stopped and dropped, along with the man who held it. Even in the dark of night, the Reb saw the astonished look on the Provo's face, and the point of the dark blade that had perforated the medulla and come out through his Adam's apple.

A dark shape materialized behind the Provo, slowing his inert body on its way to the ground so that it wouldn't make noise as it landed. The shape then slid away as quietly as he had appeared, moving a finger to his mouth in the universal signal for silence.

Jude back-tracked the infiltrator's route from the Zodiac, and then turned toward the boulder that had held the chopped finger. He halted when his eyes took in the Provo messenger negotiating the shrubs and arriving at the rigid rubber craft. He observed the prone operatives get up in a crouch, maintaining sector cover while the gofer dropped the package into the foot well and pushed the Zodiac into the water.

The gofer climbed in, followed hurriedly by his companions who took up the oars and paddled away from the shoreline. There was no hesitation. None of them looked for or waited for the infiltrator. The normalcy of their movements was meant to mask the infiltration. They had carried out the mission, and they were heading back home. The infiltrator was on his own.

Jude ran back in a crouch to where he had left the dead infiltrator and the intercepting Reb. The Reb was plastic-tying the dead body's hands and feet, with the dexterity of a special ops operative. Even the deadest of bodies should be handled as if it could get up and kill you. He signaled the Reb to stay there; that he would be back.

Jude approached with extreme caution the boulder where his LED flashlight still shined. When he was sure the gofer had not left any traps, he extinguished the light and put it in his pocket. Jude worked from behind the protection that the boulder offered against a potential Provo sniper from the Maryland coastline. When he was through sanitizing the scene, he moved back towards where the infiltrator's body was still being guarded by the Reb.

When he got there the Reb looked at him and smiled. The shock of seeing Kate's face when he finally focused froze Jude in place momentarily with an eruption of unexpected emotions. What was she doing here?

Why did she take that risk? How did she know infiltration detection techniques? What if the asshole had killed *her*? What if he lost her too? Wait until he got a hold of her! And yet, why should he care if she got herself killed?

They looked away from each other. They searched through the Provo's equipment and pockets, not really expecting to find anything useful, but just to do something mechanical before the confrontation they both expected took place. Jude crouched and took up perimeter security while Kate retrieved the Provo's weapon and cleared it. Then it was Kate's turn to guard the perimeter while Jude took off the Provo's harness and back pack.

It was SOP to minimize the number of people who were aware of any infiltration attempt and its successful interception to maximize intelligence exploitation. They dragged the corpse toward the pickup truck, bypassing the guard platoon's position. When they got there Jude lifted it and dropped it on the truck bed while Kate secured the Provo's equipment. Jude clicked his transmit button twice to let the guard platoon commander that they were leaving. They shut the truck's rear gate and walked around to the truck's cab. Once in the cab they sat silently for what seemed like an eternity.

Jude looked at the steering wheel as he asked her, "What were you thinking taking on a trained infiltrator all by yourself?"

And so it began.

"I didn't know I had to ask your permission to do my job." The words came out in a hard staccato.

"You could have gotten killed. In fact, he would have done you if I hadn't gotten there in time." The reproach in his tone swelled along with his anger.

His last word was still coming out when she told him, "And so what if I had gotten killed. I'm a soldier and shit happens."

"Shit doesn't happen when you know what you are doing." The cadence and power of his words had risen exponentially.

"And what the fuck should you care if I live or die?"

"I'm not about to lose you, too." The intensity died off toward the last word. His head was almost touching the steering wheel. His eyes still glued to its center.

Suddenly they faced each other and threw themselves at one another in a desperate embrace that turned into a deep kiss, which lasted not nearly as long as they had expected.

They tore at each other's clothing until each of them was buried against the other's skin, grappling, caressing, pushing and pulling, releasing a gush of pent up emotion. They moved against each other and fell into a love rhythm that ended moments later when there was nothing left but a sweaty embrace in winter, rapid breathing, the dark of the night, and the hope that no one from the guard platoon had witnessed the moment.

Later, they straightened out their ACUs silently and back to the AC camp. They were both lost in thought. Neither of them could recall how they made it back to the Old Dominion Drive entry point to the trail. Kate broke the silence with a phone call to get someone to retrieve the body from the pickup and send it to S-2 bunker for Intel processing. They then walked through each challenge point robotically, avoiding each other's eyes on purpose. And then they were there.

CHAPTER 31 — The Torment

"Love give me strength and strength will help me through." Said by Juliet, Romeo and Juliet, William Shakespeare

1915 hours, January 11, 2018

When they dropped into the CP bunker, Ed noticed the seriousness in Jude and Kate's faces and knew something had gone down. The guard platoon had maintained radio silence except for the prearranged clicking signal that the operation had been completed. The duo gave Ed a detailed briefing on the infiltrator's elimination in short, terse sentences. They left no detail out of the incident. Jude including how the infiltrator had overpowered Kate and Kate narrating how Jude had saved her bacon, all delivered in business-like words.

Jude went into more detail when he described the Provo special ops operatives and the tactics used. He described their demeanor, training and equipment; dumping on the CP's floor at that point the equipment they had retrieved from the dead infiltrator, including the satellite phone.

Ed asked them, "So what do you think his mission was?"

Jude looked briefly at Kate and then launched into an explanation. "I think they sent him to snatch or kill someone whose loss would help with the hostage trade. If I had to guess, I would say you were the target, especially after your conversations with Greco. It's just like Greco to make such a move."

"And you Kate?" Ed searched her face.

"I'm inclined to believe that he was going to hit someone. Maybe you, like Jude said. This was definitely a hit. A snatch takes more than one guy. Good as he was". Her words trailed off in recollection of her near death encounter, hoping to salvage a little bit of her self-respect.

"These guys were Agency, Ed. The jury is still out, but he could have been the point man for a snatch too, calling in reinforcements once he was ready. I won't put my hand in the fire for either option. What Kate says makes sense, except that he did not have a sniper rifle, and he wasn't all that good at personal combat."

Jude did not want to contradict Kate, but the mission indicators were not all that clear.

"OK. Clear as mud. So what do we do about him?" Ed took the opportunity to sit against the bunker's wall, grabbing a cup of hot coffee and gesturing to them to do the same. Kate and Jude served themselves and sat crossed-legged in front of their boss, who took a hip flask out of his pocket and "blessed" their cups with the elixir.

Jude took a sip, measuring his thoughts and told them, "I say we let it play its course. Let's not acknowledge that we know about the infiltrator, much less that we killed his sorry ass."

His 'we' was a statement of inclusion that gave Kate credit for her part. After all, she had seen the infiltrator and gone out to intercept him before Jude had noticed him. In reality, Jude had been impressed with Kate's use of tradecraft and intended to ask her about it as soon as they had a quiet moment.

He still wasn't sure he could or should bring up their lustful bout. He didn't know what to think about it, except that the physical release had felt very good. The problem was that this was the first time he had been with a woman since Angie died.

Kate must have been lost in her own thoughts because it took her a few seconds to agree with Jude's recommendation. "I also think that's the best option, Ed. I say, keep Greco guessing as long as possible."

And Jude continued, looking at both Ed and Kate, "He had a satellite phone. We need to assume that he was going to check in at some point: whether to ask for a team to support a snatch, or to report the success of his hit.

Whatever; it's better to play it close to the vest and not do anything that lets them know that we know about the infiltrator. So, maybe he forgot to call, or he lost his phone. Greco's uncertainty is our friend. But at the end of the operation, when the exchange is made, we should clear our throats and tell Greco that we foiled his move. At that point the guy's death will buy us a psych advantage, but not before" concluded the Ranger.

"There is only one thing scarier than how both of you agree with each other on this."

Ed paused for effect.

"The fact that I also agree with both of you," said the Kentuckian looking deeply at his cup of coffee. And then Ed spoke to the switchboard operator, who was also manning his cell phone. "Son, I'll take the next call from across the river."

1945 hours, January 11, 2018

Jude and Kate climbed out of the CP bunker in silence. There was comfort in the silence. They headed to

Jude's hutch and jumped into it without so much as gazing at the other. Kate's eyes landed on his.

"I don't want to talk about it," was his response to the unasked question.

"Why? Are you afraid to deal with your feelings?" was her challenge. It was too quick coming out, too uncertain to be forceful.

He climbed on one side of the sleeping platform slipping under his thermal blanket, leaving ample room for her on the other side as an acknowledgement of sorts. She followed suit, ensuring that no part of her body touched him.

Silence. There was a distant artillery exchange, someplace south. But, silence.

His night thoughts went to Angie, to that day. He held her cold, limp hand in his mind one more time. He caressed the lock of hair that fell on the bloody right side of her face. Her eyelids were closed, but he imagined he could still see her very light gray eyes staring at him with amusement, like when she was about to scold him for something silly he said or did.

He had tried very hard to be a nonbeliever, or at the very least an agnostic, until she died. Ever since the moment he held her hand and cried out to the heavens there was suddenly a reason to believe. She had to be somewhere. She couldn't be gone forever. They couldn't be gone, her and his baby boy. He had to believe that he would see them again in an afterlife. There was no way he would ever forgive those who took them away from him.

And now! Now he had sullied her memory. Their memories, by letting the animal in him do to another woman what belonged only to Angie. And the night took pity on him.

Kate's eyelids were closed but there was a storm brewing inside her. It was so powerful it hurt. The turmoil had shaken up her thought processes, and there was damage, lots of damage. She had hurt him. Somehow she had hurt him real bad with her love. She had taken advantage of the moment to fulfill her wanton desires, not thinking for one moment what it would do to him. What it would do to her. He had provoked her, how, by saving her life one more time?

She had known this was coming. She had known for so many years that the cauldron in her soul would at one point rage over. There had been the pimply boy and a string of meaningless encounters to just relieve the pressure in her belly. She had remained strong. But she just knew that there would come a time when she really would want it to be meaningful, when she had found 'the one,' when she would really mess things up. She had felt her strength crumble inside her at the moment he spent himself in her womb. And the night took pity on her.

At one point during the early morning, still dark, their eyes opened in unison and just stared at the poncho ceiling that lined the underside of the timber roof. They were afraid to look at one another, afraid of what the day had in store for them. There were no dreams. They knew when they turned to that first ray of sunshine that came through the side of the overhead log cover that there had been no dreams. The dreams would have been a welcome outlet for their feelings. It was sort of a roadmap for what they ought to do next.

And then the light that filtered through the side of the poncho ceiling pierced whatever internal peace was left in their heart. The morning crushed their musings and lanced their hopes.

CHAPTER 32 — The Respite

"In seeming contradiction of physical laws, time is heavy only when it is empty." Trevanian, <u>Shibumi.</u>

0600 hours, January 12, 2018

Jude was the first to get up and go out of the hutch. He came back as she was coming out and said, "I'm going to make coffee."

Kate was more surprised at the fact that he had spoken to her at all than at the meaning of the words. Was there a meaning? Was that an assumption on his part that she would return? What if she just kept walking away and didn't return?

She came back into the hutch as the water started to simmer and sat beside him, just staring at the bubbles in the canteen cup, the brown bubbles from the coffee she had "confiscated" from the mansion at Chain Bridge Road. The smell was powerful, the aroma intense.

He split the contents of his canteen cup into hers, letting the coffee rest and the grounds fall to the bottom, in the Turkish fashion. Shit, in the Greek fashion. If his Greek friends would have heard him calling that brewing style 'Turkish' rather than 'Greek' they would have banned him for life from the Hellenic peninsula and Astoria, New York.

"Thanks," she said, finishing the coffee, grounds and all, and rising to leave. She didn't look at him. He didn't look at her but he also stood up and walked beside her to the CP.

They stepped down into the Command bunker just as Ed was shouting on the phone "…and I woudda sent you some bigger body part, if only it wouldn't have spoiled the merchandise. You ready for the next piece of her, or do you want to talk turkey with me, sailor?"

He looked at Jude and Kate as he said the last word, acknowledging their presence with a grin.

Not giving Greco time to reply he went on explosively, "I just faxed you the detailed proposal on how to deliver them, and how the exchange is gonna take place. I ain't discussing it no more. That's the way it's going to be."

And then in a calmer voice: "It's not as if we expected to ever see them POWs again. Far as we knew your Militia had killed them all."

"You kill them all now. It makes no never-mind to me. I kill your bitch and throw her corpse in the river, but not before chopping her into smaller pieces while she can still feel it. The time and places are in the plan I faxed y'all. All I need to get from you is a 'they're underway'. I'm going to hang up now and I don't want to hear your fucking slimy voice until 1500 hours on Monday. At that time, the only thing that is going to come out of your mouth is that the operation will begin in three hours or less. I hear anything else and your whore's a goner. Out!"

He turned fully toward them and arched his eyebrows in a silent question 'how did I do?'

Jude smiled at him and said, "Very convincing, boss. If I had been Greco I would have been shitting in my pants by the time you told him how you were going to chop her into small pieces. Did he question the finger?"

"Yeah. He began asking how he could be sure it was hers since the fingerprint was conveniently obliterated. I knew where he was going with that and I took a chance. I told him to run a DNA check on the finger. I knew that would take days, and chances are they would have to run it against hair on her brush or something like that because there was a snowball's chance in hell that they had her DNA on file." And then he continued 'smug as a bug', as his wife liked to say.

"He bought it, lock stock and barrel. So, all we have to do now is wait for the call back Monday at 1500. That gives us three days, roughly." Ed signaled the end of his spiel by reaching for his coffee cup and taking a big gulp, then grimacing because it was cold.

Kate took the opportunity and said, "If you agree, Ed, I'd like to coordinate quartering, medical attention and debriefings for the returning POWs. I want to get members of their former units to ID each one of them as early as possible to make sure they are who they say they are. I thought we'd keep them all together at Langley High School track and field bleachers for in-processing. It's a good place out in the open to identify and weed out infiltrators, if there are any. And speaking of infiltrators mixed among the POWs, it would not be helpful for you to show up there until it's safe." Ed looked at her funny. The girl had gumption to tell her boss what to do, he thought.

She continued, "Woodbridge can set up a field dispensary at the track to deal with first aid and identify contagious diseases early on. And the abandoned school can serve as temporary quarters for their families while they wait to be reunited."

She was aware that what she was proposing would keep her away from the CP and Jude. It was a good time to force some space between them. She didn't know if the relationship was going to go somewhere, but they needed a break just about now.

Jude could tell what she was doing, and thought that it was probably a good thing. He also needed time to think about all that had happened.

Was he ready to let go of Angie? That thought brought a glob of stomach acid up his esophagus. Or was it Ed's coffee? Whatever. He had things to do and Kate was becoming a distraction, to put it mildly.

It was his turn. "Ed, I thought I'd take a look at the fresh meat, like you asked, and put together a replacement commando team as soon as possible. I have a couple of objectives in mind that will put Greco in a world of hurt. First, I'd like your permission to access personnel files from the S-1 shop at Camp Dawson."

Ed looked into Jude's eyes and knew that something was up. Jude would let him know in due time. The Kentuckian decided to play along and followed up with measured words, "How long do you figure it's going to take you to put your team together?"

"Don't know. I have to see if we have the right type of troops. Depending on their level of training and the mission ahead I'd want them to go through some team-building stuff on this side of the river. Why? Did you have something specific in mind?"

"Well, Judeman, it would be great if we could take advantage of the distraction of the POW delivery to infiltrate you and your team behind the lines. But, I guess that putting it together in two days is probably too much to ask. Ain't it?" Ed was baiting Jude. There was no way that he could have a commando team ready to operate on such short notice. Especially if he wanted to run trust-building exercises and get to know the troops personally, as he preferred.

Ed pushed him anyway to give his friend a definite goal quickly. More to help get him out of his funk than to advance military objectives. He knew that Jude was a "management by objectives" leader. If he had a goal he would bust balls to get it done.

Jude was also a leader whose unit was massacred as a result of faulty intelligence. Rebel intel failed to apprise the Ranger that the Militia was guarding the Greco compound at Gettysburg, and that they were supported by helicopter gunships. Losing all your men, especially if you survived, could seriously damage a leader's confidence. Ed would have to keep a close eye on his friend and the new unit.

"That's just what I would like to do. But there are too many things to do before the exchange and we are really short on time. I'll see what I can do, but, no promises." said the Ranger, his objections weakening as the challenge jacked him up.

CHAPTER 33 — Evil Attacks the Weak

"It is by its promise of a sense of power that evil often attracts the weak." <u>Eric Hoffer</u> *(1902-1983) American philosopher and author.*

1030 hours, January 11, 2018

G-3 Operations Staff Officer, General Jason Jackson put his entire shop to verify the names and location of each of the Reb POWs. Just another onerous task from "Little Caesar". Frankly, he was more interested in recouping from the catastrophic probe into Reb territory than in getting Greco's wife back. The asshole would not even negotiate. He was ready to return 100 fighting men and women to the Rebel ranks with no questions asked. So the policy had changed from "we do not negotiate with terrorists" to "we give terrorist all they want with no questions asked."

But Jackson was a regular Army officer, a proud West Point graduate, and he still remembered the motto of "Duty, Honor, Country". He would follow his orders and prepare a credible plan for the prisoner exchange. He'd rather look at it as a prisoner exchange than what it really was: a cowardly capitulation for the personal comfort of the man who had usurped the National Command Authority.

By 1000 he had a verified list. It was going to be a problem. 32 of the 114 identified POWs were dead, and another 11 were hospitalized as a result of Militia interrogation and torture. So he could only send back 71 walking POWs, and 11 more on gurneys or wheelchairs.

And there were going to be two problems with that: he would have to explain to "little Caesar" why he could not comply with the Rebel demands. And he would have to demand answers on POW maltreatment from the fucking Militia. He needed to take immediate action so that he could spin this additional failure to his boss.

Jackson was as irritable as the situation called for. He summoned Assistant G-3 Steven Marlin. No sooner had the two-star walked into his office when Jackson exploded. "General Marlin, it has come to my attention that 32 Rebel POWs have died while in your custody and that an additional 11 are injured from torture administered by your interrogators. What do you have to say for yourself?"

"Jason, you knew that the Militia had been put in charge of POW's. Why are you laying this on me?" answered his fellow West Point grad.

Jackson distanced himself physically and in tone when he responded gruffly, "I believe it's way past the time when you could take the liberty of addressing me by my first name, General. This situation has just come to my attention, and I want to know why you took it upon yourself to relinquish your responsibilities to that rag tag bunch." the last phrase was delivered with sophisticated venom. It was a clear signal that he did not intend to be at fault here.

"But General you chopped on the NCA decision memo to put the camps under Militia command," said Marlin. He was grasping at straws. He could not believe that Jackson would do him this way.

"General Marlin, the decision memo you sent me stated, and I quote, 'I recommend that POW internment duties be assigned to the Militia in order to free regular

Army troops for combat'. It's right here in black and white," said Jackson throwing a copy of the memo at Marlin.

"If I cannot trust that my subordinates have every contingency under control, I cannot run this shop. What you did not say in that memo was that you were not going to properly train and supervise the Militia on POW internment requirements of the Geneva Convention."

And injecting a tone of fake concern he finished, "General, I have no choice but to relieve you from your duties. I will do this much for you. I will not sign the memo until tomorrow evening to give you a chance to put in your retirement papers. Accompanying your request for retirement I want a separate memo owning up to your negligence and its serious repercussions on the conduct of these operations. That's all."

"I see, General. Someone had to pay for your failed, unprofessional choices. And that's me this time," retorted Marlin more candidly than his training and tradition allowed.

Jackson spoke calmly. "General, do yourself a favor, own up to your mistakes and go retire quietly somewhere for the good of the 'long gray line'. This counseling session is over. You are dismissed."

Jackson finished his harangue with an allusion to the honor of West Point, the "long gray line" of the Corps of Cadets made famous in General of the Army Douglas MacArthur's farewell speech at the academy. It was a warning that unless Marlin played along Jackson would ensure that fellow West Pointers would shun him. That meant that he would not be able to supplement his pension with post-retirement work opportunities.

Marlin closed the door behind himself a little too loudly, and Jackson picked up the phone to call the G-1 Adjutant. "Charlie, I've just relieved Steve Marlin for dereliction of duty. Have your staff prepare the memo for me with the appropriate safeguards so that he may retire honorably and discreetly. Put tomorrow's date on the memo. And Charlie, get Joshua Wesleyan here from Bragg. I'm going to offer him Steve's job. I like how fast he sent his troops here when we needed them. You might also start to draw up his appointment papers too. I don't think he'll turn down the job. That's all."

He hung up before the G-1's "Yes, Sir" could enter cyberspace on the Provo VOIP network.

1300 hours, January 11, 2018

At the appointed time, General Jackson was at National Command Headquarters to give Greco the bad news in person, and proffer an attenuation plan accompanied by his written resignation accepting responsibility for the actions of his subordinates, should the Commander in Chief chose to accept it.

Greco, ever the politician, knew that he could not accept Jackson's resignation right then and there because the G-3 controlled the informal but very influential West Point 'ring knocker' network.

Moreover, Greco could not hold Jackson responsible for the catastrophic probe into Rebel held territory, where half of his force had either surrendered, deserted, or been killed or captured by the enemy. General Marlin would play the role of sacrificial lamb for the botched attack, despite the fact that Greco had personally forbidden the preparatory artillery fires that doctrine called for. He would take care of Jackson later. He could bide his time for now since 'revenge is a dish best served cold.'

"Sit down, Jason. Let's take a look at what you have here. And put away that letter of resignation. I appreciate your sense of responsibility and honor, but I can't blame you for what your Assistant G-3 did."

Greco layered the honey thickly. He took several minutes to scan the documents Jackson brought.

"Thank you for your trust, Mr. President." After playing to Greco's ego with the presidential title, Jackson explained his attenuation plan for the POW exchange. It included a full disclosure to the Rebs on the dead and injured POWs – as if they were dealing with a real enemy Army and not 'those mutant hillbillies'.

They would repatriate what remains they could recover and deliver the wounded using Red Cross/Green Crescent escorts. And finally, to sweeten the deal, they would surrender to the Rebs the two Militia POW camp commanders responsible for the torture and summary executions.

"I like it, Jason. The hillbillies can't walk away from it. This strategy shows initiative, talent and good judgment on your part. I only wish that I could ask you to do the negotiations for me, but these assholes are just tickled pink to have me over a barrel personally. Please thank your team from me.

Now, as far as Steve Marlin goes, please make sure he doesn't fall too hard. Be discreet. We can't buck the academy system, you know?"

Greco added that last part as his personal acknowledgement and support of the "old boy" network.

A mollified and reassured Jackson told Greco, "That's all taken care of, Mr. President. He will be retired honorably before the end of the day tomorrow. And I'm bringing Joshua Wesleyan up from Bragg to take his place. Frankly, I should have done that a lot sooner. Marlin was too personally invested with the Militia. You do recall that his wife is Moslem, don't you?"

Two could play the subtle warning game. By bringing up the former Assistant G-3's 'personal investment', Jackson was telling Greco that, should he need to do so, he would play the Greco wife angle to the hilt within the establishment. Jackson may have attended the Hudson School for Wayward Children (West Point's epithet) but he was nobody's patsy.

Greco digested the West Pointer's feistiness. Hmm, maybe he would wait for a super-solid occasion to get rid of him. There was enough blame to dish out in this operation. The Virginia probe was a disaster because Greco would not let them use doctrinal fire support in the attack to protect his wife, his 'personal investment'.

"I hear you, Jason. We all make mistakes. Some more costly than others. So let's not stir the pot too much. We have a war to win. And, don't forget that I still need some plans drawn to coordinate operations with the Chinese. That pedantic General Wang keeps pushing for a date to start operations against the Rebels in Colorado."

"I have Commander Sumter on the line, Mr. President," buzzed his aide. A brief conversation ensued, ending with Greco slamming the phone on the table before him.

Jackson knew when to withdraw. "I can see you are very busy Mr. President, so I'll go back to my shop and wait for your call to resume our conversation, if you wish to do so."

"What?" responded Greco distractedly "Oh sure, sure, General. I'll give you a call later on."

As the general stepped out Greco told his aide "Ernie, please bring me that CIA file".

CHAPTER 34 — Traitors Must Expect Treachery

"The Ass and the Fox, having entered into a partnership together, went out into the forest to hunt. They had not proceeded far, when they met a Lion. The Fox approached the Lion and promised to contrive for him the capture of the Ass, if he would pledge his word that his own life should be spared. On his assuring him that he would not injure him, the Fox led the Ass to a deep pit, and contrived that he should fall into it. The Lion, seeing that the Ass was secured, immediately clutched the Fox, and then attacked the Ass at his leisure." Aesop

0600 hours, January 12, 2018

"That son-of-a-bitching incestuous hillbilly!" Greco filtered through bare teeth each and every word. His staff was within earshot and he wanted to ensure they knew how he felt. "Ernie, give him time to get to his office and call Jackson. Tell him he must be ready to start the delivery operation by Monday at 1500. Fax him the Reb plan. At first blush it didn't seem too different from what Jackson wanted to do. So tell him to adjust his plan to Sumter's. I want the operation to roll out with no glitches. If something happens to Amanda because these ring-knockers can't soldier, heads will roll.

Speaking of which, get that Agency type who recovered Amanda's finger to come see me. So far he has been the only son of a bitch around here who knew what he was doing. I want to hear how we are going to get back at those hillbilly bastards."

Greco turned to a map of the Area of Operations even before he finished with Ernie. So his last few words carried a distracted tone.

Ernie knew not to ask questions once Greco had moved on. He was a man who expected to be understood the first time. After all, the President believed his instructions to be always crystal clear. The adjutant also knew that he had to let Jackson know that Greco would not listen to any more arguments. So Ernie said, "Yes, Sir, Mr. President."

He hurried to the nearest secure phone, an ancient but reliable STU-III, calling General Jackson to give him the heads-up that the latest Reb demand was being faxed to him forthwith, and that the President expected full compliance and a rollout by 1500 Monday.

0625 hours, January 12, 2018

"Sir, Mr. Canton is outside," said Ernie coming through the door after knocking and finding Greco lost in a thick bound document with a Top Secret cover sheet.

Greco responded distractedly, "Who?"

"The CIA guy who recovered the mutilation. You asked me to get him for you," said Ernie, more defensively than he probably should have. Greco trusted his aide almost implicitly because the guy knew how to kiss ass well, and he always carried out the Admiral's instructions correctly and on-time.

"Oh, yeah. Let him in, Ernie. And you come in too. I want you to take notes of our conversation," said Greco putting down the Top Secret document he was reading and ensuring that there was nothing on his desk that the spook could read.

These guys were tricky. Greco believed in having a witness and a written record of anything he told anyone from the Agency. With today's technology, recordings could be altered seamlessly. You never knew when you had to prove something you told one of these guys.

Greco was still checking the top of his desk and its surrounding for relevant material the spook could read when Ernie and Canton walked in. Canton proceeded to sit down without invitation, which hit a sour note for Greco. But he let it go because the man seemed to be a breath of fresh air in a building full of incompetents. Greco even smiled when he said, "Thanks for coming by so quickly, Mr. Cantos."

"Canton," corrected the CIA officer.

"Yes, Canton. Sorry about that. Is that a Swiss last name?" recovered Greco.

"I don't really know, Mr. President. My family is Jewish, and it's likely that the last name came from Switzerland or thereabouts, but the Cantons have been in America since the 1700's," replied the savvy spook.

He knew that Greco was not too happy with Israel ever since they began to help the Rebels. So, distancing himself from the Jewish State was the smart thing to do.

"You don't say," said Greco distractedly and ill-humored, "but I didn't call you here to talk about family history."

What Canton did not know was that Greco was very sensitive about his immigrant parents. They were Italians who at one point had to be Greek, hence the name's etymology. So he always felt his Americanism threatened by the daughters and sons of the American Revolution. He kept his annoyance in check and continued, "I wanted to just say thanks for accomplishing your mission so well, as morbid as it was. I also wanted to get your personal impression of the other side. You are one of the few people who have an insight on how they work first-hand."

"Thank you, Sir. The mission was only complex because of the infiltration. Retrieving the mutilation gave us the opening we needed. As far as I know our man got in and will report back as soon as he hits Sumter."

"What do you mean?" That was the question that made Canton's world turn upside down. It meant that the President didn't know about the hit. That it was an Agency initiated operation and, he had royally fucked up. Blood drained from his face and his heart skipped a beat. And no matter how he spinned it, he was really in trouble with his immediate bosses.

Why in the hell had they done something like that without Executive sanction? Worse, why hadn't they warned him when they found out Greco wanted to see him? Was he being hung to dry? There was only one way he could save his ass now: selling his bosses out like they had sold him, and showing proper contrition before the President.

"Sir, I believe I just screwed up. I would have never thought the Agency would take an action that you had not authorized. I apologize for my unprofessionalism. But you are the Commander-in-Chief and what I do know is that I don't hide things from the Commander-in-Chief."

Greco, for his part was totally dumfounded, albeit pleased that the spook showed the proper loyalty to the National Command Authority. This guy had been played by the Langley crowd, but this was not the time to raise a stink. He wasn't even sure he could still think of 'the

Langley crowd'. After all, the old headquarters on Route 123 had been destroyed by Rebel artillery. He could cook up a scheme to take revenge later, against the real culprits. Greco used the pregnant pause to recover and do what he did best: be a snake.

"Son, I don't want you to be concerned at all. You have the right instincts. You assumed correctly that a mission of that kind would have been at least checked out with me. So, I don't want you to worry. You are going to be OK. I promise.

But I need you to tell me everything you know about this mission. A few minutes ago I was telling Ernie that I thought you were one of the few people around here that knew what he was doing. And I was right, of course. Now tell me about the hit."

For the next 20 minutes they discussed the infiltration operation and planned hit in detail. The most significant revelation was that Langley had an asset in the Appalachian Command. Greco could not believe that the Agency had kept this important fact from the Commander-in-Chief. This went beyond the acceptable protection of "sources and methods." To Greco this was outright treason.

What was truly important to Greco is that a hit on the Rebel commander would get Amanda Greco killed for sure.

CHAPTER 35 — Jude's Rangers Fight Again

William Thomas Overby was one several of Mosby 'The Gray Ghost' Rangers caught out of uniform behind Union lines. Condemned to death, his Union captors offered to spare him if he gave them Mosby's whereabouts. He refused saying 'Mosby will hang ten of you for every one of us.' reported by Joe Kirby, for the Civil War News, Route 1, Box 36, Turnbridge, VT

0800 hours, January 12, 2018

Jude accessed Camp Dawson's database from the AC Headquarters in Woodbridge, Virginia. Despite the conflagration the '.mil net' was almost intact, except that each side had moved quickly to deny each other access to the parts they controlled. Camp Dawson had the geographic advantage to hold on to the former Delta Force's paper files. They also had a team of IT types from West Virginia University at Morgantown who truly defied the stereotype of dumb mountaineers.

From the day the advance to DC began, they had worked feverishly and successfully to deny Washington control over key segments of the military network and intranet. Accessing the Defense Personnel System through the existing Air Reserve Personnel Center in the Colorado National Rebel Command, they were able to duplicate all military personnel records held at the National Archives facility in St. Louis, Missouri.

Woodbridge had updated and reorganized the personnel records of units that had crossed over to the Appalachian Command. However, in an effort to deny

Greco the information they had put them in a closed system where they hoped to share it with the field someday, but the database was still only accessible through the physical AC Headquarters. So that's where Jude began his search.

Jude's target population was soldiers who had Special Operations experience. Such individuals have data base records so complete that a researcher may glean a pretty full picture of the individual, to include current psychological and aptitude evaluations. Just a question needed to be asked: are you ready to go back to the black battlefield?

Jude had personally not met any SO soldier who didn't hanker for more. By 1100, he had identified 26 top-notch SOF troops from which he would choose 23 volunteers for his commando team. He would be the 24th. He was comfortable with the functionality of a 12-soldier team; a concept battle tested through the decades by US Special Forces 'A' Teams.

The 'A' Team was not a Ranger type of organization, but Jude had begun to experiment with the concept, successfully replacing Ranger weapons such as the 84 mm Carl Gustav RAAWS (Ranger Anti-Armor Weapon System) for the more reliable M-72 LAW. Each team would also have 60 mm mortars and a .50 cal Barrett Sniper system, along with the newer XM-2010 Sniper Rifle.

Jude had decided to incorporate two modified 'A' Team structures in the new unit. He was certain that the reason why his former team was annihilated was the lack of a sufficiently large contingent to modify and simplify the fire and maneuver basic doctrine Rangers preferred. Rangers were not Green Berets. They were traditionally used to force a gap through which larger units could successfully attack.

By the same token, the current tactical situation demanded the operational independence found in the Green Beret 'A' Team, along with the brute force of the Ranger doctrine. He believed that was the key to success for his next team.

1730 hours, January 12, 2018

He had set up shop in a 7-11 on Route 1 which had been almost entirely destroyed by retreating Greco forces during the Appalachian Command's initial advance. The shop owner had returned soon after that and was doing business with what stock he could salvage from the devastation. He had welcomed Jude and lent him the almost intact back room to do his thing, also providing free coffee to the interviewees. He would do anything for the Rebels, he had such a hard on for the Greco forces who had tried to destroy his livelihood.

As the men and women began arriving from their units Jude grilled them individually. First by verifying the details of their records, and then asking them how they would handle one of three theoretical situations he had personally designed. He made them wait outside after the interview ensuring that they paid the shopkeeper for anything else they wanted other than the coffee they were getting for free. This would also be a measure of their characters.

By 2330 Jude had finished the interviews and had made his decisions. He chose all 26 of them. In total he would use 11 for the A Team he would command, 12 for the second A Team, including the team leader, and three extras. He would figure out a way to use the extra three.

Of the 26, only 14 were women since it hadn't been all that long since they had been allowed to join the combat arms. There were Rangers, Seals, Marine Recon and several former AFSOC (Air Force Special Operations Command) members who were currently fighting as infantry for the Rebels.

Jude called Ed and asked that his staff notify their former units that the chosen soldiers had been detached, effective immediately. Appropriating some of the vehicles that had brought them to Woodbridge he mounted up and drove with them to nearby Fort Belvoir where one of Ed's C-130s had just delivered the Delta Force weaponry he requested from Camp Dawson. By 0200 the weapons had been distributed and the troops had gone to crash for a few hours in Belvoir's indoor archery range.

0530 hours, January 13, 2018

Jude and his new team had a quick breakfast delivered by the Belvoir officer's club kitchen. For many of them this was the first hot breakfast in weeks, and an essential morale builder. During the breakfast Jude talked to them about their new organization into two teams, one directly under his command, and the other under the command of his newly chosen deputy, and leader of the second A Team: a crusty Marine Gunnery Sergeant from Marine Recon named Tiburcio "Teeb" Alvarez.

Alvarez had been awarded the Congressional Medal of Honor for his gallantry in Afghanistan. He had singlehandedly killed 28 Taliban fighters in a furious firefight when they had tried to overrun his firebase in Helmand Province.

Jude and Teeb had stayed up all night talking about organization and expectations. They found that they were very much alike. By the time they went out to the Belvoir outdoor archery range to familiarize with their new weapons the two men had formed a strong bond. By noon they had finished all the familiarization ammunition, some of which had to be fired into Acotink Bay due to their large caliber. They jumped into their Humvees and left for Turkey Run Park, where they would bivouac and run patrol exercises.

1300 hours, January 13, 2018

Turkey Run Park sits on the Virginia shore of the Potomac River, on the other side of the George Washington Parkway across from the CIA complex at Langley. In peacetime the park hosted picnickers and semi-serious trail hikers in its approximately 700 acres of hilly, wooded land. The insurrection against the Greco government had not been kind to the former recreational area.

The artillery exchanges that largely destroyed the CIA complex also downed a good 200 acres of woodland at Turkey Run. What made it attractive to Jude was that its visitor's center had survived the destruction and could serve as a makeshift headquarters for his team. Also, Turkey Run Park was an excellent point from which to launch the commandos' first planned mission: the destruction of the POW camp at Carderock and the liberation of any prisoners still there after the exchange.

The Carderock Division of the Naval Surface Warfare Center was one of eight such locations built by the US Navy to tackle engineering problems in ships, submarines and other naval systems. The Greco government had turned its large warehouses into an internment camp for Rebel prisoners of war. They did that to protect the existing structures that they hoped to reuse after they had defeated the Rebels and restored order. By making it a POW internment camp they ensured the site's survivability because the Rebels would not do anything that could harm their comrades-in-arms. Not to mention violate the Geneva Convention.

Who managed the camp had been a hot potato between the regular Greco regulars and the Militia. Neither organization jumped at the opportunity of being jailers. Internment camp management was universally left to low quality troops who were better kept off the battlefield. Neither the regulars nor the Militia wanted to be labeled "low quality".

Jude thought that the camp made a good first target for the new team. It was managed by the Militia, so they would not be facing first rate troops. Since many of the prisoners were being exchanged for the Greco woman, hitting that target was not likely to harm many POWs. Finding and rescuing any POWs in the facility would be a personal blow to Greco. In terms of losing control of his area of operation, and in terms of trusting his subordinates to carry out his orders to trade all POWs for his wife. The POW camp was also a good target because Jude had a personal stake. When he lost his team he had been captured and interned there, and so clearing the place was a priority to him.

The team dismounted at the former Park Police headquarters building, which was guarded by a company of Rebels. The company conducted area denial patrol and other operations on a regular basis but avoided the building itself because of its potential as a target for Provo artillery. In fact, the only usable part was its basement, where the Park Police had had its indoor pistol range. That's where they set up for Jude's mission briefing.

Jude and Teeb walked up to an easel where the team had set up a large area map that had belonged to the Park Police. Since the Park Police had been a federal protection force whose responsibilities included both the George Washington Parkway on the Virginia side and the Cabin John Expressway on the Maryland side, the map covered the entire area of operations in detail.

When Jude walked up the group went silent. Someone shouted 'Tenhut', which brought them all to their feet. Jude responded uncomfortably. "As you were!"

And they all sat down with their eyes riveted on the legendary commander.

"First, let me tell you that I appreciate your military courtesy", he continued. "That said, this unit is an elite military organization made up of battle-tested men and women who have little to prove in terms of military courtesy. So, we will dispense with it. I don't particularly care to be saluted, just obeyed. I also know that Gunny Teeb, as a good NCO, would respond to a hand salute with a gnarly "You don't salute me, troop. I'm not an officer. I work for my living.'"

They all laughed nervously at Jude's joke, but also began to assess the character of the man who would lead them into battle. They liked what they saw.

"I put a lot more weight in your ability to act as a team and to kill the enemy than in your ability to kiss ass. If you feel compelled to salute anyone while we operate I suggest you salute the cadavers of dead Militia fighters."

Having made his point he turned to the map and began to explain how they would cross the Potomac at night, under the cover of a decoy artillery barrage on Heater's Island. The barrage would probably result on the redeployment of Provo units further north to block a fake Rebel crossing. He also explained the concept of the raid on the Carderock facility, including the exchange operation that they would use as a distraction for their attack on the POW camp. It was the first time that someone had told them that Greco's wife had been captured and would be traded for Rebel POWs.

Jude broke the group into two teams of twelve with three commandos left behind to secure their headquarters. Since not a single one of them volunteered to stay behind, they drew cards from a deck they found in the game room. Low cards lost out on the Carderock mission and had to stay behind. Jude told them that for the next mission, the ones who lost out on this one would not have to draw cards. That mollified the loss a little. The team then drew equipment and assigned responsibilities within the modified 'A' Team structure that Jude had in mind.

Jude and Teeb set up a sand table resembling the AO and the target. They went over responsibilities, broke for dinner and rehearsed the rest of the night. The river crossing would take place on the night of Sunday,

January 14, so that they could be in place on the Monday of the exchange.

CHAPTER 36 — The Night Before the Exchange

"5th June, 1944 - It was the eve of D-Day and HMCS Algonquin was anchored half a mile from Ryde on the Isle of Wight. Captain Desmond Piers assembled the crew on deck and made a speech which has forever sunk into my memory. "Tomorrow is "D" Day. There will be no leave tonight and I have the great honour to advise you we have been chosen to be in the spearhead of the invasion." Everybody groaned. "Now I have something to add to this. We will be at the point of the spear." This instant, we all had the undesirable feeling that tomorrow we might all be dead. My stomach felt like a bunch of feathers. It was the most awful feeling I ever had. In retrospect, we were quite lucky. The enemy only fired a few shells at us and because we were such a small target the shore batteries raised their guns and fired over our heads. What we thought was a huge disadvantage turned out to be the safest place to be." - Memories from D-Day Eve, Ken Garrett

1900 hours, January 14, 2018

The four Zodiac F470s sat in a small tree shrouded cove on the Virginia side of the Potomac. Each was fully loaded with six commandos and their equipment. Jude gazed at his watch.

The sibilant trajectories of artillery rounds broke the silence of the night. The Leesburg battery began to lay out the fire mission on Heater's Island.

When the first explosions were heard in the distance, Jude gave the 'go' arm signal. The commandos sank their paddles in the dark river water and pushed towards the Maryland shore. The fire mission obliterated what had been left of Heater's island and masked the Rangers' infiltration. The explosions, though far away, also masked the splash of the paddles.

1900 hours, January 14, 2018

Kate had been organizing things at Langley High for almost two days and decided to get some early shut-eye so that she would be rested for the exchange. Her sleeping bag was right next to the piano in the school's auditorium. She and had commandeered the school to house the returning POWs, and the auditorium in particular for her troops and medical personnel who would tend to the returnees.

The families and selected unit members who would identify each of the POWs to prevent infiltrators had been accommodated in the school classrooms. The cafeteria was being handled by volunteers and the food had been provided by local merchants. The Woodridge headquarters had set up an aid station and a platoon of ambulances to transport the more serious cases to a major nearby hospital which was still functioning adequately.

The moment she laid her head on the winter coat that doubled as a pillow the artillery barrage on Heater's Island resounded in the distance.

She was the only one at the school who was privy to details of the commando crossing Ed had proposed. All kinds of rational ideas went through her mind: no letting up on the enemy prior to the exchange; the enemy not letting up on the Rebs; the Provos trying to cross again in a desperate attempt to rescue the bitch. But the thought that really grabbed a hold of her was Provo artillery targeting Jude. Her heart was trying to beat a path out of her chest.

She thought about calling Ed, but that would be unprofessional. She had no need to know about everything that went bang in the night. If AC headquarters decided that her mission would be impacted, they would call her. She looked around and saw the troops and the other Rebel personnel looking at each other, guessing what was going on. She decided to intervene.

"OK, guys. It's OK. Go back to sleep if you can. That's a planned Rebel fire mission. No Need to worry. Carl and Esther, take your guys into the classroom area and calm down the families. I screwed up and forgot to tell you that this was going to happen. Everything is OK."

She then set the example by laying down her head, closing her eyes and pretending to go to sleep. When the artillery mission died down, her eyes just refused to open back up again; she was that tired. Her last conscious thought was about Jude. Her reputation as a cool leader had been carved in stone.

1905 hours, January 12, 2018

Ed's mobile rang. When he answered he was surprised to hear the metallic Provo voice asking him to hold for President Greco.

Greco began "I'd like to know what you-" but Ed broke in "Didn't I tell you not to call me until tomorrow at 1500? This time I'll let you choose wart part of the bitch you want me to send you, Squid."

"Nooooo, wait" screamed Greco in terror as he lied to cover for his untimely call "Your artillery is firing on the barges that hold your POWs for tomorrow's exchange. You have to stop them. Please don't hurt Amanda."

This last plead was accompanied by a sob, "Please".

"Listen to me, asshole, and listen good. The barges are nowhere near the fire mission. We have eyes on the barges on your side of Little Falls Dam from where they are going to come across tomorrow. We got a report that you tried to cross troops over Heater's Island and I had my "red legs" remind them that it ain't healthy, you double crossing bastard.

I don't wanna hear this phone ring again until 1500 tomorrow when, I say again, when you will tell me the precise time those barges are going to come across, and I will tell you the precise time the bitch's rubber dinghy is going to carry her fat ass across to your side."

Ed disconnected, wondering how long it was going to take Greco to figure out that "red leg" was the Army's nickname for artillery troops.

Ed had suspected that Greco would call when the artillery diversion started and had concocted this response to be able to speak credibly on the reason for the fire mission. He didn't lie altogether. The Provos *had* sent SOF troops across, *possibly* as a spearhead for a battalion...*four days ago*...so it was sort of true. And it would do the job.

For his part, Greco could not be sure that his field commanders had not tried to cross on their own initiative. "The fucking idiots," he thought.

2015 hours, January 14, 2018

Jude's commandos moved inland as they had rehearsed and split into the two teams. Moving alongside the river would have been too dangerous since the Provos were out in force in preparation for tomorrow's exchange. There were some close calls as they rushed across some of the roads, but by 2300 they were on their assembly areas: Jude's team behind an abandoned McMansion on Anchorage and MacArthur, and Teebs was in a copse on Vendome, across from the facility's Atlanta Road gate.

The raid would take place the next day.

CHAPTER 37 — The Exchange

Honorable alike in what we give and what we preserve. We shall nobly save, or meanly lose, the last, best hope of earth."
President Abraham Lincoln, message to Congress, 1862

0800 hours, January 15, 2018

Ed Sumter's morning thoughts had turned to personal accountability; not a good sign for a cheerful outlook the rest of the day. He would have to think really hard about a justification for kidnapping and ransom. Yep, it didn't bode well for the rest of the day.

"A man's gotta do, what a man's gotta do," he heard himself say aloud in a bad imitation of John Wayne. His combat staff just looked at him

"Charlie, please ask Lieutenant O'Connor to come see me," he said staring at the ground. The S-4 supply and logistics officer would do as he asked, although he too felt the pall that had descended on the CP that morning.

He would have chosen Kate to escort Amanda Greco back to Provo lines. But Kate had to coordinate the entire prisoner exchange operation from shore. So Ed chose his old friend from the Kentucky National Guard to be the escort.

Ed needed someone he could trust implicitly in handling this important chess piece; funny how he could think in those terms about a hostage.

The lanky lieutenant showed up 'by and by' with a straw poking out of his closed lips in the worst imitation of a country bumpkin Ed had seen in a while.

"If I didn't know you got yourself a PhD in Physics I woudda taken you for someone who just fell off the turnip truck, Jimmy Joe" joked Ed. "Get yourself a cup of coffee and let's sit down on the exchange. I wanna go over the finer points, my young lieutenant."

"Sure thang, Commander. Can't wait to hear you teach me how to suck eggs", smiled Jimmy Joe, not wanting to remind Ed that he was 40 and the father of six kids.

1500 hours, January 15, 2018

Greco called at precisely 1500. He had learned not to mess with the Kentuckian. He kept his message short and to the point because he didn't want to go into last night's artillery barrage. His field commanders had sworn up and down that they had not tried to go across *this time*…those two words had told Greco everything he needed to know. He pressed General Jackson and the G-3 'admitted' that part of the reason he had fired General Marlin was his sending an unauthorized reconnaissance in force across Heater's Island. Jackson added that Marlin had acted with the best of intentions. Greco looked at him in ominous silence, contemplating the West Pointer's fate.

General Jackson had felt compelled to fill in the silence, so he told Greco how Rebel artillery had stopped the attacking force on its advance. Greco had wanted to tell the general that describing the details of his incompetence was just digging the hole deeper.

"Commander Sumter, this is President Greco. My troops inform me that they are prepared to ferry your people across no later than 1700 hours. There have been developments, however," said Greco.

"And what developments would those be, Mr. Greco?" he could not make himself call the usurping Provo Mr. President. The word 'developments' had raised a huge red flag.

"We are prepared to take across everyone on your list. Unfortunately, 32 of the 114 POWs you identified are deceased, and another 11 are so badly injured that they will be transported in gurneys and wheelchairs. But we have provided the best available equipment for them."

A painful few seconds of silence passed until Greco heard the Rebel commander's voice again.

"How did that happen, Greco?" Ed did not raise his voice. In fact, he lowered it to a deep threatening bass.

"It seems that the Militia camp management exceeded their authority in the areas of interrogation and summary executions. What I can tell you is that we have apprehended those responsible and they will also be sent over on the barges your disposition."

Greco's words sounded hollow and detached, ending on a high note, as if the Admiral expected Ed to congratulate him. Anyone who knew the Kentuckian would have assured the Provo that Ed's blood would be boiling.

Ed broke the silence. "So, Mr. Greco, do I understand correctly that you will be coming across on the barges to surrender to my troops? You did say that you had apprehended those responsible; right? You do understand that YOU are ultimately responsible for those war crimes. Don't you?"

His voice had risen in a menacing crescendo that put the fear of God in the Provo.

Greco was about to ask Ed to be reasonable when a click told the Provo that it was too late. For the next 30 minutes he tried unsuccessfully to get Ed to answer his phone.

1507 hours, January 15, 2018

For the first time in his life Ed fell into a complete depression. He was really in an impossible situation.

On the one hand, he had a chance to bring home dozens of his soldiers; soldiers who had gone through a savage regime of torture and maltreatment for what they believed in. Bringing them back safely was a commander's responsibility, and a point of honor.

On the other hand, he couldn't let Greco get away with what he had done to those men and women. Taking it out on Greco's wife would have seemed a satisfactory response. It was also an abominable thought to an honorable man.

Lost in his despair he hardly noticed Kate dropping into the CP bunker "Hi, Ed. We're all set at Langley High and I thought I'd come by and find out if there is any news on a firm delivery time."

Ed looked at her up and down and gave her a sad inquiring smile. "You coudda called and asked me Kate."

Looking at the ground he continued more seriously than the moment called for. "You are really here because you wanna know if Jude's OK, right? Last night's fire mission scared the bejesus out of you; didn't it?"

Kate briefly opened her mouth to deny it but she stopped herself short and admitted her guilt with a low voice and pleading eyes. "Is he OK?"

"'Course he's OK. I woudda told you by now, wouldn't I? I got his radio click signal. He's lying low to hit the objective tonight."

"Then he went across after all? His team is ready?"

"He didn't tell you? Heck, I know there's 'need-to-know' and all them spooky concepts. But a guy who's sweet on a girl will find a way to warn her not to worry if he was gonna do the sort of stuff he's doing."

Kate did not even think about denying it any more. Ed looked at her and his head angled down in a 'what's up' kind of way. "What gives, Kate? What's happened between you two? I mean, you can tell me to mind my own business. But it don't work that way. I'm in charge and I need to know what goes on with my troops. Hell, I'm your friend and I *have* to know. So, spill it." That last command brought back the affable hillbilly persona.

"Ed, I wish I knew. Well, I sort of know it's maybe too early since his wife got killed. Sometimes at night and other quiet times he looks away, lost in thought. Then sometimes when he is talking his words come out unduly harsh, as if he had just noticed that he was doing something wrong and couldn't justify it. When that happens I also wonder if I've done something wrong. Or if he is just angry, or worried, or just thinking about something really awful. He's so hard to read.

"That's it for him, I think. Now, on my side, I can't quite put my finger on it but I think I may have a problem committing to a man with his kind of baggage. Every little girl dreams about finding a knight in shining armor who will fall in love with her, and who has never belonged to another girl. The thought of him in someone else's arms is repulsive."

She looked down at bunker's floor.

Ed put his massive hand on her shoulder "Let me tell you about guys, Kate. The thought of you in someone else's arms don't do much for a guy's ego. And Kate, far as I know you didn't spend your life in a nunnery, did you? So let's cut out the double-standard stuff, OK? But, you are in love with him, ain't you? So what's the deal?" said Ed with poster-boy logic "Grab him by the nuts and twist'em until he comes to his senses. Listen, I could lose either one of you at any moment; heavy shit happens when you are at war. Why not be happy while you can? You guys need to have a serious conversation or two. You want me to talk to him?"

Kate hurriedly shook her head, still looking down "No, Ed, I'm a big girl. I can do my own talking. Sometimes a girl needs her mom to hold her hand, talk about things and set her mind straight. Sometimes" and she sort of smiled at the Kentuckian. "It takes a big hillbilly to take my daddy's place, explain guys to me and make me come to my senses, that's all."

Her embarrassment was so obvious that Ed turned his head and reached for a cup of coffee to pass to her.

Infusing his down-to-earth humor into the serious situation Ed guffawed "And now the girl takes me for her Paw…well I'll be…" said Ed to no one in particular, but in a good imitation of Aunt Bea in the Andy Griffith show." OK. So that's out of the way. Now it's your turn to help me get something in perspective."

He sat down on one of the wooden crates and motioned Kate to the one next to it; and he told her about his dilemma on the POW situation.

1545 hours, January 15, 2018

Ed had the RTO reach Greco. When the Admiral answered the phone, Ed told him gruffly "Move them across".

The Provo couldn't leave well enough alone and asked, "We still have a deal, then?"

An incredulous sounding Kentucky accent boomed over the airwaves. "It's obvious to me that you didn't get into Annapolis because of your high IQ," and then yelling full blast "Of course we have a fucking deal, Squid. Just get them on the fucking barges and move them fucking across. I'll do the same for your fucking bitch. Do I have to paint you a fucking picture?" and he looked at Kate, who nodded and moved her hands palms down in a calming motion.

Ed disconnected.

"OK, Kate. Go and do your thing" said the Kentuckian trying to regain his composure.

Kate started to walk away, but then turned her head towards him briefly. "You gonna be OK?"

"Sure. And, Kate thanks for talking this out with me." He went from seriously subdued to more humorous. "You see? Even great military minds like mine can get in between a rock and a hard place."

He regained his seriousness and continued, "One more thing, Kate, I want to be the one to break the news to the families of the KIAs. So call me when you and your troops have sorted out the living from the dead. I'll do the deed personally. It's my job."

Kate had listened to Ed's agonizing thoughts. If he had known about the dead POWs in advance he would not have let the families go to Langley High School along with all the other POW families. The storm in his soul didn't have an outlet. He wanted to hit something, someone. He wished he could get his hands on the sumbitch across the river and drag his carcass behind his Humvee until all the skin peeled off!

Kate's emotions were not all that different. Yet, she was an outsider looking into the 'loneliness of command' that weighed on Ed. It let her see things more clearly.

Greco had played Sumter, no doubt about it. There was nothing Ed could do except wait on a chance to make Greco hurt really bad for this.

As their commander, Ed felt responsible for the lives of the surviving POWs. He could not throw these lives away just to satisfy his rage or his need for revenge. He also could not kill a non-combatant woman in cold blood. It was just not in him. Ed felt he had lost this round. It was as simple as that.

Kate made him see that he had not really lost. Each one of the fighters he could return to his or her family was a major victory. Any one of them was more valuable than the Greco woman. "Concentrate on that," Kate had told him.

And he did.

She looked at Ed again, turned around in silence and ran for her Humvee to go back to the school.

Ed went to his corner of the CP and began to put on his combat gear for want of something to do with his hands.

1650 hours, January 15, 2018

Nothing builds tension better than anticipated combat. Jude and his men were tense. They carried out a silent buddy check on each other to ensure that the equipment was put on correctly and that the crew-served weapons had at least one operator and one assistant. They reviewed in their minds each fighter's role in the upcoming assault: the coordinated attack that they had rehearsed the day before. They felt ready for what was coming.

Jude stared at his watch intently. When the digits changed from 1659 to 1700 hours, he raised his right hand and lowered it toward the Carderock POW camp, giving the 'go' hand signal and mouthing a silent 'move out'.

1647 hours, January 15, 2018

Kate and Jimmy Joe O'Connor arrived at the Virginia shore by the Little Falls Dam in separate vehicles but at the same time. Jimmy Joe opened his front passenger door and helped a bound and hooded Amanda Greco get out of the truck. He looked at Kate and Kate nodded. He then led the hostage to the motorized Zodiac that would take them across the river and helped her get in.

Kate lifted her arm signaling the Provos across the Potomac that her side was ready; the exchange could begin. When the Provo across the river also signaled their readiness, she turned to Lieutenant Jimmy Joe O'Connor and nodded.

At precisely 1700 hours, the barges chugged out of the Maryland riverside, just as Jimmy Joe engaged the

Zodiac's outboard. The Potomac at Little Falls Dam is not all that wide, but it seemed like hours until the Provo barges and the Rebel Zodiac reached their landings simultaneously.

The Rebel shore

On the Virginia side, Rebel fighters and medical personnel rushed the barges to help move their precious cargo to firm land. The POWs were in pitiful shape; evidently suffering from malnutrition and physical and mental torture. The swarm of Rebel medical personnel and armed fighters used gurneys, wheelchairs and a lot of pushing and shoving and shoulder-lending to help the POWs reach the ambulances over the rough terrain.

Kate's MPs took charge of the handcuffed Militia prisoners and rushed them to their vehicles, sometimes through unavoidable POW gauntlets intent in taking revenge.

The Provo shore

Touching ground on the Maryland side, Jimmy Joe killed the outboard motor, got out of the Zodiac and helped the still hooded Amanda out of the boat. They walked up the shoreline arm-in-arm toward where a small group of people waited. All of a sudden a woman detached herself from the group and ran towards Amanda and Jimmy Joe.

Some in the Provo group yelled, "No, Martha".

Reaching Jimmy Joe and his hostage, the woman ripped the hood off Amanda's head. Locking eyes with the hostage, she drew a pistol and pointed it at Amanda's head.

In a gallant move befitting the stereotypical old-fashioned Kentucky gentleman, Jimmy Joe shoved Amanda aside and jumped in front of the bullets meant for the hostage. His head and chest took the full and fatal impact of the first three shots. As the Rebel officer collapsed, the first Mrs. Greco went around to the petrified Amanda and emptied the rest of the pistol's magazine into the second Mrs. Greco, just before the others from the Provo group got to her. When they finally subdued the assassin, she offered no resistance, but she did have a strange smile on her face.

"Take your hands off me," she said. "I am the real Mrs. Greco."

The Rebel shore

From the Virginia shore Kate saw Jimmy Joe fall lifeless at the feet of the hostage he was protecting. When Jimmy Joe's body touched the ground she mechanically brought up her hand held radio and spoke a code phrase. It was the order to launch the pre-arranged final protective fire mission.

Having moved within range of the exchange site the night before, the Leesburg and Woodbridge batteries responded immediately. Four murderous high explosive barrages rained against the Provo positions.

Even before she heard the incoming shells' sibilant warning, Kate yelled to the troops and POWs: "Incoming".

The troops rapidly shepherded the POWs and medical personnel to the defensive positions that the Rebel combat engineers had prepared for just such a contingency. Kate dived into the nearest fox hole. The 155s and 105s lit up the Maryland shore at Little Falls Dam until it was no more.

Glossary

AC – Appalachian Command

AC (forward) – Headquarters of the Appalachian Command on the battle field.

ACU – Army Combat Uniform made of 50% nylon and 50% cotton in digital camouflage print. It succeeded the camouflaged BDU and the earlier fatigues.

ATN PS22 – Night vision rifle scope which allows the shooter to see in the dark.

Army of God – Paramilitary group organized by American mullahs to capitalize from the terrorist act that brought down the American Republic.

CFC – Civil Forces Commander, a liaison officer between local governments and the Rebels.

CNS – Committee of National Salvation.

CONUS – Continental United States.

Ghillie blanket – Camouflage tarp with strips of cloth imbedded to resemble vegetation.

Humvee – Military vehicle used to transport personnel and light weapons.

OCONUS – Outside the Continental United States, abroad.

XM-2010 sniper rifle – Experimental sniper rifle designed to replace the current M-24.

Zodiac F-470 – Tactical rubber boat used by Special Operations Forces.

Made in the USA
Charleston, SC
24 October 2013